Her body was saying things she never could

"Body language," he informed her. "Your cheeks are glowing, your lips are parted...."

Classic signs of sexual attraction, thought Mallory. She brought one arm across her chest to rub her shoulder absently, protecting her breasts from his view.

"And you want very much to be touched," he said.

She was beginning to feel exposed, extremely vulnerable. Her eyes wandered from Colt's face to his hand, which was tracing a lazy circular pattern around the rim of his glass.

"Now look what you're doing," he advised.

Mallory looked at her own glass just in time to realize that her fingers were moving in a slow stroking motion up and down the stem of her glass. The sexual implications were startling and blatant.

"When I move my fingers faster, yours move faster," Colt explained. "We've been communicating in perfect rhythm all evening...."

Dearest Friend,

A good romance novel is like a diamond—you can never have too many! *Dreamweaver* is one of those diamonds.

My very first published novel is a story about the heartbreaks, successes and failures of glamorous Hollywood life. Believe me when I say I know what that is all about. Rebecca Flanders and I have collaborated on this story, where passions, fantasies and desires are more brilliant in the lives of Mallory, Colt and Jake than in their films.

Dreamweaver discovers love, questions love, discards love, then finally reaffirms love.

I do hope you will enjoy reading the book.... Thank you...all of you...for your support, your love and your friendship.

My love,

Felicia Gallant

Dreamweaver

FELICIA GALLANT

WITH **REBECCA FLANDERS**

Harlequin Books

TORONTO • NEW YORK • LONDON
AMSTERDAM • PARIS • SYDNEY • HAMBURG
STOCKHOLM • ATHENS • TOKYO • MILAN

First published November 1984

ISBN 0-373-97012-9

Chapter One

MALLORY EVANS awoke feeling wonderful. There was no particular reason for it; it just felt like a great day. White-yellow sunlight streamed over her bed through the sheer curtains that covered the one glass wall of her bedroom, seeming to bounce and dance in the air like a shower of diamonds. Mallory loved that huge window. To her it was the epitome of Southern California. She loved her entire obscenely large bedroom. She loved the triple-size bed, the delicate curves of the brass headboard, the white wicker sitting group before the window, the lush green plants in every corner. She loved the lace edging on her sheets and pillowcases—real cotton lace, not synthetic factory-woven—and she loved not even knowing how much she'd paid for them. And she loved the delicate white-and-pale-yellow color scheme of the room. On the bedside table a small ivory clock ticked out a comforting, repetitive rhythm. All was light and space; there was nothing dark or threatening.

For a moment Mallory lay there, stretching drowsily in a state of sensuous contentment against the bed of yellow daisies, but suddenly she sprang out of bed and to the window in a single motion, pushing back the curtains.

The window looked out on an enclosed garden
and one corner of the stylish kidney-shaped swimming pool. The light shimmered on the emerald
green lawn; the sky was a wedge-shaped slice of
yellow-blue between her redwood fence and her
neighbor's roof. Mallory's contentment soared. Blue
skies in Los Angeles were reason enough for anyone
to celebrate, she supposed. Bright red peonies and
brash fuchsia begonias glowed in neatly manicured
flower beds around a central arrangement of three
healthy orange trees, and the water in the pool lay
like a shiny piece of blue cellophane. It was like a
painting, an ad campaign for The Good Life. But it
was hers. Her orange trees, her garden, her pool.
And she was surely the luckiest woman in the world.

Mallory hummed to herself as she made her way
to the kitchen, going out of her way to pass through
every room in the house, pausing now and then to
admire the decor or lovingly touch one or two ob-
jects of which she was particularly proud. Sunlight
flooded every room through multiple oversize windows, and every room in her house had at least one
clock, all carefully wound and never allowed to run
down. Grandfather clocks, Swiss clocks, delicate
French ormolu clocks, all ticking in unison. The
sound was as soothing as the pulse of a mother's
heartbeat heard from the womb. There was reassurance in the tick of the clocks, the illusion of control over time, the reminder of deadlines and limits.
Mallory liked to know her limits; she liked the
security of captured time surrounding her.

It was eight-thirty in the morning, and Mallory

was certain this was going to be the best day of her
life. By nine o'clock, she was sure it would be the
worst.

She took her coffee and the newspaper to the
poolside—something she rarely did because lingering over morning coffee in the luxury of the sun
seemed an almost sinful indulgence. Mallory was
perfectly aware that she was one of the Puritan work
ethic's most tragic victims. Sometimes she chuckled
at herself over it, but despite a few words of reproof
from friends, no one had complained yet. Not the
producers or directors for whom she had supplied
scripts for three blockbusters in five years, not the
millions of moviegoers who thrilled to the *Nestar*
trilogy; certainly not her agent, her accountants, or
her attorneys. Sometimes Mallory had to pause and
shake her head in awe that there were so many people who cared about her, whose lives she affected.
Her agent, *her* accountant, *her* attorney.... And
sometimes her power frightened her. But work was
Mallory's panacea, and as long as she was working
she did not think about anything else. That was the
advantage of being a workaholic, and that was why
she only laughed when her friends tried to get her to
slow down and enjoy life. They did not understand
that working, the privilege to work, was more than
Mallory had ever asked for from life.

But today she was ready to take a little of their
advice. Her latest script was in the hands of her
agent, and though this one was a risky divergence
from the trilogy that had made her name in this
business, Mallory knew without a doubt it was the

best thing she had ever done. The first elation of a finished project had passed. The second stage of uncertainty and doom had also passed—that three-day period when she had to practically tie her hands together to keep herself from rushing to the phone and begging Jake to return the script because it was too horrible for anyone to see. Now was the waiting period, and though she usually weathered it in alternating states of nervous exhaustion and depression, this time it settled in like an old friend. Perhaps she was, at last, getting comfortable with success.

So Mallory would spend the morning sitting around the pool with a yellow ceramic pot of coffee and a package of oatmeal cookies on the umbrella table beside her, the golden May sun toasting her shoulders through the silk kimono she wore, absently scanning the paper and doing absolutely nothing. Wars and threats of wars, murders, rapes, suicides and an alarming drop in the Dow Jones average did nothing to affect her today. The drone of traffic from a faraway highway reached her clearly on this still morning. The sound of a fast-paced life with purpose and direction was soothing. Mallory smiled to herself and settled more comfortably in the webbed-vinyl chair. The coffee was the best she had ever made. Today was going to be perfect. Today she would work in the garden. Today she would start her diet. She might even spend the afternoon by the pool with a new romance novel, or go shopping. Then the telephone rang.

Mallory reached for it lazily, reflecting with secret amusement that Southern Californians were the only people she knew who had telephones installed outside. It was all part of the contradictory life-style she found so intriguing. Hollywood types spent fortunes to live laid-back lives, but could never be more than a few feet from the telephone, which was the umbilical cord connecting them to the rat race they were trying to escape.

"Hi, babe. Are you free for lunch today?"

The familiar down-home East Texas drawl belonged to Jake, and that was when Mallory knew something terrible was going to happen. The sun was not really as bright as it had seemed at first, but was in fact slightly obscured by the perpetual L.A. smog. The orange trees looked a little wilted and the begonias dusty. Mallory's hand tightened on the yellow receiver and a lump formed in her throat around her last sip of coffee, which was a little on the bitter side after all.

"Why?" Mallory got to her feet, muscles tensing in an unconscious flight-or-fight posture, her hand going nervously to her throat. "What's wrong? Something's wrong, Jake. You never want to see me unless it's bad news." Already she had resigned herself to the worst. "It was lousy, right? You can't sell it. It's okay. You don't have to spring for lunch to tell me that. I can take it—"

His low, rolling laughter swallowed up the rest of her words, and Mallory could imagine him leaning back in his squeaky leather chair, pushing the Stetson off his forehead, eyes twinkling, gold tooth flashing as he grinned. She frowned in both annoyance and frustration even as she tried to relax.

Jake loved it when she got like this. She had resolved long ago to stop giving him so much pleasure at her expense. But her resolution never lasted very long.

"Are you finished?" Mallory inquired at length, as coolly as she could manage.

He was still chuckling. "Are you?"

She assumed her most aggressive, businesswoman-in-charge stance, as though he could be intimidated over the telephone. As though Jake could be intimidated by her at all. "Now will you kindly tell me what this is all about?"

"Calm down and get your hand away from that damn cookie jar," he replied patiently. "Fat never made anything better."

Guiltily Mallory released the cookie she had automatically reached for. The man must have X-ray vision. She frowned and repeated her request. "What do you want?"

"Why, just a little business lunch, peaches, that's all. Agents and clients do that kind of thing every once in a while, don't they?"

He knew he was driving her crazy. Mallory kept her voice calm. "The script, Jake. What did you think about it?"

"That's what I want to talk about over lunch."

"Who did you show it to?" she demanded. "Why did they turn it down? What was wrong with it?"

This time, instead of laughing, he merely sighed — a long, patient, infinitely forbearing sigh. His drawl always became thicker when he was trying to hide something. "Now, peaches, what makes you think anybody turned it down?"

"Because," she explained, ready to scream with frustration. Her hand was cramping from its tight grip on the phone. "Because if it was good news, you would tell me now. You wouldn't wait to get me drunk on white wine and lobster salad and try to break it to me gently."

"This damn paranoia of yours is going to make you crazy, you know that?" Jake replied mildly, completely unruffled. "You just meet me at noon at Marcetti's and we'll have ourselves a nice long talk, all right?"

Mallory sighed. One thing she had learned about Jake was that the drawl was not all he had brought with him to the Golden Coast. He could be as stubborn as a Texas mule, and once he had made up his mind not to tell her anything over the phone, no amount of pleading, cajoling or tearful tantrums could make him change his mind. "All right," she agreed reluctantly. "Twelve o'clock."

"And Mallory." His voice was very serious now, commanding attention. Mallory mentally stiffened. "I want you to remember one thing, little girl. You're the best thing this business has seen in twenty years. You're a hot commodity. You can pick and choose, and do you know why? Because you're *good*, that's why. You're damn *terrific*. You just remember that, you hear? You're the best there is."

The news was bad. She was sure of it.

She stood for a moment after she had hung up the phone, anxiously chewing her lower lip as she looked around her suddenly dimmer garden. She wondered if Jake had any idea how much this script meant to her. She wondered if, in fact, it was as good as she thought it was.

Mallory's shoulders squared, and her head lifted slightly with resolution. The script was good. It was damn good. *She* was good. Jake was right; her paranoia would drive her crazy if it hadn't already.

There was no reason for it, she decided as she looked once again around the garden and tried to summon up the contentment of the morning. She was thirty-one years old, and this was all hers. An expensive ranch house in an exclusive L.A. suburb—not Beverly Hills, but very close—a white Porsche for which she had paid cash not six months ago, designer sheets and a sunken bathtub. A housekeeper three times a week. Four telephones. Her own orange trees. How many women her age could claim as much?

And how fragile it all seemed.

Five years ago this was beyond her wildest dreams. It had burst upon her suddenly, as though the sky had split at the seams and poured down all its treasures into her lap. Couldn't it all disappear just as suddenly?

Again she found herself with a cookie halfway to her lips and frowned in quick annoyance. With swift determination, she returned the cookie to the package and took it, and the coffee pot, back into the house. Mallory knew she was being stupid. She knew her insecurity was her worst handicap. She understood the reasons for it and she knew she had to do something about it. No one had *given* her anything. Everything she owned she had worked for.

She had succeeded because she was good, she was the best in the business. She was wanted. She was a hot commodity. The sky had not opened and spilled out a fortune. No god had smiled on her. She had paid her dues and everything she had accomplished had been won through maniacal work habits and superior production. She had what it took to make it to the top. No one could take it away. She knew that.

And even as Mallory dressed for lunch with Jake, she was still trying to convince herself of that.

COLT STANFORD knew immediately Mallory Evans when she entered the restaurant. There was no reason he should have recognized her—the woman shunned publicity in a way that was almost unnatural in Hollywood—but he had noticed Jake Farrow's name on the reservation list. So when the tall, uncertain-looking young woman came through the door, he knew instinctively who she was. Somehow she looked exactly the way he had pictured her.

A moment later his intuition was confirmed.

Evelyn Bouchard had her usual table with its perfect view of the door, and as Colt passed on his way to the kitchen she signaled to him. He would have ignored her, but he was close enough for her to touch his sleeve, and when she did he had to stop.

"Sorry, ma'am, this isn't my table," he told her with a sweet smile.

Evelyn laughed lightly. The sound was as grating on Colt's ears as breaking glass. "How marvelous that you haven't lost your sense of humor along with everything else."

Colt inclined his head regally. "It's known as grace under pressure. What can I do for you, Miss Bouchard?"

But Evelyn ignored him for the moment and turned back to her friends, one hand resting against her jawline, the other toying with her glass. She widened her eyes in mock amazement and lowered her voice conspiratorially. "You wouldn't believe it if I were to tell you who this gorgeous hunk of a waiter really is. . . ." She glanced back up at Colt, eyes dancing madly. "And from what great heights he has fallen."

Colt's expression became bored. He did not like Evelyn and she knew it, a fact that earned him both her displeasure and her grudging respect. But he was one of the few people in this room today who could afford to antagonize Evelyn Bouchard. He had nothing to lose, and that must have irritated her.

"The fallen mighty have to earn their living with tips, which are growing smaller by the minute if I don't get back to work. Did you want something or not?"

Under ordinary circumstances, Colt would not have wasted this much time on her. But standing by her table gave him an opportunity to watch the woman he thought was Mallory, and as Evelyn surely must know, he wasn't all that concerned about tips.

Evelyn folded her hands demurely under her chin and briefly followed his gaze to the foyer. She looked back up at him with a smile. "A favor," she pronounced. "In return for one of my own, of course. See what you can do about seating Mallory Evans next to my table and I'll make sure nothing appears in my next column about the desperate straits that have reduced the great Colt Stanford to waiting tables at Marcetti's."

Colt couldn't have cared less what appeared in Bouchard's column. He also had no intention of delivering an innocent like Mallory Evans into the hands of the wolf. But he was glad to have his speculations about Mallory's identity confirmed, and he was feeling certain strong protective instincts toward the woman he had never met. Besides, all else being equal, he would not have done a favor for Evelyn Bouchard had the fate of the free world depended upon it.

But Colt merely smiled as he turned to go. "You must be slipping, Evelyn, or else you would have noticed Jake Farrow sitting on the other side of the room, waiting for his most successful client. I'm afraid," he added over his shoulder, not bothering to keep the amusement out of his eyes, "not even *your* considerable charms will persuade him to change his table now."

Colt could feel her eyes boring daggers into his back, and he chuckled a little as he walked away.

It was something of a hobby of Colt's to keep up with what was going on in the business, and he recognized on sight most of the people in the restaurant. A few, with the shocked dismay in their eyes with which one might regard a contagious disease, even recognized Colt, then quickly pretended not to. Colt was not offended, any more than he would have been embarrassed by yet another mention of his name in Evelyn Bouchard's notorious column. He had reached his tolerance level for both embarrassment and offense when his career had ended so abruptly and so publicly three years ago. Nothing anyone in this room could do or say could hurt him now.

Colt's life was busy and more or less rewarding. He rarely thought about his "fall from greatness," as Evelyn had put it. When he did it was always distantly, without remorse or pain, but rather with the detachment of one who has long ago learned acceptance.

It might have been the return to Marcetti's, where once he had dined in luxury and comfort along with the stars and the starmakers, dishing out fame and fortune between courses and changing destinies with a sweep of his hand. It might have been the presence of Mallory Evans, looking so lost and out of place in this meeting house for the crème de la crème of Hollywood's finest. Whatever the reason, Colt was stricken by a sudden nostalgia, and he could not help thinking about the past.

Perhaps it was because a lot about Mallory Evans reminded him of himself.

Colt Stanford was a typical casualty of Hollywood's own particularly ruthless brand of politics. More than talent was needed to make it in this business, but with the determined naïveté of a young man on the rise, filled with ideas, ambition and enough enthusiasm to revolutionize the industry, Colt had refused to recognize the more unsavory ingredients needed for success. All he wanted was to be the best there was at what he did.

And Colt was that. With the ink barely dry on his degree in filmmaking and enough awards to impress the most jaded producer, Colt got his first chance as an assistant director and climbed quickly up the ladder. He directed his first major motion picture at age twenty-five. It was an unqualified success. For the next five years he had everything he had ever hoped for, expected or needed.

Colt had made the films he wanted and each was better than the last. He had married a beautiful young starlet who adored him. He had maintained his own high standards of honesty, fair play and artistic integrity.

But Colt had not learned that success in the fast-paced world of Hollywood's illusion-brokers had little to do with honesty or fairness. Success relied far more heavily upon who was sleeping with whom, who was slipping money under the table to whom and in what amounts, and who had the guts to play the dirtiest for the highest stakes.

In his years as Hollywood's fair-haired boy, Colt had already gained a reputation as "disgustingly straight." He was faithful to his wife. He wasn't interested in party drugs or other assorted fringe benefits of celebrity. He demanded a fair day's work for a fair day's pay, and he didn't court the media. Worst of all, he didn't play games.

Looking back on it now, Colt realized he had been setting himself up for professional assassination. But even had he known then what he knew now, he would not have done anything differently. Being Colt, he couldn't have.

One moment he was in the middle of the biggest film of his career; the next he was released from his contract, surrounded by controversy and unemployable. The wife he counted on for support turned her back on him. The trade journals told the story of his "failure" in bold print. And all the principles upon which Colt had built his life came tumbling down around his feet.

Had Colt been a different sort of man disillusionment and bitterness would have eventually destroyed him. But Colt managed his life too efficiently for self-indulgent weaknesses. He was hurt, he was sorrowful, and yes, he was even scarred. But he took the experience, learned from it, accepted the fact that there was nothing he could do about it, and he went on.

Within six months he was building a new career for himself, one that, while it was a far cry from satisfying his talents, he found nonetheless rewarding. Less than a year after that, the woman he once had loved was married to the very producer who had cost Colt his dreams, his wife and his career. Colt had learned his second bitter lesson: all he thought he knew about his wife was only illusion. She had never loved him, only his success, and it was in the nature of the power-brokers to go with a winner.

Colt had followed the career of Mallory Evans closely, not only because she was possibly one of the most brilliant new screenwriters of the decade, but also because her appearance on the Hollywood scene had coincided roughly with the decline of his own career. And because, from what little he knew of her, she appeared to be what was an absolute rarity in this business—a genuine artist.

She shunned publicity, she worked long hours, she produced quality material. She was not to be found among the glittering guests at celebrity parties or whiling away time on some well-known yacht; she did not frequent sushi bars or health spas. She appeared to have no social life at all, and *her* name was never splashed across Bouchard's column.

Mallory Evans had always struck Colt as the type of person who, like himself, did not care to play the game. Seeing her now in person only confirmed that impression. He felt a little sorry for her, and he thought about warning her that Bouchard had Mallory in her sights.

That was why, instead of heading for the kitchen when he left Bouchard's table, Colt wandered instead toward the foyer where Mallory was standing with the lunch-hour crowd waiting to be seated. At the last minute he remembered that, although he knew who *she* was, Mallory Evans was not likely to appreciate advice from an impertinent waiter. That reminded him that leaving his station was a firing offense at Marcetti's, and the job was not his to risk.

Colt started to go back to the kitchen, knowing that, because Jake Farrow was sitting at one of his tables, he would more than likely have a chance to speak to Mallory before lunch was over. . . . But just before he turned, the movement Mallory made caught his attention out of the corner of his eye, and he knew the opportunity to meet her had come sooner than he expected.

Chapter Two

MALLORY EVANS had never considered herself one to stand out in a crowd, certainly not in a crowd as glittering and outrageous as this one. Jeannine, her best friend, said it was because she had no style, which was probably true because, taken separately, Mallory had all the features and assets of a truly striking woman. Yet somehow those features never came together to create the dramatic effect that was her potential.

She was of moderate height, but her slim neck and delicate arms gave the impression of height and grace. Her complexion was strikingly fair, for her dedication to her work kept her away from the sun her counterparts worshipped. Her face was a make-up artist's dream — perfect oval shape, straight nose, eyes well spaced and a mutable hazel color, lips easily defined. But Mallory was no makeup artist. Jeannine had recently persuaded her to have her strawberry-blond hair clipped just above the shoulder blades into a smooth pageboy style. Her hair was also beginning to be quite an annoyance since her hairdresser had threatened Mallory with her life should she ever again wind it into the careless topknot Mallory had become accustomed to.

There was a breeze today but only enough to create a strong draft every time the door swung open to admit another body into the cheerfully overcrowded foyer. With each opening of the door the wind caught Mallory's baby-fine hair and scattered it across her cheek. As she reached up for the third time to brush some strands off her face, she was jostled by a grinning child actor and she caught her watchband on the shoulder of her bouclé knit dress.

It had come from Jeannine's exclusive Rodeo Drive shop. Mallory cared little for fashion and even less for Jeannine's prices, but she wore the outfit because its waistless lines were very useful for disguising the pounds she had a tendency to put on while in her "waiting and worrying" state. Now she swore softly under her breath as she struggled to free her watchband and remembered exactly how much the garment had cost. She felt incredibly foolish with her arm crooked over her shoulder and her elbow sticking straight out, and a warm flush crept over her cheeks. Above all else, Mallory did her best to make herself invisible in a crowd. It would be just her luck —

"Ah, Miss Evans," the bustling maître d' exclaimed cheerfully, as he returned to his station and spotted her. "Mr. Farrow is waiting for you." All eyes turned toward her.

It was no use. She was going to have to tear the dress. Keeping her eyes lowered and her head ducked, Mallory prepared to give that fatal jerk that would either rip out the shoulder seam or break the watchband. Instead, she felt strong fingers slip beneath hers. In one deft movement the material was disentangled. Mallory looked up in some confusion to meet a pair of gently dancing male eyes.

They were hazel and surrounded by tanned features that were both unremarkable yet vaguely familiar. The man's face was fringed by a fall of dusky brown hair that seemed inclined to tumble across the forehead despite a cut that was designed to brush away from the ears and taper to the collar. It was not a famous face, but Mallory felt in that one quick second of eye contact as though it were a face she had known a long time. Perhaps that was because his expression was so friendly, in the midst of what seemed to her at that moment to be a hostile crowd.

He was wearing jeans and a polo shirt with a small mint stripe. As her eyes uncomfortably wandered away from the amusement in his she noticed three things — the hint of a strong chest with its sprinkling of light brown hair where the collar of the shirt was left casually unbuttoned, a nicely shaped arm muscle that curved very close to her body as his fingers lingered on her shoulder and a very definite and unmistakable personal attraction in his eyes. Mallory was both surprised and titillated. Until that moment she had not realized how much time had passed since she had elicited that expression from a man.

His fingers lingered against the knit material perhaps two seconds longer than was necessary, but long enough to send a tingle of confusion to Mallory's cheeks. Then he smiled at her and stepped away as she turned to follow the maître d'. The entire episode, from the time she had caught her watchband on her dress to the time the crowd made room for her to pass, had lasted no more than thirty seconds and not a word had been exchanged, but Mallory was strangely elated. She was reminded of how much she missed that sensation. The memory of twinkling male eyes looking down at her lingered like a pleasant secret.

Marcetti's was a small restaurant far off the beaten path, which boasted authentic Sicilian dishes and terrifyingly unrealistic prices. The decor was haphazard, the service intensely personal and the clientele exclusive. The waiters did not wear uniforms, but that was something Mallory had never noticed before today.

There was always a crowd at Marcetti's, another testament to the contradictory philosophy of Southern Californians. Marcetti's had become the gathering place for the very rich and very famous solely because of its inaccessibility. Actors, musicians, producers and directors were among the powerful elite whose names were household words, and they chose the small, relatively obscure restaurant precisely to avoid recognition. Yet by the very nature of its clientele, Marcetti's was *the* place to be seen. They came seeking privacy and ended up posturing for the media. It was, indeed, a strange world.

As Mallory made her way to Jake's table she almost forgot to dread the meeting. He looked so relaxed lounged back in the trendy leather bucket chair, his battered gray Stetson perched precariously on one knee as he sipped his drink, that surely nothing could be wrong. Then she noticed the absence of the champagne bucket and her spirits sank again.

"Margaritas," Mallory said dully as she was seated. "You're drinking margaritas. You always drink margaritas when you've had a bad day. What's wrong?"

Jake fastened his pale blue gaze on her with an expression that was typically inscrutable. "Sometimes, peaches, I drink margaritas because I'm thirsty," he informed her lazily. "I ordered one for you," he added unnecessarily, nodding at the salt-rimmed glass of tequila before her. "What took you so long?"

"I hate tequila," she said despondently, but took a sip anyway, for fortification.

In the past five years Jake Farrow and Mallory Evans had become one of the most formidable teams in the entertainment business, yet there was more to their relationship than the simple symbiosis of an agent and a client. Mallory would never have made it without Jake. Jake in turn had garnered a small fortune from Mallory's talent. And that was where any similarity to an ordinary agent-client relationship ended.

First and foremost a businessman, Jake had recognized Mallory's talent and made his decision to represent her based solely on that. But after the decision was made, the subtleties that bound them together quickly became more complicated.

For his other clients, Jake made shrewd deals for

top dollar, took his percentage, turned the files over to his secretary and forgot about them. But Mallory was different. His treatment of Mallory was not quite so cut-and-dried. Jake took care of her, protected her, guided her, encouraged her. He shielded her from the unpleasantness of the business in a way he never bothered to do with anybody else. He helped her through the rough times and he celebrated her victories. She depended upon him, and he was always there for her. Jake knew her strengths and her weaknesses, her fears and her secret dreams. He was a silent and understanding ear when she needed to talk; he was supportive and unshakable during her battles with self-doubt. If asked, Mallory would not have known whether to best describe him as her professional representative, or her very best friend. Jake knew that, and accepted it. For Jake had been in love with Mallory for the better part of five years.

Mallory never knew, but it was within the nature of the relationship—and Jake's cautious, studiously alert personality—that she would not. Jake dealt with his personal life, as well as his professional one, in his own inimitable fashion, and he would not be rushed. Mallory would understand, when she was ready. And when she was ready to turn to him, he would be there, waiting. Meanwhile, they had nothing but time.

Jake Farrow was a man straight from a John Wayne movie, from the top of his dishwater pale, thinning hair to the squared toes of his scuffed rattlesnake-skin boots. Lanky with slow and lazy movements, he had a leathery face not given to the expression of strong emotions. He had the frame of a rodeo rider and the countenance of a high-stakes poker player; his personal style belied the fast-paced business world in which he moved. That was precisely what made him the best agent in the business. His laid-back manner and slow drawl disguised a mind that was as sharp as a razor; nothing escaped the alert blue eyes that were in constant assessing motion behind heavily hooded lids. When he gave his ingenuous, perplexed little grin, accompanied by a disarming gesture of scratching his head, the sharpest producer or the hardest budget manager in the business didn't have a chance. Mallory was not his only client, but she knew she was his favorite. He went above and beyond the call of duty for her, a labor of love disguised in the name of profit. He had never failed her yet; it was ridiculous to think this might be the first time.

Yet still Mallory worried. She worried so much that her strongest inclination at that moment was to leap out of her chair and fasten her hands on the throat of the man who had made her a fortune and made her a star and forcefully shake the truth out of him. The very image almost made her giggle, so she concentrated on the margarita again. Most likely, the unflappable Jake Farrow would merely brush her aside, rebalance the Stetson on his knee and finish his drink without once blinking. No, there was no point in pushing him. He would sit there with lazy eyes moving around the room, appearing to notice nothing and cataloging everything in the minutest detail, wheels turning in his mind while he cogitated the kindest way to break it to her. . . .

Then his gaze wandered briefly to her, he took another sip of his drink, and he murmured, "Smile pretty, peaches. The vultures are descending."

Mallory looked up and straight into the sweetly smiling face of Evelyn Bouchard. "Well, well, well," the woman said brightly, quick eyes going first from Jake to Mallory without ever missing a beat in the breadth of her smile or the airiness of her dialogue. "Hollywood's latest girl genius and her agent in conference. Could this possibly be the first hint of another multimillion-dollar deal in the offing?"

Bouchard, like Jake, was another classic example of the Hollywood syndrome: no one was what he appeared to be. Evelyn Bouchard had the looks of a twenty-year-old college cheerleader — long blond braid, fresh-scrubbed face, preppy skirt and loafers. Her shirt had an alligator on the pocket. Her smile was genuine and her eyes twinkled a lot; her directness was so disarming that she could convince anyone that she was his best friend within five minutes. She was also the most vicious trade columnist in the business.

This was not Mallory's first encounter with Bouchard. Their paths crossed occasionally but never before had Mallory been the recipient of Bouchard's direct attention. Mallory had always assumed that she was too dull for the stuff Bouchard columns were made of. Now she began to wonder if the woman, genius that she was, had only been playing out the line with Mallory, waiting for the right moment to reel her in.

Mallory smiled rather distantly, waiting for Jake to rescue her. He did not. Evelyn laughed, a sweet, self-effacing sound, and glanced at Jake. "Oh-oh, looks like I've tripped right over one of those top secret things I'm constantly being warned to keep my mouth shut about. Don't worry, I'm not in the mood for letting any cats out of any bags today." She lifted her glass toward the sunny view from the opposite window. "In fact, on a day like this I'm not in the mood for much of anything. Isn't it funny how we live 365 days a year in a state known for its sunshine, and the first time we get a real glimpse of what the sky looks like without all that nasty smog we all go a little crazy. It makes you want to run out and capture some of that color in a jar, doesn't it?"

Mallory couldn't help smiling at that—she felt the same way. She was beginning to wonder if they shouldn't ask the woman to join them, rather than have her stand there holding her glass while engaging in what appeared to be no more than a friendly conversation. "When I was little," Evelyn continued, turning pleasant gray-green eyes on Mallory, "we used to catch lightning bugs in Mason jars on summer evenings.... Did you ever do that? You're from Mississippi, aren't you?"

Mallory was making a monumental effort to overcome her natural aversion to newspaper people. It was a phobia, pure and simple, a leftover from the past, like her paranoia and her insecurity, that surely had no place in her present life. Was this Jake's silent signal that it was time she let go of mean-

ingless fears and faced the fact nothing could
threaten her now? Mallory was trying.

"Of course," Mallory replied, forcing a warm
smile. "Then my brothers would sneak the jars in
the house under their shirts and put them on the
dresser after they were supposed to be in bed. The
whole room would light up. Are Southern kids the
only ones who do that?"

"Goodness, yes." Evelyn laughed. "Other kids are
too busy playing stickball in the streets and lifting
water pistols from the five-and-dime to learn the
finer cultural points of growing up. How many
brothers do you have?"

If there was a warning look from Jake, Mallory
missed it. "Two," she replied. "Where are you
from?"

"South Boston, Virginia."

"I didn't know that." Mallory's surprise and delight
were genuine. "One of my brothers lives there now."

Evelyn's pleasure couldn't have been feigned. She
rested her hand on the back of Mallory's chair and
prepared to settle in for a cozy little chat. "Really? I
still have family there. What's his name?"

This time Mallory caught Jake's bland but richly
meaningful look. He sipped his drink and said not a
word, but Mallory decided to ignore him. After all,
this was certainly better than sitting in ominous silence waiting for him to break the bad news. What
difference could it possibly make if this woman
knew her brother's name? She told her.

"What does he do there?" Evelyn seemed genu-
inely interested.

Mallory told her that too, and she was aware of a change gradually making itself known in her that had begun with coffee by the pool, was somehow related to the touch of a stranger with forward-tumbling brown hair and appreciation in his eyes and was now culminating in an uninhibited conversation with a woman Mallory would have, at another time, frozen dead. Maybe Jeannine was right. Maybe she should change her image, start coming out more. After all, what was she afraid of?

"I'll ask my aunt if she knows him," Evelyn was saying. Her expression was warm. "You know, we've met so many times, but we've never really talked before. I mean, here you are the biggest phenomenon in the business and I don't know the first thing about you." She smiled. "Is that deliberate?"

Subtly the conversation had shifted from girl talk to interview. Not unaware of it, Mallory thought she could handle it. It was even kind of fun. "Hardly," she said, laughing. "There's just not very much to know."

"*Everybody* has some story to tell," Evelyn reminded her gaily. "And secretive people usually have the most interesting stories of all."

Now Mallory was becoming uncomfortable. It was simply not that easy to cut the ties that bound her to a nightmare. Newspapers weren't the problem; Mallory knew that. They were only symbolic of something worse.... In retrospect, the most unbearable part about the hell she had endured seemed to be seeing her picture splashed all over the front page of Mississippi newspapers and her story put into words for thousands of strangers to read . . . making it real somehow, making it immortal. Mallory knew her reaction was irrational—reporters did not make the news, but only wrote it—yet she simply did not want to be the subject of another story, not ever again. She had a right to protect her privacy, whatever her reasons.

She fingered the stem of her glass and kept her smile in place, though she could no longer meet the woman's eyes. Silently she telegraphed Jake to rescue her. "Not secretive," she assured the other woman quickly, "just boring."

"Oh, I really doubt that," Evelyn responded, and Mallory knew that she was being privileged to witness the famous Bouchard technique at work. She also knew she would have been much happier watching it from a distance. "I for one think your story is fascinating. I mean, to have reached such a pinnacle of success in such a short time—what's it been, four years?"

"Five," Mallory corrected, wincing automatically. She could sense the self-satisfied smile that Evelyn was too much the professional to let show. She had Mallory in her net and could take her time bringing her in.

"Well, how in the world did it all begin?" That was no mystery. It was common knowledge how Jake had received an express package from an unknown writer who was too unschooled to know that successful Hollywood agents did not read unsolicited scripts. The package had accidentally gotten past his secretary, and he had opened it before noticing the error. Being in a particularly good mood that day, he had started to read it. . . .

Unconsciously Mallory lifted her shoulders. "All the stars in the right places, I suppose." This was not what the woman wanted. She was digging for larger treasures, and Mallory began to experience a mild panic.

"Isn't it amazing the way these things happen sometimes?" Evelyn's voice was easy and well paced, almost mesmerizing her victim into confidence. "Some of the biggest success stories in history seem almost capricious—everything coming together in the strangest way at the most absurd moment." She laughed. "I used to feel that way about my ex-husband. I mean, our entire romance was too unlikely to be believed. One accident right after the other kept throwing us together until we had the biggest accident of all and got married. . . ." She stopped and looked at Mallory, eyes widening in amusement. Mallory suddenly knew exactly what the woman was digging for. "Why, I don't even know if you're married. Good heavens, and I thought I knew the marital status of at least everyone within fifty miles of this town!"

Mallory's hand tightened on her glass in a quick, convulsive motion; she felt a coldness in her cheeks. For just a second the air-conditioned restaurant and the draining heat from her limbs gave way to a suffocating July afternoon in a still Mississippi town, motes of sunlight drifting through a dusty windowpane, the steady tick-tick of a clock in the background and air that was thick with the silent helplessness of terror.... With a jerk, Mallory forced herself back to the present, a friend on one side of her and an enemy on the other, and she answered much too swiftly, "No. I'm not married."

Mallory did not have to look up to know that she had just given Evelyn Bouchard a piece of bait she was not about to let go. Again, Evelyn was too much a master to let it show. She merely laughed and said, "Now that I can't believe! *Everyone* in this town has been married at least twice."

That was the opening, of course, for Mallory to deny having said she had never been married, which would lead to more and more questions, each one more subtle, each one more revealing.... *Damn it, Jake,* Mallory thought in a mixture of anger and despair, her hand tightening even more on her glass. *Help.* Jake did not look up, and Mallory did not know what to do.

She was floundering far over her head, and no rescue was in sight. Mallory prepared herself for the worst.

Chapter Three

"EXCUSE ME, SIR, can I take your order now?"

Mallory had been dimly aware of the waiter hovering discreetly in the background, but the waiters at Marcetti's were so well trained they would stand for hours if necessary, waiting to be noticed. They *never* interrupted a conversation. Mallory's surprise at this breach of protocol was mitigated by an overwhelming relief, and she could have kissed the man's feet at that moment. She looked up in swift and silent gratitude... and met the soberly composed face of a man with fluffy brown hair and a mint-striped polo shirt. The man from the lobby.

Jake glanced at Mallory and she quickly unfolded her menu, almost upsetting her cocktail glass in the process. Though her eyes scanned the list of food, her mind was tumbling in confusion.... Why did she feel that peculiar disappointment to see him standing there in polite deference with an order pad and pen in his hand, a waiter? Why was there a twinge of embarrassment? It was all quite ridiculous. She must have imagined the brief flare of attraction she had felt when he had freed her watch from her dress. Pushing these thoughts aside, Mallory realized the most important thing right now was his perfect sense of timing. Twice in less than half an hour he had rescued her from a potentially disastrous situation, and she was grateful.

Mallory's reaction when she recognized him did not escape Colt's notice. He was both amused and sorry for deceiving her, even so unintentionally. Now that he had met her — not formally, of course, but on a much more basic level — he was more fascinated by her than ever. And his protective instincts had come out in full force.

She was a pretty woman with the most unusual color of strawberry-blond hair he had ever seen. It was styled so simply and unpretentiously, swept back from her forehead and curving just under her chin. . . it reminded him of an advertisement for baby shampoo. Her eyes were wide and hazel, expressive and vulnerable. Her complexion was gardenia-delicate, completely devoid of any traces of the famous California tan. She was small-boned and fragile looking. Everything about her made him want to take care of her. And that, for today at least, was exactly what he was going to do.

Quickly, Mallory ordered the first thing she saw and then did not remember what it was. The minute she folded the menu, Evelyn turned to speak to her again.

"Will that be with shrimp sauce or garlic sauce, ma'am?" the waiter asked politely.

Startled, Mallory opened the menu again. This man had a beautifully modulated, strangely sensuous voice that commanded attention with no effort whatsoever. In fact, everything about him commanded attention, and she understood why she had not taken him for a waiter before. In some indiscernible way he just didn't look . . . or speak like a waiter. But Mallory did not want to think about how attractive he was. Still trying to remember what she had originally ordered, she answered, "Shrimp sauce."

Evelyn tried to start the conversation again and again he interrupted without giving her a chance, "What type of salad dressing would you like?"

Mallory caught the quick flash of annoyance in Evelyn's eyes, making it hard not to smile. "House," she replied, and this time ventured a closer study of the impudent, ill-trained waiter. His face was perfectly composed and his eyes friendly as he wrote down the full order. Yet Mallory felt as though a bond of conspiracy had been established between them. Was he doing this on purpose?

Evelyn waited a few seconds to be certain of no more interruptions, then began cheerfully, "Now, as you were saying—"

"Coffee with the meal or after?"

This time Mallory had to smile. "With," she replied, handing him the menu.

It would have been generous to say that the sixth sense that made Evelyn the best she was at what she did told her when to make a graceful retreat, but Mallory was certain nothing had saved her from the woman's relentless clutches but one interfering and very determined waiter. Evelyn glanced across the room, smiled at Mallory and said pleasantly, "I'd better get back to my table. My friends are waving at me. Let's talk again later, okay?"

"Of course," Mallory was able to reply politely. As she watched the woman go, Mallory's relief was only slightly dimmed by the dreadful assurance that Evelyn Bouchard had not gotten to where she was today by giving up quite so easily.

With far more efficiency than he had demonstrated earlier, the waiter took Jake's order and promised to be back with a carafe of wine in a moment. He flipped his pad closed, and just as Mallory was turning away from her cautious survey of Evelyn's retreat, he caught her eye. To Mallory's astonishment, he winked at her, then turned and was gone.

"A, Evelyn Bouchard is from North Boston, Massachusetts," drawled Jake, still keeping his eyes lazily fixed on the goings-on across the room. "B, if that woman ever caught fireflies in a Mason jar you can be damn sure she forgot to poke holes in the top and took great pleasure in watching the bugs smother to death one by one...if she didn't pull their wings off first. And C, you know as well as I do, peaches, that she dishes up little darlings like you for breakfast."

It took Mallory a moment to refocus her attention from the outrageous behavior of the waiter to the deadly significance of what Jake was saying. When she did, it hit her hard. A lump settled heavily in her stomach, and the warmth that had been in her cheeks only a moment ago abruptly deserted them again. Her voice was strained and she could not meet Jake's eyes as she said in a low voice, "Do you think she knows about Larry?"

She could feel Jake's gaze rest upon her. His reassuring glance backed up the quiet confidence in his tone. "Nobody knows about that, honey, except the people you want to know," he said gently.

Mallory's stricken eyes were a reflection of the emotional turmoil she was trying very hard to conquer. Her voice was a little unsteady. "Then why did she pick on me? She must smell a story somewhere. Why did she ask about my marriage? Oh, Jake, why didn't you stop her? How could you let me go on talking to her?"

"Because, peaches," he drawled easily, "I just love watching you make an ass of yourself. Rowntree Productions wants the script. At our price," he said without a change in inflection or tone, not missing a beat.

Mallory's mind was working rapidly and in flashes on three different levels, each of them of equal significance. Part of her was shying away from the remembered horror of five years ago and trying to brace herself for the possibilities of a renewed nightmare, which the encounter with Bouchard had suggested. Another part was almost absently looking for the waiter who had rescued her, as though his presence in itself were a talisman. He had *winked* at her. He had known exactly what he was doing with Evelyn. Like a knight on a white charger he had sallied forth to rescue the lady in distress, and having completed that task, he disappeared casually into the sunset. Part of her, perhaps a very large part, was thinking about him and wondering about him with a secret contentment, and only a small part of her attention was directed at Jake, at what he was saying and why she had been summoned here. It took a long time for the shock of his words to sink in.

Mallory stared at Jake in frozen-faced incomprehension, unable to believe what she thought she had heard. After all this anxiety, all the terrible possibilities, how could he utter the pronouncement in such a flat, matter-of-fact tone and how could she almost miss it? Had he said they *wanted* it?

"You look like you could use this," the waiter said, pouring a generous amount of wine into her glass.

Mallory hardly noticed. "Did you say . . . ?" she faltered, wanting to make sure.

The waiter moved around to fill Jake's glass, and Jake lifted it to her in a toast. "Piece of cake, peaches," he responded.

Still cautious, Mallory inquired, "What is our price?"

"A quarter of a million."

The waiter disappeared.

Mallory had to let that sink in. The money was too much for her to comprehend; its meaning was lost on her. What struck her was that they wanted *Day of the Last* — her baby, her best. They wanted it, and they wanted it badly. The significance washed over her, as it always did. Someone was actually going to give her *money* for what was to her second nature, someone was going to pay her for the privilege of bringing her characters and her story to life. The thrill that coursed through Mallory from head to toe was so powerful it was almost sexual. They loved the script.

As if by magic the waiter appeared before her with two glasses and a bottle of champagne. "Congratulations." He grinned and the bottle opened with a muted pop. "On the house."

Mallory laughed out loud and lifted her brimming glass first to him, then to Jake. For a moment her dancing eyes met the warmly crinkling ones of a single innocuous waiter and held. In that moment the joy of her triumph was only a shadow to the swift bubble of pleasure that burst through her. She did not stop to analyze why. She did not remark to herself how silly it was. She was a child unquestioningly accepting a gift. An attractive man smiled at her and appreciation sparkled in her eyes and she was on top of the world.

The interlude was so brief that not even Jake noticed. Then the waiter clicked his heels together smartly, gave her a dramatically exaggerated bow and left them. Mallory laughed again, fully and delightedly. It felt as if it was the first time she had laughed in a long time.

When she met Jake's eyes again she was a little flustered. "That was nice," she managed after a moment, gesturing to the champagne. *Can this be you, Mallory Evans, flirting with a waiter,* she wondered. *Wouldn't Jeannine love to see you now!* But the thought only made her feel like laughing again, the encounter leaving her warm all over. It was good. However ridiculous the interchange between her and a nameless waiter was, it was good.

The glow in Jake's eyes grew warm with appreciation as he studied her; he touched his glass to hers. "To the best in the business."

Mallory returned the toast with a quiet, ecstatic gratitude that needed no words. Jake knew.

"Well, you certainly look a lot better than the first time I was here," the waiter said cheerfully as he set their salads on the table. "A quarter-of-a-million-dollar deal will do that every time, I suppose." Mallory laughed, enjoying the personal nature of his smile. "When will the latest creation of the Mallory Evans genius flash upon the silver screen?"

"Oh, a year or two yet," Mallory assured him, eyes still sparkling. "These things take time." She was acting as though this was the first time she had received adulation from an unknown fan. . . . It felt like the first time. Mallory did not get out very much—she had very limited contact with what Jake loved to call her "adoring public"—but she should by now have been used to the surprised widening of the eyes and the admiring tone that accompanied, "So *you're* Mallory Evans. . . ." Perhaps she would never get used to it. Or perhaps there was something about this man that made his response seem special. Something more than an admiring fan's.

"Do they ever," he agreed, the tiny lines next to his eyes crinkling endearingly. "The question is, can we wait?"

"No," she returned laughingly, "the question is, can *I*?" It was just silly conversation, the same kind she would conduct with her hairdresser or a shop clerk if she were in a particularly good mood. Nothing of importance had passed between them, but he'd made the situation seem meaningful. Personal. It was in the way he looked at her, she was sure—not offensive, but certainly not deferential. Mallory realized with a small jolt that was not entirely unpleasant that they had both felt the same attraction.

"If I can make it, so can you," he assured her with another wink that was almost too quick and too subtle to be perceptible.

No, Mallory decided as she watched him leave, he was only an extraordinarily good waiter. He had mastered the art of dealing with the public and that was the first prerequisite in a profession such as his. He made everyone feel unique, the goal for all that effort being nothing more than a large tip. After all, no one in Hollywood was what he seemed. Not Jake, not Evelyn Bouchard, not a dynamic and extremely personable waiter who made Mallory feel as though she were the most attractive and interesting woman in the room.

Still. . . there was something about him that went beyond his performance of his duties, and that was what both puzzled and fascinated Mallory. He simply didn't belong here. The waiters at Marcetti's, like most other restaurants in Los Angeles, were all young—college age or slightly older. They were aspiring actors or out-of-work actors who fought for the chance to linger on the fringe near the famous and powerful. In the exclusive restaurants of New York City a man could make a career out of serving tables; in L.A. accruing tips of up to five hundred dollars a day was simply something one did while Waiting to Be Discovered.

But this man did not fall into that category. He was too old, for one thing, in his early to mid-thirties. And too confident, too casual. Though the behavior of the other waiters was by no means for-mal, they were all poignantly aware of the line of other fame-and-opportunity seekers forming behind them to ever do anything so brash as offending a customer like Evelyn Bouchard or ordering champagne on the house without permission. No, this man definitely did not fit into the mold. Everything about him proclaimed loudly and without reservation that he did not belong here.

Besides, there was still the annoying little suspicion that she should have known this man. When Mallory had first encountered him in the lobby she'd been struck by something familiar about him. The shape of his face, the unruly cut of his hair, the crinkling lines at the outer corners of his eyes.... Maybe he was a bit actor filling in between parts, she decided with a mental shrug. Actually it really didn't matter because whoever he was and whatever he was doing here he had contributed largely to making her day. He had gotten her to enjoy an innocent flirtation with a stranger, and that, when Mallory took time to think about it, would surprise her. Mallory Evans did not even speak to strangers, much less flirt with them. The changes were coming, slowly and subtly. She was trying to learn how to relax. She had even tackled and almost survived an interview with the most notorious columnist in the business. And for the first time in recent memory Mallory had let herself respond to the attentions of a man—never mind who the man was, or how lighthearted his attentions were. For another person those simple accomplishments would have been silly, even laughable. For Mallory, they were a milestone. Maybe she was finally ready to do something about her life.

The salad platters were removed, the main course served. Mallory was almost too embarrassed to meet the waiter's eyes — as though she had been having obscene fantasies about him behind his back — but he did not give her a chance to retreat into the safety of her shell. He bent close to her, though surely no closer than was necessary in the course of pouring her coffee. "The Dragon Lady is now on her third cup of coffee," he murmured. "I think she's lying in wait for you."

Mallory shot him a brief, grateful glance, and had the presence of mind to keep her eyes from wandering in the direction of Evelyn Bouchard's table. The smile he gave her in return was gentle and quietly encouraging. Absurd as it seemed, Mallory was suddenly convinced that he understood all the undercurrents between a ruthless reporter and a reluctant interviewee, and all the reasons for them. She was attributing to him perception and sensitivity beyond the depths of human ability and wisdom outside the range of logic, but that didn't matter. It was simply one of those rare and unexpected moments of human communication — a flash of empathy as warm as a handshake, a bracing look as quick as a wink. It was like finding a friend in the midst of an empty sea, and Mallory was elated. It didn't matter if it was all superficial and illusionary. It didn't matter if it was no more than a trick of the trade because it worked. She felt strong and protected, cared about and courageous, all from no more than a smile. The man certainly knew his business.

Through the entrée, which was delicious despite the fact that Mallory still did not know what it was, she luxuriously basked in the glow of success. She paid scant attention to the desultory trade talk Jake made. Instead, she grew strong in the certainty of her own triumph and heady with daring glimpses into the future she allowed herself. She had done it. Again. The one and only most important project of her life. Everything was coming together today like magic; she was on a roll. Changes were happening and all the signals seemed to indicate they were good ones. Nothing could go wrong.

Then Jake poured the last of the champagne, leaned back in his chair and gave her a slow, satisfied smile. Not once in the course of the meal had the Stetson been dislodged from his knee. "Well, peaches, my lovely, do we sign?"

It was a formality, nothing more. Never had Mallory refused his advice or even mildly questioned his judgment; in return, Jake never asked for praise. That was their agreement. She created the product and he created the demand and both profited hugely. Before today, Mallory had never even considered reading a contract.

She took a deep breath. *Change your image? All right, Mallory, my girl, here's your chance....* Calmly, she said, "No."

Only the very slightest quirk of an eyebrow—too small to be noticed by anyone who did not know Jake's deadpan expression as well as Mallory—was his reaction. He waited.

And Mallory held his gaze. "I won't take a quarter of a million." Jake said nothing. "I'll take two hundred thousand, with final cut. . .and I want to choose my own director."

Not until she actually heard her own words echoing did Mallory believe she had really had the courage to say them. She had known from the moment she finished the script that she wanted to see this one through to the end, that she had to have her hand in every phase of its production, that she would trust no one else to fulfill the potential of her project. Not until this very moment had she realized how badly she wanted that control. Only now could she admit to herself how much of what she was had gone into the making of that screenplay, how much love and pain and personal energy had been taken from her and woven into its pages.

Mallory had made her fame writing fantasy. But *Day of the Last* was at the opposite end of the spectrum—a hard-hitting, brutally realistic look at the truth behind the Hollywood illusion, the unvarnished and sometimes sordid stories that lay just beneath the veneer of the industry's most polished dreamweavers. Just as Mallory herself found the fragility of dreams like happiness, love and security too frightening to hold on to, the script chronicled how easily and unfairly those very dreams could be snatched away.

It was a story of bitter compromise, senseless destruction and the ruthless ambition that drove people to success, and of the desperate lengths to which they were driven to hold on to it—only to discover that all they had ever held was an illusion. It was the story of the courageous struggle between principles and practicality, between honor and survival. It was truth in a way that was painful for Mallory to write, but it was a story that had to be told.

And it had to be told in exactly the right way. That was why Mallory could not abandon it now. She would see it to completion, her loving hand would guide it every step of the way; she would see it become the best it could be.

"That's all," Jake said flatly. Not one muscle of his face twitched, not an eyelash moved.

Mallory swallowed hard and nodded. She also knew what she was risking. Final cut—the right to approve the final edited version of the film—was not given to just anyone. And as far as a studio's allowing the screenwriter her choice of director. . . . That may not have been completely unheard of, but it was not, on the other hand, exactly something that was done every day. How much was she in demand? How badly did they want her script? If they called her bluff what would she do—abandon the project? She could lose it all.

"You didn't like the way the last three were directed?" The question was redundant. He would not have taken the trouble to argue with her if he thought there was a chance of giving her what she wanted. Jake was offering her an opportunity to back out.

Mallory couldn't believe what she was doing. Her throat was dry and her stomach was queasy, and this was only Jake. How would she ever pull it off in front of a boardroom of studio executives? "Nothing major," she admitted, and was surprised at how even her voice sounded. "But this is different, Jake." A statement, not a plea for understanding. "It's important. It has to be done right."

She could see his mind whirling like the wheels of a computer. Behind those blank eyes, Jake was reviewing the probabilities, amassing figures, assessing the odds, plotting strategy. But the bottom line was that what Mallory wanted, Mallory got, if there was any way the forces of heaven, hell or Jake Farrow could arrange it.

At last he lifted the hat from his knee with a slow and deliberate movement, stretched his long legs out before him and took his time about arranging the Stetson on his head. Every muscle in Mallory's body stiffened as he fastened watery blue eyes on her. "You could blow it, peaches," was all he said.

Mallory nodded. Her throat was too tight for a reply.

He got up from the table. "Catch you later, little one. I've got appointments to keep."

Incredulously, she turned in her chair to watch him as he walked away, and all she could think of to say was, "You're leaving me with the check!"

Jake grinned and tipped his hat to her. "You can afford it, sweetheart."

When he was gone Mallory simply sat there, letting the significance of what she had done wash over her. She felt a little shaky, somewhat numb and totally in awe of herself. Was she crazy? She couldn't go up against a major studio and demand rights that even those who had been in the business for years were sometimes denied. Not even Jake could sell anyone on the idea that she was qualified to choose the director — how would she begin to judge?

And what *was* Jake going to do? If Rowntree turned down her offer, would he take the script to another studio? And if they turned it down.... Oh, God, Mallory thought in one terrible moment of sickening despair, she was being greedy. She should have been grateful for the huge offer Jake had been able to negotiate. This was the biggest deal of her life, and she was going to blow it with outrageous demands that would be sure to label her as a prima donna in the business and make every producer in town wary of dealing with her. She wondered if it was possible to catch Jake before he left the parking lot.

But she made herself sit still and slowly finish her champagne. All right, it was a big risk, but if she could pull it off it would be the most important move Mallory had ever made. And it was worth the risk. To bring her story to life in the way she had intended when she wrote it. Her demand was necessary for both the integrity of the film and her own artistic satisfaction. She could make of this film everything it was meant to be, and no one else could. There was no choice — any sensible producer could see that. Who else could read between the lines, who else could interpret every movement and inflection of tone, know exactly what camera shot and what background setting would deliver most effectively the unspoken theme Mallory had conceived? Her demands were not outrageous at all. She had to do it.

She was so wrapped up in her own thoughts that she jumped at the sound of the voice. "I take it your meeting went well." Evelyn Bouchard slid into the seat Jake had just vacated.

This was all Mallory needed. She had pushed her luck with Bouchard earlier and Mallory had too much on her mind to deal with the woman now. She smiled her best coolly disinterested smile and said, "No comment."

Evelyn laughed lightly. "Come on, Mallory, no games, okay? I'm not interested in what Jake Farrow had to tell his most successful client over lunch. . . I know about Rowntree and I know about the quarter of a mil. Small potatoes."

Mallory effectively disguised her astonishment at that announcement while guarding herself against the disarmingly open smile that lightened Evelyn's childlike gaze. She looked around futilely for the waiter. Where was he when she needed him?

Evelyn rested one arm casually across the back of the chair as she leaned forward slightly, encouraging confidence. Her expression was still friendly and innocent, but her bright green eyes reminded Mallory of those of a cat outside a mousehole. Mallory was too flustered and distracted to deal with this now. She had too much of more importance on her mind. Why in the world had the woman singled her out—now, of all times?

"No, I'm not in the mood for business today," continued Evelyn easily. "Let someone else get the scoop. I'd really like to get to know you better, Mallory. You keep so much to yourself—a regular mystery lady! No one ever sees you hanging on the arm of the latest heartthrob at the poshest parties, no studio bashes, no intimate tête-à-têtes. . . . Why, you don't even attend your own premieres! Now you've got to admit, that's bound to make a person just the least little bit curious."

"I see my films at private screenings. I don't have to attend premieres." She could have bitten her tongue. Why was she encouraging this viper?

Evelyn looked neither encouraged nor discouraged, merely interested. "But you were up for an Academy Award last year and you didn't even go to the ceremonies. Are you shy?" she teased.

"Yes," Mallory said shortly. "I'm shy. And I really don't have time for an interview right now, Miss Bouchard."

Then, blessedly, the waiter appeared with the check. Perfect timing, as always.

Evelyn laughed endearingly. "Goodness, is my reputation that bad? This isn't an interview—just natural curiosity. You know," she said, her voice lowering reflectively, her expression becoming wistful, "it's always sad to see people get on the defensive the minute they see me coming. It makes for a very lonely profession. You don't have to be that way with me."

Mallory reached for her purse while the waiter stood politely by, a patient sentinel who appeared and disappeared according to her needs. She tried to smile at the woman. Mallory did not like to be rude. "I'm sorry, Miss Bouchard—"

"Evelyn, please."

"Evelyn," corrected Mallory automatically, taking out her wallet. "It's just that it's been a busy day and about to get busier."

"I understand." Evelyn smilingly waved the excuse away and Mallory almost, for one brief moment, liked her again. Mallory Evans was very gullible. "It can't be easy, keeping up a schedule like yours. I can't tell you how I admire you. I mean, marching right into Hollywood and taking the business by storm like you did—and smack on top of a divorce too. Most women would have. . . ."

But Mallory heard nothing else. The credit card slipped from her fingers and a jerky motion of her hand almost knocked her purse off the table. The waiter caught it a second before the contents scattered all over the floor. Evelyn Bouchard knew.

Mallory was aware that Evelyn had stopped speaking and was looking at her peculiarly. "That is the way it happened, isn't it?" Her manner was light and her smile friendly. "I mean, don't let me fictionalize your life. It's only that the whole story fascinates me. I keep thinking that if I study women like you long enough I might have a success story of my own to tell one day that's equally spectacular." Then her face softened in pretended chagrin. "Am I being a pest?"

Mallory couldn't respond. She couldn't even move. She felt like a butterfly stretched out between two pins on a slab of Styrofoam. Her mind was spinning back, back into an abyss where dark terror still lurked. . . .

She could feel the rounded tube of metal pressing

into her neck. After a while the gun barrel had grown warm with her heat and slippery with her perspiration and seemed to throb in time with her own pulse, becoming part of her. The stale, decaying odor of alcohol and sweat surrounded her, seeping from his pores into hers and blending into every gasping breath until it seemed the scent was coming from the walls, the carpet, every fiber in the house and permeating her very being. It had taken three years before Mallory could even stay in the same room where alcoholic beverages were being served, the power of that scent was so pervasive. There was a green-bottle fly trapped against the windowpane, fluttering its wings, but no matter how hard it flung itself against the glass, no matter how furiously it beat its wings, it could not escape. Above it all, was the ticking of a clock, as strong and as steady as the sound of Mallory's own heartbeat, assuring her that time did indeed move forward, that there was an end to this somewhere up ahead, and as long as she could concentrate on the tick of that clock. . . .

Colt had seen the beginning of the interchange from across the room. Out of concern he gradually worked his way over to Mallory's table. He saw her cheeks pale, her eyes darken, and the drawn look around her lips that told him she was repressing some emotion he could not begin to imagine. She was deep in her own dark thoughts now, unaware of him or Bouchard or anything else that was going on around her.

He wished he knew what had put that expression of trapped terror on her face, and he wished he could do something to make it go away and never return. But he did know that whatever it was that was upsetting Mallory was related to Evelyn Bouchard, and that he *could* do something about.

"I think that's a reasonable assumption," Colt said politely, directing eyes that were much less than polite on Evelyn, "since Miss Evans told you not three minutes ago that she wasn't giving interviews."

The strong, smooth male voice snapped Mallory back to the present, and she turned slow and mutely grateful eyes to her cavalier. She saw a response of kindness, confidence and satisfaction mixed in his. Someone was on her side. Things didn't seem so bad anymore.

For perhaps the first time in her life, Evelyn Bouchard was speechless. In the wake of the welcome interruption, Mallory took up the pen that accompanied the check and signed her name on the bottom with a hand that was hardly shaking at all.

Evelyn cleared her throat slightly and rose with a graceful, unhurried movement. "We'll talk another time, Mallory," she said pleasantly, the promise loaded with venom. "Have a good day now."

"You too, you bitch," murmured the waiter under his breath, almost causing Mallory to choke on an unexpected bubble of slightly hysterical laughter. She quickly controlled herself with a sip of ice water. When she looked up into the waiter's eyes with relief and amusement brimming in hers he was smiling warmly at her. "You can't let people like that intimidate you," he advised. "She makes her living off other people's blood, which in any honorable person's book entitles her to no respect at all. You just remember that."

Mallory released a long breath of pent-up anxiety and calming resolution. "You're right. Thank you. . . ." She quickly turned the check over and saw the waiter's name was scrawled at the bottom — Mark. She looked up at him. "But you shouldn't have done that. You were risking your job."

The laugh lines around his eyes crinkled as he took the tray with the check and her credit card. "Wrong. I was risking *Mark*'s job. I'm just subbing for a friend. My name is Colt. Colt Stanford."

The twinkle in his eyes lingered like an embrace as he left her, and that only added to Mallory's confusion. What an upside-down day it had been. From tragedy to victory, from nightmare to gaiety. As she walked out into the sun-splashed afternoon she was feeling like a schoolgirl again. Add schizophrenia to paranoia, she thought wryly, a thirty-one-year-old woman whose moods bounce back and forth like a tennis ball all because of a good-looking waiter's smile.

Suddenly Mallory stopped short as it struck her. Colt Stanford. She half turned back toward the restaurant in open-mouthed amazement. She *knew* he looked familiar. . . .

During the drive back home she forgot about Evelyn Bouchard and Rowntree and mammoth career decisions; she forgot about Jake and the script that was the most important thing in her life and not once did the figure $250,000 cross her mind. She was thinking about Colt Stanford, and shaking her head in wonder with each renewed thrill of excitement.

In the land of illusion, nothing was ever quite what it seemed.

Chapter Four

"WELL, IF I HAD KNOWN I would have brought champagne." Jeannine Chase swooped down upon the sofa with much fluttering of her paisley caftan and clanking of jewelry, kicked off her sandals and swung her feet over the back of the couch. "Sounds like you had quite a day."

Mallory's laugh was a mixture of dazed exhaustion and wondering contentment. "I'll say! And forget the champagne—one more drop today and I'll float away." She spoke over the butcher-block divider where she was chopping vegetables for what Jeannine assured her was an absolutely infallible recipe for mu-shu pork. Once a week they got together for another experimental no-fail recipe, left a mess in the kitchen for Mrs. Horscht to clean up and usually ended up eating out. Mallory held up an unlikely-looking specimen with an expression of cautious distaste, and inquired, "Is this gingerroot, do you think?"

"Either that or rutabaga. I hate it when they put the signs in the produce department so close together you can't tell one vegetable from another. I can't believe you actually turned down a quarter of a million dollars." Jeannine lowered dramatically mascaraed lashes in a gesture of wistful imagining. "And you stood up to Jake Farrow, demanding your rights. . . ."

"I stand up to Jake a lot," Mallory protested, thought about it briefly, then capitulated. "Well, at least I would, if he ever gave me anything to stand up to him about. I didn't demand my rights, exactly. . . ."

"And you didn't even run and hide in the bathroom when you saw Evelyn Bouchard coming," continued Jeannine in exaggerated awe. "You survived a battle with Attila the Hun of show business. Mallory, babe, there's hope for you yet."

Mallory carefully followed the instructions for dicing what she only hoped was gingerroot, shrugging as she divided her attention between the recipe and the knife in her hand. "I don't know about surviving. More like being rescued at the last moment from a fate worse than death."

Jeannine sat up with more jingling and fluttering, tucking her slim legs beneath her and propping her chin on crossed arms along the back of the sofa. "Ah, yes, the ever vigilant waiter in disguise. Who was he again?"

"Colt Stanford," Mallory replied, and devoted more concentrated attention to the food preparations. She was almost certain that what she had just dumped in the bowl of crisp bamboo shoots, carrots, bean sprouts and water chestnuts was not gingerroot. "You know, the director."

Jeannine shook her head. "Sorry, Mal, it's bad enough having to live in this squirrel cage without trying to keep up with every name that ever flashed across a screen. Doesn't ring a bell."

"Oh, you know him, all right," Mallory assured her, and briefly refreshed her friend's memory.

Mallory had carefully followed the entire fiasco in the papers as it had happened five years ago, partly because, film buff that she was, she had always admired Stanford's work, partly because of a sense of horror that such a thing could happen to any member of their profession. Brilliant beyond his time, Stanford had been part of the tide of young and innovative creative geniuses that had revolutionized the industry in the fantasy wave of the late seventies. He had been among the first to employ special effects on a broad basis and had pioneered the use of Dolby NR on the sound track. A Stanford film was a larger-than-life experience. One not only saw the scene he created but was transported into it, becoming a part of the setting, the story, every emotion of every character on the screen. But technical expertise was only part of his magic. Actors who had worked with him raved about him. He knew the secrets of motivation and manipulation; he knew how to get exactly what he wanted from all the performers. He worked some mysterious sorcery that involved everyone on the set in his world of fantasy and they did more than give a convincing performance—they lived it. He was, indeed, a legend in his own time.

Then it all toppled down on him. The exact details were never clear because there were many conflicting stories. Colt was signed to direct a film with a history-making budget, one that had been years coming to production and had been surrounded by controversy every step of the way. It was not a film designed for commercial success, but rather one of those stories that simply needed to be told—thus the surprise and the outrage in the industry when it was awarded such a high budget. A group of dedicated artists were gathered under Colt's direction to do the film, and the production was under way. Then, in the middle of the project, Colt Stanford was dismissed and another director was assigned.

At that point the stories diverged. Some said Colt, who was notorious for refusing to work with certain artists—most notably those who considered their party time more important than being prepared for early-morning calls—had attempted to fire one or more of the major actors. Some said a huge part of the exorbitant budget had gone directly into Stanford's pocket. Others said that Colt was challenged on his directorial expertise by the producer and, like a prima donna, walked off the set. Other accounts—and Mallory, who had studied Stanford's career so closely, found these the most credible—related that there had been an argument in midproduction over changing the film from its original concept to something more commercial. Colt, in challenging the decision, had made them choose between him and the film. They had chosen the film.

It was released as a commercial venture, and bombed at the box office. Even Mallory had been able to tell immediately that the problem with the film was the absence of Colt Stanford's directing, and the popularization of a concept that, had it been produced as originally intended, would have been powerful. But the backers needed a scapegoat, and Colt Stanford filled the part nicely. Investors lost a fortune, the production company lost esteem, it was an embarrassing situation for all concerned. The industry shunned Colt Stanford like the plague. No one would touch him after that.

"So now he's waiting tables at Marcetti's," mused Jeannine thoughtfully, then she flashed Mallory a grin. "Somehow that story sounds familiar to me."

Mallory smiled. Jeannine prided herself on being Mallory's first sounding board for every new story idea, and of course she recognized a similarity between the story of Colt Stanford and *Day of the Last*.

"I suppose, since it was such a famous case, Stanford's story must have been in the back of my mind while I was writing the script," Mallory admitted. "That, and a dozen other stories like it."

"Poor Mr. Stanford," Jeannine observed quietly.

Mallory nodded soberly, brushing her hands across the front of her oversize chef's apron. "It just makes you realize how fragile this whole business is—how transitory. One day you're on top and the next you're standing in the welfare line, and what can you do to prevent it? I mean, what can you really do?"

"Simple." Jeannine rose and stretched gracefully, winding her frizzy blond hair into a knot at the base of her neck for a moment before allowing it to tumble over her shoulders again. "CYA—cover your ass.

Something your friend Mr. Stanford apparently forgot to do."

"Okay, I fixed the vegetables, you do the pork." Mallory bent to retrieve a bright orange wok from the cabinet beneath the sink. It had been a Christmas gift from Jeannine, who blithely informed her that the only truly reliable sign that You Have Arrived was owning a wok. Usually, the very sight of it made Mallory smile, but tonight her features were creased with a preoccupied frown. "I don't know," she decided with a shrug. "That's part of it, I suppose, but it seems to me the best thing you can do to protect yourself is to stay in control. Just don't open yourself up for anything."

"There you go, kid. Give 'em an inch and they'll take your heart."

Mallory lifted an eyebrow. "Well, that's a switch. Isn't this the woman who is famous for her two-hour lectures on the Modernization of Mallory? Let's see, how does it go again...." She mimicked her friend's low-pitched, sensuously modulated voice. "Darling, you're twenty years behind the times. You've got to get out more, get in touch with the real world, find out what's *happening*. You can't keep yourself wrapped up in that papier-mâché world of yours forever, you know."

"What, are you kidding?" Jeannine kept her expression perfectly deadpan as she obligingly began to slice pork strips into the required bite-sized pieces. "You've got it made. No complications, no challenges, everything perfectly predictable. You sit around all day and grind out millions of dollars

worth of predictably successful scripts, stash away
money in predictably secure C.D.'s, have nicely conservative business luncheons with Jake, the outcome
of which, of course, is always utterly predictable
triumph. I repeat, you've got it made. No one is
ever going to see *your* face splashed all over the
front page of the *National Enquirer*. No one is ever
going to burst through your front door and sweep
you off to heights of passion—good heavens, that
would be much too disorderly. And no one will ever
find you sobbing into your pillow over a broken love
affair or pacing the floor at night because you just
blew a wad in Vegas and the mortgage is due. Oh,
no, you have things much too much under control
for something like that. Though why anyone would
want to be in control of a life as dull as yours, I can't
imagine."

Mallory stifled a giggle. "Dull, but relatively
secure."

Jeannine shook her head in subdued impatience
and dropped a handful of lightly floured pork into
the sizzling wok. "Nothing is all *that* secure, no matter how hard you try to make it. Okay, so for five
years you dug in and worked your little buns off and
I say, great going, good for you—but now you've
done it. You're a flaming success and it's party time.
Let go and relax a little."

Again Mallory laughed, although a bit dryly. "I
think I'd have a nervous breakdown if I even tried to
let go." The experiment beside the pool this morning had been just that, an experiment. Because
what had she done the moment she had a chance?

She had put herself up for the biggest project of her career, one that would demand more time and effort than even she was sure she was capable of. It was no use; she was hopelessly addicted to working. It was her great love affair with life.

"Really, Mallory, I don't see how you do it. I know you're an artist and artists are supposed to be eccentric, and dedication is all very fine and good, but there really should be a compromise somewhere. *Everyone* has to have some social life. Just think of what you're missing!"

"Oh, sure," replied Mallory airily, giving the golden pork in the wok a desultory shove with a wooden spoon. "Exposure to rape, burglary, social disease, extortion, kinky sex. . . ."

Jeannine fastened her bright, dramatic eyes upon her friend with a gentle understanding. "Are you really that afraid? After all this time?"

Mallory thought about that. Briefly, images that had flashed through her head under the expert grilling of Evelyn Bouchard recurred and were still. A room in a once tasteful upper-middle-class house, now all but devoid of furnishings, its carpet stained with liquor and cigarette burns, its walls scuffed from careless boots and dirty hands. A room that once had been echoing with emptiness and now grew smaller with each minute it imprisoned Mallory. A fly trapped in the dusty sunlight of a windowpane. A clock on the mantel that had been her only link to sanity during the endless ordeal, the hands of that clock that had moved so slowly, by inches and fractions of inches for the space of one woman's eternity.... Sometimes Mallory wondered if she had ever really escaped that dingy room and the horror that had imprisoned her there? Was she still being held hostage to her own fears?

Mallory thought about the absence of what Jeannine had euphemistically termed a "social life" and realized she had been thinking about that more and more lately. Mallory thought about how, on one recent rainy night, she had fantasized about going to some faraway town where nobody knew her, walking into a bar and picking up a man and spending a night of wild, uninhibited passion with him.... Then dressing the next morning, driving back home and resuming her work schedule without ever a word being exchanged. She also thought about how things never worked out quite that conveniently outside fantasy. Then she shrugged. "No, not afraid," she replied honestly. She gave a little grimace that was half amusement and half derision. "Just pressed for time."

Jeannine turned away with a sound of exasperation and began cutting more pork.

Mallory realized that she was probably something of a phenomenon. There had been no man since the nightmare with Larry, not even in the most casual sense of the word. Not a touch, not a kiss, not even a meaningful look. She had not even held a serious conversation with a member of the opposite sex other than Jake and, via long distance, her two brothers. For the first two years the trauma was so fresh and the relief so great Mallory had not wanted to be around anyone who might remotely represent a sexual threat. She reveled in her newfound freedom and found constant delight in the smallest details of life—furnishing her own place, fixing her own meals, choosing her own friends. And working. And being paid enormously for it. It was like being born again into a whole new world filled with magic and promise; the cresting of her unexpected success was a mind-boggling bonus. Those first years, trying to get used to it all, she had loved being alive too much to share the experience with anyone. . . or to risk any of what she had so recently come to claim as her own.

But yes, more recently, Mallory had begun to think about what she was missing. She had not been a virgin before Larry; she knew what it was like to be loved and caressed. Sometimes, briefly, she still hungered for a man's touch. Once in a while, in her innermost thoughts, Mallory even resented the life she had built for herself that kept her so well insulated from human contact. Yet those were only very morose, very down moments that did not last long. When she was honest with herself Mallory admitted she loved her life and wouldn't change one part of it. She had worked too long and too hard and paid too dearly for the contentment to risk it now. Quite simply, her life-style did not allow room for other people. She didn't need the hassle.

"I'm saving myself for Mr. Right. You know, the Big Romance That Will Change My Life," Mallory said flippantly.

"And other assorted fairy tales," Jeannine snorted, dumping the bowl of chopped vegetables on top of the pork, eliciting a sizzling sound and a gush of steam.

Mallory rescued a carrot. "I don't know," she protested, munching. "Hasn't my life been pretty much a fairy tale these past few years? Anything is possible in the land of glitter and make-believe, you know."

Jeannine gave her a shrewd, amused glance. "Flirting with a waiter, huh? Maybe you're right. . . anything is possible."

Mallory got a brief flash of smiling eyes and was surprised by a tingle of remembered excitement. Yes, she thought, maybe it was. . . . And she shrugged. "Good practice, anyway."

"For the day you finally get the courage to fling yourself before the first man who crosses your path and cry, 'Take me, I'm yours'?" Jeannine enacted the drama with a flourishing sleeve and a hand pressed across her forehead in an exaggerated gesture of abject surrender that made Mallory dissolve into giggles. "Say, kid—" Jeannine recovered her posture to poke curiously at the simmering mixture in the wok "—this might even turn out to be edible."

"Smells weird." Mallory poured two glasses of rice wine. . . sparingly, because it smelled weird too.

"It's supposed to."

Mallory handed Jeannine her wineglass and they wandered into the living room. "Do you think I can do it, Jeannine?"

Jeannine lifted her eyebrows as she curled her bare feet beneath her on the sofa. "Fling yourself in front of a strange man and offer your body shamelessly?"

But Mallory was serious. The slightly perplexed, vaguely preoccupied furrow of her brow gave her face a suddenly youthful, very vulnerable look. Her fingers absently tugged at the gold chain around her neck and she gazed unseeingly into the clear liquid in her glass. "Take the responsibility for this film. Choose the director, oversee the final cut. My God, I don't have any experience at all! Can I really do it?"

Jeannine knew and valued her friend too much to play the game. She sipped her wine. "Dear heart," she said frankly, "I haven't the faintest idea. What do you think?"

"I don't know," worried Mallory. "I know what has to be done—I know what I want—but whether I can do it right or not is another matter. I probably never should have mentioned it to Jake."

"Probably not."

"I could lose the whole deal."

"I guess you could."

"They'll never go for it."

"No, probably not."

"And if they did, I'd probably do all the wrong things and make a mess of it."

"Quite possibly."

Mallory looked up and grinned. "I did good, didn't I?"

Jeannine returned the grin with a lift of her glass. "Kid, you did terrific. Go for it."

Mallory clinked her glass to Jeannine's in an unspoken toast, sipped her wine and gasped.

"Hits the spot, doesn't it?" Jeannine grinned mischievously, and Mallory nodded, blinking watery eyes.

"Smooth," she choked, then abruptly jumped to her feet in alarm as the first hint of something gone wrong in the kitchen wafted through the air. "I thought you said it was impossible to burn food in a wok!"

The dinner was rescued just this side of scorched and put on a warming plate while Jeannine wrestled with a pancake batter that had a tendency to be a little stringy and Mallory tried to keep the sauce from thickening too fast.

"All kidding aside, Mal," Jeannine said when the crisis point of the pancake batter had passed and she was able to concentrate on conversation again. "Things are going great guns for you now. You're just hitting your stride, just starting to find out what you can do...and I don't think I can stand to sit back and watch you turn a once-in-a-lifetime, top-of-the-world experience into a scene out of *Pilgrim's Progress*. Do you have any idea what it does to me to sit here and watch you *wasting* it all? Do you have any idea how many women in this world—myself included—would fight to have your talent, your name, your money...." Jeannine was only beginning to get wound up on her favorite subject. "You're living in the most exciting city in the world, lady! You're paying taxes on all that golden California sunshine, you know. Why let it go to waste? You've got an eight-thousand-dollar pool and a thirty-thousand-dollar car, and they just sit there growing algae and rust, respectively." She dished up four pancakes with particular enthusiasm and Mallory made a great ceremony of pouring the sauce over each one. "Some of the most famous beaches in the world, Mal. The hottest nightlife, the most interesting people. . . and what do you do? You chain yourself to your typewriter from sunrise to sunset and go to bed at nine o'clock. Your idea of a hot weekend is catching *Love Boat* on Saturday nights." They carried their plates into the dining room. "I mean, it's really embarrassing. Here I am, best friends with a celebrity, and you're so damn boring I can't even gossip about you." Jeannine swept aside her voluminous sleeves, seated herself gracefully and folded her hands under her chin imploringly. "Won't you *please* let me take you out and reintroduce you to planet Earth?"

Mallory smiled in secret amusement. She was thinking how much she liked sleeping alone. That huge bed, the enormous room, all that space to do with as she pleased. Keeping the light on all night if she wished, sleeping in the middle of the bed or either side, using both pillows or none at all, stretching out from one corner to the other, not worrying about sharing her space with anyone. "Where would you take me?" she teased, while unfolding her napkin. "God knows, it would take a lot of dressing up to make me presentable."

"Well, that could be a problem," Jeannine admitted thoughtfully. "But, as we all know, only the rich can afford to be beautiful, and it just so happens I know the perfect place for you to start."

"A little boutique on Rodeo Drive?"

Jeannine winked. "Right."

The routine was so familiar it had become a joke between them, but for the first time Mallory didn't laugh. Maybe Jeannine had been nagging her too long, or maybe it was simply an idea whose time had come. If this deal came through—and that was a possibility so enormous in impact that she could not let herself completely absorb its significance— Mallory would need all the self-confidence she could get. A change of image definitely appeared to be in order. She might just take that next giant step after the Porsche and give her friend all the business she could handle.

But Mallory certainly wasn't going to rush into anything.

The mood shifted to somber as they each gave the dish before them the moment of respect—not entirely devoid of skepticism—it deserved. "It doesn't look exactly like it did in the last Chinese restaurant I was in," Mallory ventured.

Jeannine courageously waved away any doubts. "When was the last time you were in a Chinese restaurant?" she said disparagingly. She surveyed the shredded crepe, overdone vegetables and gooey sauce that was splattered over her plate with an impressively manufactured enthusiasm. "It looks delicious."

"It does smell better," Mallory admitted. Their eyes met in a moment of mutual decision before they lifted their forks in unison.

Their eyes widened with the first nauseating taste and held during the difficult process of swallowing.

There was no longer any question about the ingredient Jeannine had so innocently mistaken for ginger-root. For a prolonged moment there was only silence, then as one they gasped, "Rutabaga!" and rushed to the kitchen.

They were gulping glasses of water, wiping streaming eyes and trying not to choke on laughter when the phone rang. Mallory stumbled toward it, draining the last gulp from her water glass. Her voice was thick and hoarse with laughter when she picked up the receiver.

"Mallory?"

Her heart jumped and caught even before he identified himself. That voice, deep and masculine, but as soft as a caress. . . . How could she mistake that voice? Even the intimate use of her first name seemed somehow to be an identifying mark. Not Miss Evans. Mallory. Perhaps it was that signal, very subtly and very naturally moving the most casual of relationships onto a different level, that caused the swift pleasant warmth in her cheeks. Maybe it was simply the sound of his voice.

"It's Colt Stanford." He said it as an afterthought, as though he was perfectly aware she had recognized his voice. As though he thought she might have been expecting his call, which of course she most certainly was not. She had never expected to see or hear from him again. Why should she? Yet why was her heart beating so ridiculously fast?

"Y-yes." Mallory cleared her throat. "Hello."

"Hello, yourself." There was a low chuckle in his voice that communicated itself over the telephone like a charge of electricity. "You left in such a hurry this afternoon I didn't get a chance to talk to you. I wanted to make sure you were all right."

Mallory was aware that Jeannine had grown very still behind her. The whole world seemed to have grown suddenly still, waiting for Mallory Evans to respond to the first man who had approached her in five years.

Well, Mallory knew how to deal with the public. She knew how to discuss rewrites with men whose names were legends in the entertainment world. She knew how to demand an explanation of her tax statement. She knew how to gracefully fend off shop clerks and delivery boys who eagerly wanted to know whether Garth and Trista would ever find each other and return to Nestar. She could be polite but distant, aloof yet charming. She could handle it.

But there might have been just a little too much warmth in her voice as she replied, "That's kind of you. Thanks, I'm fine."

"I was worried about you." His voice was so smoothly modulated and perfectly pitched that Mallory was convinced for a moment that he truly was.

"Oh." Why did she feel as though she were glowing? Her eyes must surely have been sparkling. She cradled the phone close to her body with both hands and half turned from an alert Jeannine. Her own voice grew softer without her realizing it. "There was no need, really." And she gave a small self-conscious laugh. "All in all, I had a very nice lunch."

"Glad to hear it. I'm only sorry we didn't get a chance to talk more."

Mallory's heart was pounding again, and she didn't quite know how to respond. Part of her was wondering, was this man coming on to her? Very likely he was, she decided. Other realizations, equally surprising and equally clear, were flashing at her. She was sorry they hadn't had a chance to talk more too. She liked this man. Even if he had remained a nameless waiter Mallory would have liked him, but how many times would her path cross that of a man like Colt Stanford? She had admired his work for years, and now she actually had an opportunity to speak to him, to get to know him. What perfect timing, just as she was about to take on the responsibility of choosing her own director from the dozens of qualified professionals. . . .

"I also didn't get a chance to return your credit card," Colt was saying.

Mallory blinked, having a moment's difficulty in adjusting to the mundane nature of the conversation. That was not at all what she had been expecting him to say. "Oh, no." She kept the disappointment out of her voice very effectively. "I walked out and left it again, didn't I? I'm always doing that." At least now she knew the purpose of the phone call. Not a personal contact at all as he had made it seem at first, but merely a perfect professional doing his job. Why had she expected anything else? Mallory gave another little laugh, simply to make sure Colt knew she hadn't read anything into his previous conversation he had not meant to be there. "You didn't have to follow up on it personally. Most restaurants are used to me by now. If you'll leave it at the desk, the maître d' will mail it to me in the morning."

"Well, as I told you, I was just there for the day, and I didn't want to take a chance on someone else following through for me. I'd rather return it to you myself."

Mallory's attention quickened again. She could feel Jeannine straining behind her for some hint of what was being said on the other end of the line. But Mallory was cautious. Was he still just being polite, thorough and professional? Could he possibly want to see her personally? Why would he?

He was only being polite. She was sure of it.

"I'd like to return it over dinner tomorrow night," Colt continued easily, then he chuckled. "Anywhere but Marcetti's."

Mallory's mind went completely blank. She was not even aware of how long the telephone silence went on until he prompted, "Mallory?" Embarrassed color rushed to her cheeks. Mentally she cursed herself. She used to be so much smoother than this. He was going to think this was the first time anyone had ever asked her for a date.

A date. She didn't have time for this, Mallory had told herself repeatedly. Going out, doing the night-life, being "in circulation." That was not what she wanted. The awkward first-date small talk, the un-easiness, the strain to be charming and attractive and interesting—who needed it? She didn't have room for another person in her life.

One date. A simple dinner. A chance to spend

the evening with an interesting person. "I'd like that," Mallory said; her voice actually sounded natural. "Thanks."

"Fine." Colt seemed pleased, but not surprised. "Seven tomorrow night."

When he started to hang up, Mallory interjected quickly, feeling like a sixteen-year-old, "My...my address...."

"That's all right." There was a smile in his voice. "I have it."

Mallory felt silly. Of course, if he had her credit card and her phone number, of course he knew her address. "Great," she responded, and even managed to come across as graceful. "I'll see you then."

Mallory hung up the phone very slowly, as though slightly shell-shocked, and turned to face her expectant friend. "I can't believe what I just did."

Chapter Five

JEANNINE CHASE AND MALLORY EVANS had been roommates in college, and though two more dissimilar personalities could not have been found had they searched the world over, the friendship was one of those destined to last a lifetime. Mallory was intense, hard-working and dedicated. Her future depended upon the scholarship that allowed her to work for her degree in education, and she devoted every ounce of energy toward that purpose. Jeannine was flighty, careless and fun-loving. Her father owned a fleet of luxury liners, and the only thing Jeannine ever worked hard at was having fun.

During their college years, Mallory pulled Jeannine through each crisis period before final exams, covered for her with the housemother, lied for her to jealous boyfriends and could always be counted on to pull her out of whatever scrape she found herself in. Jeannine, in turn, dragged Mallory away from the books for an all-night pizza party when her eyes became so tired she couldn't read the words anymore, fixed her up with the most eligible men on campus and was constantly revamping her wardrobe.

Jeannine hated to study and did so as little as possible, but she would stay up to all hours of the night coaching Mallory. Jeannine, who to all intents and purposes had never had a serious thought in her life, proved to be a surprisingly perceptive and sympathetic listener when Mallory had a problem. And Mallory, who was not much of a party girl herself, was always ready with unexpectedly astute advice on Jeannine's perpetually chaotic love life. They were perfect examples of complementary opposites. The bond of friendship formed in those college days continued to link them through the separation of time, distance and divergent lifestyles.

When Jeannine, typical of her impulsive nature, invested a huge chunk of daddy's money in the Rodeo Drive boutique and settled down in sunny California, and Mallory, also typically, returned to her hometown to teach high school and marry a conservative young man on his way up, the two women never lost touch. It was Jeannine who, through long-distance support, helped Mallory survive those last awful months of her marriage, and afterward it was Jeannine who had flown to Mississippi and had bodily taken Mallory back to California with her, insisting that Mallory live with her until she was on her feet again.

A lot had changed since those early college days. The two women were closer, somewhat wiser and far more in control of their lives. But some things would never change. Mallory was still hard-working, determined and hopelessly naive. Jeannine was still exuberant, free-spirited and incorrigibly independent.

And Mallory still had absolutely no sense of fashion or style.

Jeannine stood at the dressing-room door now, her hands on her silk harem-pants-clad hips, and shook her head helplessly. Jet drop earrings bounced against her neck and her very expensive cloud of curls floated around her shoulders as she did so. "My girl," she pronounced in disgust, "you're hopeless." She marched forward and unfastened the shoulder clasp on the very slinky gold cocktail dress Mallory was modeling. "You've got it on *backward*."

Mallory's eyes widened in amazement. "Are you kidding me? Do you mean all *that* —" she turned for a side view in the mirror that revealed an enormous amount of skin in the back "— is supposed to be in *front*?" She grabbed the dress protectively as Jeannine attempted to shimmy it around Mallory's body. "Oh, no. Not for me, thanks. I haven't shown more than an inch of cleavage since I turned thirty. I'm not about to make up for lost time by showing it all in one night. Don't you have any *regular* clothes?"

Jeannine gave a pained sigh as she watched her friend slip out of the exquisite little dress and return it with much ceremony to the hanger. It had taken all the resources at Jeannine's command to drag Mallory down there that morning, and now it looked as though all the effort was going to waste. You can lead a horse to water, but....

"If by 'regular,'" she retorted, "you mean that ragged collection of bargain-basement specials you have in your closet — no. Come on, Mal, this is your first chance to score in five years," she pleaded. "You've got to knock his eyes out, you've got to—"

Mallory choked on a laugh, turning to stare at her friend in incredulous amazement. "Score? What is this, a hockey game? In that case, I have an old gray sweat suit at home that will do just fine."

"You know exactly what I mean," Jeannine replied with an airy wave of her hand. "Woman does not live by bread alone." She moved purposefully to the hook that held Mallory's discarded selections. "Have you tried all these on? What did you think of this little suede number?"

"Perfect for Cher. Ridiculous for me." Mallory reached for the sundress she had worn into the shop. "Sorry, Jeannine, you're just going to have to resign yourself to the fact that I'm not the high-fashion type. I'll find something at home. It's just a date, after all."

Jeannine stared at her as though she had just committed a sacrilege. "Just a date? Just a *date*? There's no such thing as 'just a date.' Now you listen to me, old girl," she said severely, crossing her arms belligerently over her ribbon-spangled chest. "Times are hard in the old boy-girl game. You've got to make every shot count. How often are you going to come across a man like this Stanford dude? Good-looking, under fifty, smart, nice manners, not addicted to anything that we know about and, best of all, heterosexual? Come on, wake up, you've got a gold mine here! And when you open that door tonight you've got to be the best thing he's ever seen—"

A subdued chime announced the entrance of

another customer. Sparing a glare for Mallory, who was by now almost doubled up with laughter, Jeannine peeked around the dressing-room door. "Speaking of the best thing you've ever seen. . ." she murmured, and Mallory knew the customer must be male.

Jeannine looked back at her severely. "You stay right here," she commanded. "Don't move a muscle. I'll be right back."

The man who stood casually perusing Jeannine's collection of handmade jewelry was something straight out of a crystal ball. He was tall, slender and dark-haired. He was wearing a charcoal-colored suit whose body-hugging lines proclaimed that it had been tailored for him at great cost. Everything about him exuded grace, elegance and refined taste, and nothing about him was a common sight in Jeannine's avant-garde shop.

Jeannine ran a finger along the pelvis-hugging waistband of her harem pants, fluffed the dangling ribbons that decorated her nearly transparent halter top and slipped behind the counter. "Looking for anything special?" she inquired brightly.

He glanced up. His face was gently sculpted yet well defined, lean and beautiful like the rest of him. His complexion was fair, and he had the most heart-stopping gray eyes Jeannine had ever seen.

"Yes." His voice was smooth and well modulated, like his slow smile, and his accent was British. "A souvenir. Something very typically Southern Californian." As he spoke his eyes swept over her, lighting with appreciation and what might have been gentle amusement on the shape of her face and the gold halo of ringlets, on her eyes and sweeping across her lips, brushing the well-shaped bosom barely disguised by the confection of chiffon and ribbons she wore. The instant contact she felt with the touch of that gaze was almost physical, and she responded to it immediately and powerfully.

Jeannine was not a woman of vacillating moods or uncertain desires. She had never labored over a decision in her life. The idea of playing coy had never occurred to her. She knew what she wanted and she usually got it; it was as simple as that.

Jeannine knew within thirty seconds of meeting him that she wanted this man. Perhaps more than she had wanted anyone or anything else in her entire life.

Her smile was an answer to the subtle light she saw in his eyes, and it hid nothing. "For your wife?" she inquired, and added frankly with a slight twitch of her eyebrows, "I hope not."

One corner of his smile deepened, causing the most intriguing bracket to form at the side of his mouth. The spark in his eyes was definitely amusement now. "No."

"In that case," Jeannine responded, leaning forward to place both elbows on the counter, resting her chin on her folded hands, "I have just the thing. The perfect typically Southern California souvenir—me."

Delight danced in his eyes as they swept over her again, lingering longer this time on her eyes than on the by-now delightfully fascinating view of her cleavage. But he kept his tone sober as he informed her, "It's for my fiancée."

Jeannine dismissed that piece of information with an airy wave of her multibraceleted arm. "Fiancées!" she scoffed. "They're a dime a dozen. Genuine artifacts of Southern California are much rarer," she assured him. "And much more interesting."

He cocked his head in a charming pretense of fascination. "Is there such a thing, I wonder?"

"As what?"

"A genuine artifact of Southern California — genuine being the operative word. This is the land of plastic and tinsel, isn't it?"

Jeannine straightened up, settling back with her arms folded across her chest, regarding him with frank wonder and appreciation. "So," she murmured. "There's a philosopher behind that *Esquire* pinup body. A bonus."

He lifted an inquiring eyebrow. "Does *Esquire* have pinups?"

"Pedantic too," Jeannine observed, and he laughed. His eyes seemed to shoot off multicolored sparks when he laughed.

"Miss —"

"Jeannine," she supplied quickly. "Jeannine Chase."

"Miss Chase," he said deliberately, eyes still dancing with restrained mirth, "you are truly delightful, but I do think for now I'd better stay with a nice pair of earrings or perhaps a necklace."

"Better yet," Jeannine said, unlocking the cabinet and carelessly scooping up a pair of amethyst earrings, "send your fiancée earrings and take me out to dinner." She placed the jewelry on the counter for his approval. "These are rather nice, don't you think?"

"Quite." Amusement still played in his voice, and she could feel those wonderful eyes on her. "Precisely the color of your eyes, I think."

Jeannine looked up at him, and her smile softened into what felt very strangely like the beginnings of a blush. Quickly she reached for tissue paper with which to wrap the gift. "Are you just visiting Los Angeles, or do you plan to stay?"

"It depends, actually." Jeannine could still feel his eyes upon her, and the gaze was actually making her nervous. She could not recall the last time a man had made her nervous. "I'm buying some property here."

Jeannine looked up brightly. "Oh? Whereabouts?"

He laughed, little lines forming about his eyes as he did. "I do love the American language. Whereabouts? As, in what area? Bel Air, actually, among others. I'm not too familiar with the neighborhood, however, so I'm not terribly sure where to begin."

"I'm a marvelous tour guide," Jeannine volunteered, flashing him one of her bold smiles as she presented him with the boxed and wrapped earrings. Then, glancing down at the package in her hand, she added, "You are going to take these, aren't you?"

"Yes." His hand closed over hers and lingered there for a moment as he took the package, and Jeannine actually felt her breathing become shallow. When she looked up at him, his eyes seemed suddenly serious and very deep gray.

"To both?" Her voice sounded a little husky. "The tour guide and the earrings?"

He smiled slowly and retrieved the package from her limp fingers. "We'll have to see, won't we?" he suggested softly as he reached for his wallet.

He paid cash, so that Jeannine did not have the advantage of learning his name from a credit card. On inspiration, she said, "I have to fill out a sales slip. . . ." She gave him an innocent look. "Procedure, you know." She scrambled under the counter for a sales slip and a pen — Jeannine rarely took care of clerical matters herself — and tried to look very professional as she asked, "Name?"

The look he gave her told her he knew exactly what she was up to, but he seemed amused. "Byron Warnham. That's with an *n*." He watched her copy the name. He continued smoothly, "555-4830. I'm usually in before noon on weekdays, but if not, you can always leave a message with my houseboy. I'm leasing a place for the summer."

Jeannine was so startled she almost forgot to write down the number. When she looked up at him again her pulse was racing, but nothing in her flirtatiously suggestive smile showed any sign of her inner war with exhilaration and confusion. "You realize of course, that giving information of that nature to a woman like me could be dangerous," she advised him.

He studied her for a long moment, then unexpectedly he smiled. "Perhaps I'm counting on it," he remarked before he turned and left.

Jeannine stood in a dreamy-eyed reverie until Mallory's impatient call from the dressing room pulled her back to reality.

Jeannine found Mallory, with a disgusted look on her face, struggling out of a pair of skintight evening pants. She paused to lean against the door, closed her eyes blissfully and declared, "I'm in love!"

"And I'm in a hurry," Mallory retorted with a glare. She started sorting through the various costumes that hung from the hook and spilled over onto the dressing bench. "What did you do with the dress I wore in here? Did you hide it?"

Jeannine spared one more dramatically yearning look toward the door by which Mr. Byron Warnham had just departed, then marched forward to take her friend in hand. Jeannine was wondering if she should give Byron until tomorrow to call. Mallory was wondering how much longer this could possibly take.

It took, in fact, another hour and a half. Jeannine besieged Mallory with yet a second mountain of slinky cocktail dresses, some of which were quite flattering, but Mallory could not imagine herself wearing any of them out of the store. Jeannine finally relented by suggesting a more tailored outfit that still had an expressly feminine air with its softly pleated skirt and bowed and ruffled blouse. But the price tags only made Mallory feel as though she were making far too big a deal out of this whole thing. Three hundred fifty dollars for one evening? It was not as though she ever expected to have a chance to wear the dress again. Who was she trying to impress anyway? It was only a dinner date, more business than pleasure really. Just one evening to spend talking with a man legendary for his expertise in a field in which she was interested. The very thought of her coming on like a femme fatale in four-inch heels sent Mallory into such peals of laughter that she almost fell off those same heels in front of the dressing-room mirror.

Finally tired enough of the game to stand up for her rights, Mallory firmly purchased no more than a pair of designer jeans—which she needed anyway—and a pale blue silk shirt devoid of ruffles or frills. Even Jeannine reluctantly agreed that black denim and silk could go anywhere in Southern California, but insisted that Mallory borrow a pair of her silver-and-turquoise earrings and a small matching bracelet for the evening. To that Mallory did not object. She looked good in hoop earrings, and the turquoise brought out matching flecks in her eyes she had never realized were there. She left feeling very satisfied with her purchases, if a little guilty for not spending more money in her friend's shop. But Jeannine waved her on gaily.

"I'll get you next time . . ." she insisted.

Mallory replied by laughing. "There probably won't be a next time. But on the off chance there is, I'll keep you in mind."

A moment later, Mallory was on her way. It was going to be a busy day, but she had never had trouble scheduling her time before. She had appointments with her banker and her accountant. She had grocery shopping to do and a quick stop to make at the office-supply store for paper and typewriter ribbon. Worst of all, she had to take her Porsche for its six-hundred-mile check. That was never fun.

Mallory had never wanted the Porsche and didn't like it. The command console made her feel as though she were in the cockpit of a space capsule and the speed the car was capable of terrified her. She had owned it for six months and to this day refused to drive it if there was the slightest threat of rain because she had not yet figured out how to work the windshield wipers. But Jeannine had insisted it was good for her image. Her attorney said it was a good investment. And Mallory had purchased the car without giving a second thought to what she really wanted.

If she had known, however, how much trouble the upkeep was going to be on such an expensive toy, she might not have allowed herself to be so easily railroaded. She hated taking it in for checkups. The mechanics always made her feel inferior and defensive, as though a woman who had no more reverence for a machine such as this had no right owning it. Today her mechanic was at first amazed, then slightly offended at the low mileage. By the time she explained how little she actually needed to drive and listened to his lecture about a high-performance engine needing high speeds and plenty of use, she was quite a bit behind schedule.

It was after five when she got home. When she had unpacked her purchases and sat down with a cup of herbal tea for her customary fifteen minutes of relaxation before settling down at her desk, it was a quarter to six. Mallory examined the clock with some perplexity. It wouldn't take her long to get dressed, but she decided it was better to go ahead and get ready now, and use the extra time waiting for Colt to arrive by starting on her next outline.

Again Mallory had underestimated the amount of time and effort involved in dressing for a date. Her hair had to be washed and carefully blow-dried. Powders, perfumes and lotions that she rarely ever used had to be selected in complementary fragrances and applied appropriately. Her nails had to be polished but Mallory had forgotten they took forever to dry. Then the dressing process began.

Jeannine had done everything but get down on her knees and plead with Mallory to purchase a new and extravagantly styled set of underthings. Mallory was not very impressed with undergarments—no one ever saw them anyway—so her collection, though in good repair, was sparse and utilitarian. Now she wished she had taken Jeannine's advice. The silk shirt obviously required a more delicate bra than she was accustomed to wearing. She tried on every one she owned without finding one that didn't show a seam or a bit of lace edging where the first button of the shirt began. Having spent a good ten minutes trying on and discarding options, Mallory finally decided the shirt would look better without any bra at all. Her bosom was not her most prominent feature, and chances were no one would notice she was braless anyway.

The jeans, she decided, looked better with panty hose worn underneath them. Though Mallory had always thought it a silly affectation to wear full-length panty hose beneath pants, she couldn't find in her tangled collection two knee-high stockings that matched, and her ankles were a little too white against the black denim to go bare legged.

Then there was the makeup. Mallory hardly ever wore makeup—she so rarely went out of the house. She didn't realize how much trouble it was to choose the right foundation, coordinate blusher with lip gloss, match the color of her eye shadow to the color of her blouse and apply mascara without smearing it. Doing the job right seemed to take forever.

At three minutes to seven, she was ready. She looked nice. The dangling hoop earrings added exactly the right festive note to her casual attire, the matching bracelet was a touch of class. The shirt was perfect. She had never owned anything one-hundred-percent silk before, and she resolved to add more to her wardrobe. The pale color was flattering; the blouse's simple lines were dressy but not overstated. Not even she could tell she wasn't wearing a bra. The jeans, which she had been afraid would show unflattering lumps and bulges that were the result of two weeks overindulgence in oatmeal cookies and frozen pizzas, had exactly the opposite effect and smoothed her figure into sleek lines she hadn't known she possessed. "God bless Gloria Vanderbilt," she murmured, placing her hands on her hips and twisting toward the mirror to better examine the whole effect. Just then the door chimes sounded.

Mallory's gaze flew in a mixture of amazement

and despair to the clock on the dresser, the minute hand of which was squarely in the middle of the twelve. She had thought she would have at least five or six minutes to relax and gather her thoughts— *nobody* was that punctual. What had happened to the hour she had saved at the end of the day for work?

Oh well, she thought as she hurried to the door, how long could dinner take, anyway? A couple of hours. She would be home by ten at the latest and there would be plenty of time to catch up on her writing and still get enough sleep to be fresh for a new day tomorrow.

One advantage to the surprise flight of time was that Mallory had been so busy all day she had not had much opportunity to grow anxious about the upcoming date. Adrenaline was now pumping, her eyes and her cheeks were brightening, and as she flung open the door a little breathlessly the only thought she had was how strange it looked to have a man on her doorstep.

Chapter Six

COLT KEPT HIS EXPRESSION FRIENDLY and his stance casual as Mallory opened the door, but his eyes were sweeping her from head to foot and he felt an appreciative catch of his breath at what he saw. He knew that to the ordinary eye there was nothing particularly breathtaking about her appearance, but to Colt, she was beautiful.

She looked good in jeans, as most shapely women did. The blue blouse picked up the color of her eyes, and the turquoise earrings highlighted her peaches-and-cream complexion, giving her an added sparkle that Colt found captivating. The soft-as-silk rosy blond hair was pushed behind her ears with a few baby-fine strands fluttering around her jawline. Colt found himself wanting to tuck those tendrils away, to feel the texture of her hair against her skin. But of course he didn't do it.

"Right on time," she said, greeting him with a smile.

"One of the leftovers from my studio days," Colt returned lightly and removed a white envelope from his jacket pocket. "Business first."

"Oh, my card. Thanks." As Mallory accepted the envelope, she took a quick moment to study him without seeming as though she were obviously assessing him. She was glad to see that he was dressed as casually as she was, in a burgundy sports coat and dark slacks, his shirt the same pale blue color as hers and opened two buttons at the neck. He was well groomed and seemed very much at ease. His dark hair fell in its perpetually tousled way across his forehead and his lightly tanned face appeared friendly. Mallory was suddenly very glad she had said yes. This might even be fun.

She put the envelope on the table by the door and picked up her purse at the same moment. Colt did not invite himself in, but waited politely for her. Mallory liked that.

"I've been trying to guess what your favorite food might be," he said as he walked her to his car in the lingering daylight. "But I must confess I'm at a loss. How about a hint?"

Mallory laughed. "Anything but Chinese!" And before she knew it, she was telling him about the fiasco of last night's dinner with Jeannine, talking to him and laughing easily with him as though she did this sort of thing every day of her life. She had never imagined it could be so simple.

Colt drove a ten-year-old TR-7 in immaculate condition—also, apparently, a leftover from his studio days. Once inside he announced with decision, "How about a good old-fashioned American steak? We're not likely to get many surprises with that."

"Perfect," agreed Mallory. "I think I've had enough surprises to last me awhile."

The look Colt gave her was intimate and teasing; it made her feel warm. "Now, I don't think *anyone* ever has enough surprises. It takes all the fun out of life."

Mallory laughed. "Not for me, I'm afraid. I pretty much like to know what to expect."

Colt turned the car off the residential street and onto the main boulevard. "*That's* a philosophy you don't hear too much in this part of the world. Don't you know that the first requirement for being a resident of Los Angeles is to always expect the unexpected?"

"No," Mallory pointed out, "the *first* requirement for being a resident of Los Angeles is to have a screw loose somewhere." She couldn't believe how easily she was talking to him, how much fun she was having already. *You're doing terrifically, Mallory,* she congratulated herself, and was both pleased and, yes, surprised. "I think that sums up the whole character of the state. What kind of people would live in a place that geologists and seismologists have predicted for years is doomed to destruction? Where else in the world do you find people who treat an earthquake that measures 6.6 on the Richter scale like no more than an inconvenient rainstorm? No wonder everyone here is a little nutty—you have to be!"

"Not nutty, just accommodating to circumstances," Colt disagreed mildly. "All it takes is a little readjustment in attitude. Ask any man on the street and he'll tell you that when the Big One does come, the rest of the continent will break off into the sea and leave California standing, exactly like it always was, business as usual."

Mallory laughed, liking him more and more. "Nutty," she informed him, and he chuckled as he maneuvered the car onto the freeway.

In a moment Colt glanced at her, a quickly observant but peculiarly tender look. "Nervous?"

He was studying her hands, which were clasped lightly in her lap. Immediately she unfolded them. "No," she answered, and thought that was pretty close to the truth. "That's just the way I always hold my hands. Why?"

Colt shook his head slightly and smiled. "You were doing the same thing at lunch yesterday when Madame Guillotine was grilling you."

"Oh." The man *was* observant. Mallory waved his remark aside. "Those were slightly different circumstances."

Colt shot her an amused look. "I certainly hope so. I wouldn't want to think I could ever make anyone *that* uncomfortable."

Thinking about that incident took some of the gaiety from Mallory's mood, but she dismissed it with a wry twist of her lips and a shrug. "I guess I did look a little like a deer caught in the sights of a double-barreled shotgun on the first day of open season." She glanced over at him. "Thanks again for the rescue."

"My pleasure." He caught her eyes for a moment. "I'm one of your biggest fans, you know."

The delight and surprise in Mallory's eyes was felt throughout her entire body as she laughed. "What a coincidence! I'm one of yours."

Colt nodded soberly. "I knew my flair with a champagne cork would impress you."

Mallory laughed again. She didn't think she had ever felt such an elating mixture of excitement and relaxation. She didn't know why she had avoided going out for so long.

By the time they reached the restaurant they were deeply involved in a conversation that was mostly professional, but not highly technical. Colt was very careful not to make her feel as though she were being interviewed, but Mallory found herself telling him more about her work and her personal life than she would have dreamed of revealing to Evelyn Bouchard. When she realized how painlessly Colt was drawing her out, she was amazed. He did it so smoothly she didn't even resent it.

The restaurant was small, dimly lit and sparsely populated—made for intimacy. They were seated at a corner table where a single red-globed candle cast seductively dancing shadows on the white tablecloth and a lush potted plant screened their view of other guests and gave the illusion of privacy. In the background soft violin music played, and the scent of the desert wild flowers that banked the windowsills blended with that of candle wax and wine. *Just like in the movies,* Mallory thought with a barely suppressed giggle that was really generated more from nervous excitement than amusement. As her eyes caught Colt's she saw a twinkle that suggested he had read her thought.

"I'd like to ask you a personal question, if I may," Colt said unexpectedly. "You and Jake Farrow—is there anything more than a professional relationship between you?"

Mallory was startled—first that such a thing

would occur to him, secondly that he would actually ask her. She was not certain whether to be insulted or flattered. Why would he ask her about her relationship with another man unless he himself were interested in a relationship? That thought both disturbed and flustered her. Forcing a bit too much brightness into her tone, she answered, "Goodness, whatever gave you that idea? Jake and I are very good friends, if that's what you mean."

Colt smiled, a quiet and reassuring smile. "You know how trade gossip is," he said casually. "I guess no one likes to think that anybody in the industry can be completely unattached."

Mallory seemed to relax with that, and Colt was reassured. He had seen the way Jake had gazed at her during lunch. As a result Colt had begun to wonder if, for the first time, trade gossip might be right. But apparently Mallory did not think so, and that was good enough for him.

She thought this might be a good time to switch the subject from herself to him. "We've talked enough about me," she said firmly, yet keeping her tone friendly. "I don't even know what you're doing now. . . besides tending tables at Marcetti's, that is."

The waitress was waiting to take their cocktail order. Mallory ordered the first thing that came to mind—a wine spritzer—and Colt ordered Scotch and water. He turned back to Mallory with a smile as smoothly as though the conversation had never been interrupted. "I teach film editing at the technical college—" he grinned "—when I'm not waiting tables at Marcetti's. Mark is one of my students. He had an interview yesterday and I volunteered to fill in for him."

A small frown of perplexity and subdued amazement creased Mallory's brow. To think of a man of his caliber reduced to teaching at a vocational school.... "But that's not even your field," she protested.

He shrugged. "It's a job."

She shook her head sadly. "It's a waste of talent."

Again Colt grinned. "Why don't you tell the school board that? Maybe I'll get a raise."

But Mallory was serious. The drinks were served, but she hardly noticed as she leaned forward slightly, emphasizing the intensity of her thought. "It doesn't bother you? Thinking about everything you lost? You're so talented and now there's no outlet for that talent. You were on top and now...." She turned one palm upward in a gesture of confused defeat.

Colt smiled, and the slow-moving candlelight caressed the lean planes of his face. His face, strongly masculine but somehow hinting of great capability for gentleness, fascinated Mallory. Its angular shape was clear-cut and defined, suggesting strength of will and determination, but the mouth was tender, easily given to a smile. And his eyes, with the small lines at the corners and the slightly uptilted shape, described a person who was as quick to laugh at himself as at others. It was one of the most interesting faces Mallory had seen in a long time, and she hadn't tired of looking at it. "Sure, I miss it, if that's what you mean. But I think anyone who goes into this business has to be aware that the bottom can fall out at any

time. Just as with any other game of chance, you have
to be prepared to lose from the minute you start winning." He lifted one shoulder in a light, dismissing
gesture, which displayed an amazingly genuine lack
of concern. "Of course you can't ever forget that
everything—from the first words we put on paper to
the final cut that flickers across the screens of
theaters everywhere—is just make-believe, sleight of
hand, a trick of the eye. The only real trouble you
can get into is when you start believing in it too
much."

Mallory shook her head slowly, as a symbol of
both rejection and confusion. "I don't understand
how you can be so nonchalant about it."

Colt's smile was crooked and endearing, his tone
only half serious. "I can't afford not to be, can I?
That's life, Mallory. You either go with the flow or
drown in the undertow. Nobody's handing out any
guarantees for anything."

Absently stirring her drink, Mallory again shook
her head, her eyes downcast. "I don't think I'll ever
be able to look at it that way."

"Oh, you're not doing too badly." Colt sipped his
Scotch slowly, not moving his eyes away from her.
There was something almost mesmerizing about
those eyes, seeming to communicate a variety of things
from compassion and perception to confidence and
trust, and Mallory found herself falling easily under
their spell. "Having input into the direction of this
film is exactly what you need to do right now."

Her eyes widened, both impressed and surprised.
"How did you know about that?"

His quick half grin was more amused at her reaction than embarrassed or self-depreciating. "You would be amazed at how much waiters hear that no one is supposed to know." Colt leaned toward her conspiratorially and lowered his voice with that last phrase for dramatic effect. "Top secret U.N. Security Council Meeting, Eyes Only, the fate of nations rests in the balance. Full-force security guards, electronic debugging, paper shredder for the note pads, and not one word leaks out...until the guy who served the coffee goes home and spills the entire defense plan to his wife in bed." He straightened up again, eyes twinkling. "People forget they're there. Waiters, maids, busboys, the meter readers and the gardener...all part of the invisible underground." Then he glanced up with a grin at the waitress who had been patiently waiting to take their order. "See what I mean?"

Colt ordered medium rare steak and lobster without consulting Mallory, and though she knew she should have resented his making the decision for her, the authority and ease with which he performed the task only made her feel comfortable and protected. It was almost as if he knew how much she hated choosing from the menu. It was good to have someone in control. But she had to ask, "How did you know I liked my steak medium rare?"

He merely lifted an eyebrow and smiled mysteriously, but did not answer. Everything about him exuded mastery, an ease of manner, confidence—the total male. The woman in Mallory could not help responding to it.

His eyes deepened with pleasure as he looked at her. "You're sparkling tonight," he said softly.

Mallory tried to hide her surprise at the sudden intimate turn of the conversation with a careless turn of her head. "Am I? Sparkling?" Suddenly she felt sparkling. She felt as though her eyes were dancing and her cheeks were glowing and alertness was heightening every nerve in her body. It was adrenaline, nothing more. She had been so wary of social encounters like this for so long, and it was turning out to be so easy. . . . Yes, she was pumped up a little. Sure, she was sparkling. Why not?

Colt nodded soberly, though the hint of a smile lingered at the corners of his lips. "I have a feeling you don't do that very often."

The waitress returned to pour the dinner wine. Mallory wondered what he would think if he knew she didn't do any of this very often. The legendary Colt Stanford, here at her disposal. . . that was exciting enough. To actually be out on a date with a man was revolutionary and stimulating. To discover he was someone she could like and be comfortable with was an added bonus. But why had no one warned her how charismatic he was?

Colt smiled at her as he leaned back in his chair, one hand lazily moving in a circular pattern around the rim of his glass. Oh yes, the atmosphere had certainly changed in the past few moments, becoming close and personal, unpredictably intimate. . .much more like a date than the friendly meal Mallory had imagined. Something had to be done about that.

"I've been meaning to ask you," she said brightly,

"how did you get my phone number? It's unlisted, you know."

He chuckled softly, and Mallory felt an easing in the intensity that seemed to be generated from his eyes. He accepted her signal to back off a bit. "That's another one of those secrets of the servile world. The president of the United States may not be able to get your phone number, but you can bet the clerk at the A&P or the man who cleans your pool—or the head waiter at Marcetti's—has it on file. You're very careful about protecting your privacy, aren't you?"

Mallory met his eyes then, not hesitating to let him read the friendly but deliberate warning there. "Yes," she said simply, "I am."

She could not be certain whether Colt accepted her reply or not; his face was much harder to read than her own. Perhaps that was part of his fascination. And she could not be certain whether the next words were a challenge to her statement, or merely a natural extension of the conversation. "So," he invited easily, "tell me about Mallory Evans. Are you really as romantic as your films make you appear?"

She laughed in both surprise and sudden relaxation at the easing of the atmosphere of almost palpable sensuality that Colt seemed to have been generating over the past few moments. "Romantic? Hardly! I'm a diehard cynic."

Colt's brows lifted in surprise, his eyes lightened with disbelief and amusement. "Is that a fact? I find that hard to swallow."

"Why?" Mallory challenged. As dinner was served

they discussed the legend of Garth and Trista, whose love story she had immortalized throughout the galaxy over the past three years. She was comfortable now, in her own realm, discussing with authority her own work, yet still there was that undercurrent of excitement within her that made it impossible for her to enjoy, or even taste much of, what she assumed to be an excellent meal. Still she glowed. She hadn't expected to have this much fun.

The conversation moved easily toward the films Colt had directed while Mallory listened in fascination to casually tossed-out gems of wisdom from the expert. She grew comfortable with the eye contact, with his slow, subliminally suggestive smile, with the deliberate and resonantly sensuous timbre of his voice. There was the stimulation of two sharp minds, there was the confidence of professional talk, and there were undercurrents of man-woman interaction that Mallory could not ignore. He listened to her intently, he responded to her intelligently. With every movement, every smile, every unspoken gesture, Colt made her feel feminine and appreciated. It was part of his natural charm.

Although Mallory was busy relating to Colt as a professional equal, avidly absorbing every word and eagerly engaging in intellectual interchange, she was also noticing the strong appeal of his masculinity. She tried not to wonder if he was seeing anything in her besides Mallory Evans the successful screenwriter. He was certainly a charming dinner companion, never forgetting to refill her wineglass and punctuating his conversation with that endearing little smile that purposefully concentrated her attention for just a second longer than usual on the curve of his lips, but that could be all part of an act—something he did unconsciously. Mallory should not put too much importance on the fact that when Colt looked at her she often saw nothing other than the appreciation a man feels for a woman in his eyes. Mallory did not know whether she would ever see Colt Stanford again. It didn't matter. Tonight had been the most enjoyable evening of her life, and she was glad she had come.

"Those first mirror shots," Colt was saying now, "were landmarks in directing ingenuity." His gaze was serious, but his eyes held hers easily and naturally, observing and recording her every reaction. He made her feel as though her interest in what he had to say was more significant than the words themselves, and Mallory responded to it. She sat forward a little, her breasts brushing the table and her hands clasped loosely around the stem of her glass, her expression thoughtful and absorbed. She did not know when she would have an opportunity like this again. Every word he spoke was gold. "You've got to realize that directors back then worked under a handicap. They didn't have the advantages of technology we have today. Those early filmmakers were the real geniuses—everything had to come from their imaginations. Today, with superior cameras, fast film, a variety of lenses, process shots, talented film editors, technical innovations. . . ." He made a short, derogatory gesture with his hand and something peculiar flickered across his eyes, stopping his speech briefly. It was as though he had seen something in Mallory's face he did not like, and it startled him. But before she could wonder what it was or even register the strange and totally uncalled-for reaction, he continued smoothly, "Most of the challenge has gone out of it, as far as the technical ability goes. I think that makes for some very lazy directors—and some poorer-quality-than-necessary films. The smart ones, of course—" Colt leaned back and sipped his wine, and for the first time in a long while broke the eye contact, lowering his glance briefly to his glass "—learn from the masters and incorporate the basic techniques of old-fashioned illusion into modern films." In his smile now there was nothing more than a friendly—and to Mallory, a very generous—offer. "I have a whole library of early filmmaking techniques at home. It's at your disposal, if you like."

Mallory's eyes widened in eagerness and delight. Quickly she accepted. "Could I? I can use all the help I can get. There is so much I don't know about editing. Everything I can learn about the technical side of the business will help. Maybe you could pick out a few of the most important books. I'll take very good care of them. . . ."

"My pleasure." There was nothing he would not have done to please her, to put that childlike look of excitement in her eyes. Moment by moment, her happiness was becoming all-important to Colt.

Usually Colt moved much more carefully in affairs of the heart. The experience with his wife had taught him how easy it was to be taken in by appearances, how unwise it was to trust in first impressions. But with Mallory the hard-learned lessons did not seem to apply. She was real, genuine. She evoked emotions within him that no one else ever had before. On a deep and as yet to be admitted level, Colt knew that this woman was someone who could last forever.

His smile deepened, and the atmosphere changed subtly again. "Are you glad you came? It wasn't an easy decision for you, was it?" She was so very fragile and readily hurt. Nothing could come easily for her. Colt wanted to change that.

Mallory refused to let him see how taken aback she was. How had he guessed that? She thought she had handled the episode so well, had been almost blasé, even.... But she only smiled and dropped her gaze to the tabletop, hoping, perhaps, to hide some of her confusion from him. "Yes," she said softly, and met his eyes again. She knew her eyes were glowing. "I'm having a very good time."

"Not resenting one very impudent waiter for interfering in your business lunch?" he teased.

Mallory laughed. Colt was leaning back in his chair again, one arm crooked nonchalantly over its back, causing his jacket to part and thus emphasizing the way the material of his shirt hugged and defined his chest muscles. The other hand traced an absent pattern on his wineglass. Mallory's gaze touched briefly on the portion of bare, hair-sprinkled chest and collarbone above the buttons of his shirt, moved upward along his throat, fastened for the smallest part of a moment on his lips. She wondered what it would be like to be kissed by him. She wondered if he would try.

"I've been meaning to ask you," she said, perhaps a little too quickly, "how you knew I was in trouble yesterday? Bouchard pulls her routine on everyone who comes in there at one time or another, and I was handling it as well as anyone else. How did you know I needed rescuing?"

A quick, secretly amused smile twitched at one corner of Colt's mouth. He lowered his eyes briefly, as though examining all possible replies, rejecting the most outrageous and finally considering the truth.

"Another trick of the Secret Society of Waiterdom?" Mallory prompted.

The amusement in Colt's eyes was directed partially at her and partially at himself. "You might say that," he admitted. He still hesitated just a little, watching her, as though unsure whether she really wanted to hear the complete answer. Then he shrugged very lightly, and still keeping his eyes on her face, Colt said, "Simple observation. You were sending help signals so loudly they practically bounced off the walls." At Mallory's perplexed expression, he continued, "When Bouchard came over the first time, you looked up to talk to her, but you turned your body in the opposite direction — away from her. You were smiling and holding a polite conversation, but the longer she stayed, the farther away from her you twisted, until I thought you were going to fall out of your chair — or be seeing your chiropractor in the morning, at the very least. Your hands were like this." He closed both his hands into fists on top of the table. "A closed mind if I ever saw one. Every time she spoke to you, your eyes would shift to the left—she was hitting you on some pretty deep emotional levels. Those were the signs of more than just a person in an uncomfortable situation, you were damn near desperate, and losing control of the situation fast. So. . . I saw my duty and I done it."

Mallory was both fascinated and puzzled. "But—"

"Body language," he informed her. "One of your most valuable tools. Remember, Mallory, human communication is made up of two parts—language and motion. What is said and what is unsaid. That unspoken communication is going on all the time, sometimes reinforcing our words, sometimes contradicting them, sometimes filling in the gap. And we're always reading and responding to it, whether we consciously realize it or not." He grinned. "Like now. Did you see that?"

Absently, Mallory smoothed her hair behind one ear, her eyes curiously fascinated. "What?"

Colt's glance moved from the place where Mallory's hand still lingered at her neck to her face. There was a hint of mischief and self-satisfaction in his smile. "I just winked at you—very fast, so that your conscious mind didn't even register it. But your subconscious saw and reacted in the instinctive way—with a grooming motion." Self-consciously, Mallory moved her hand back to her glass, and Colt laughed at the tinge of color in her cheeks. "Oh, yes, right now you're telling me a lot of things about yourself you'd probably prefer I didn't know."

"Like what?" Even though Mallory tried to force belligerence into her tone she could not get past the warmth in Colt's eyes to do so. The words came out as more of a coquettish challenge, and that seemed to delight him. The mastery Colt exuded was awe inspiring, but the gentleness with which he exercised his control was soothing. Mallory should have felt guarded or intimidated; instead she felt protected and privileged. And excited.

Colt's smile was as secret as a caress as his gaze moved over her face, touching and cataloging each of her features one by one. The sensuous masculine timbre of his voice registered in a nerve center deep within her. "Your cheeks are glowing," he said softly. "Your lips are parted...."

Classic signs of intense sexual attraction, thought Mallory. And why not? But she laughed. "Too much wine," she said, and she brought one arm across her chest to rub her shoulder absently, protecting her breasts from his view.

She thought it was a defensive gesture, for she was feeling very defensive at that moment. She was surprised when he added softly, his eyes resting on the caressing motions her fingers were making against her silk-clad shoulder, "And you want very much to be touched." Mallory immediately unfolded her arms from the self-embrace and took a self-conscious sip of her wine. She was beginning to feel very exposed, extremely vulnerable, yet the personal shift of the conversation was accelerating... almost too much, like the mixture of anticipation and anxiety that forms in the pit of the stomach right before the roller coaster lurches into motion. She smiled a little nervously, and the gentle amusement she saw in Colt's eyes was reassuring. Cautiously she relaxed.

"Look what I'm doing," he said then, holding her eyes with that same teasing warmth.

Though she was at first confused, Mallory's glance wandered from Colt's face to his hand, which was engaged in nothing more startling than tracing the same lazy circular pattern around the rim of his glass that he had been doing all evening.

"Now look at what you're doing."

Mallory looked at her own glass just in time to realize that her fingers were moving in a slow, stroking motion up and down the stem of her glass. The sexual implications were startling and blatant. Colt laughed at the expression on her face. "When I move my fingers faster, yours move faster. When I slow down, you do too. We've been communicating in perfect rhythm all evening." Mallory deliberately clasped her hands on top of the table, laughing in both embarrassment and amazement. Exposed was a mild word for what she felt right now—stripped naked might have been a more accurate description—but strangely she did not resent it. Perhaps because Colt teased her so lightly, amusing both himself and her. Perhaps because Mallory found him so mesmerizing. Or perhaps because he did no more and no less than point out the truth, and she could not find an appropriate defense against that. "You make me feel as though I should sit on my hands!" she protested, and she was surprised by the sudden softening of Colt's features.

"Oh no," he said, and his own hand drifted very lightly to cover one of hers. The teasing vanished. Instead it was replaced by something gently enigmatic that unsettled Mallory perhaps simply because she was caught so off guard. "I wouldn't recommend that at all. There are too many more interesting things to do with them." For a moment their eyes locked, and Mallory's throat went dry. Then Colt squeezed her hand very briefly, and said in a more normal tone, "Shall we go?"

Mallory nodded and licked her lips nervously as she slid out of her seat. He followed the unconscious motion with a decreased intensity in his eyes and paused in the process of laying bills on the table. "I like that too," he said softly, and again Mallory felt that confused and delighted surge of color to her cheeks. She did not know what to say.

Chapter Seven

MALLORY WAS FEELING A LITTLE LIGHT-HEADED — no lunch, very little dinner and too much wine, she decided — and Colt somehow sensed it. His hand rested lightly and supportively on her elbow until they were out of the restaurant, then moved very naturally to enfold hers. His hand was strong, warm and dry, and the simple feel of it covering hers sent an odd little jumping motion from Mallory's throat to the pit of her stomach. What a wonderful thing it was, a woman's hand resting inside the strong clasp of a man's. What a protected, innocent and cared-for sensation, yet by its very innocence hinting at stronger and more forbidden pleasures. Touching. Closeness. How very much Mallory had missed it.

There was magic in the California night as they walked in silence across the shrub-lined asphalt to the car. The moon was a hazy sliver in a blue velvet sky; there were no stars. The elusive scent of wild flowers blended in the clear air with the subtlety of Colt's cologne; it was a fragrance Mallory would never forget. Warmth and masculinity emanated from him and seemed to be absorbed into the very pores of her body. Yes, there was magic — in the night, in his touch, in his presence. She reveled in it.

"You see, Mallory," he said as he started the car, easy and businesslike once more, "you've got to use every tool you know when you start to put a film together. Your knowledge of people—how they act and react, what they perceive and how they perceive it—is your most valuable asset." Though Colt had shifted the conversation to the impersonal and his tone was casual, none of the lingering intimacy that had been established in the restaurant was lost. It was as though he was just giving Mallory a chance to get used to the feeling, bringing the relationship back onto the conversational level with which she was most comfortable. But still everything about him exuded awareness of her and drew Mallory into awareness of him—the low, easy timbre of his voice, the way his arm muscles moved against the material of his coat as he turned the steering wheel, the lazy smile in his eyes when he glanced at her. Colt had drawn a web of closeness around them that Mallory was incapable of breaking—nor did she particularly want to.

She turned in the bucket seat to look at him as he spoke, shifting moods as easily as he did from the sensuous to the intellectual. At that point, both were equally stimulating to her. "Now, in film," he went on, and Mallory watched in quiet fascination the play of streetlights on the clean angles of Colt's face as he turned onto the highway, "we're communicating on three levels—with dialogue, with action and with *what the camera chooses to reveal.* The trick is in making all those levels work together." His expression was intense with concentration on the subject he knew so well, his tone serious but not lecturing.

Mallory realized at that moment how much she liked Colt Stanford, how deeply he intrigued her, how much she really hoped she would see him again. He stimulated her in so many different ways. He was generous and open, he had so much to give that she needed. She had never imagined it would be like this. Her first venture into the world of social encounters and he had succeeded in making it perfect. Did he have any idea how special this night was to her?

As Colt continued, Mallory listened with contentment and avid interest. "Every motion, every blink of an eye or shift of the head an actor makes is telling the viewer something about that character. It may be something we want him to know, or it may be something best left unrevealed at that point of the story. . .or it may be the actor's personality coming through, in which case we want to eliminate it entirely. The camera has an awesome power. It can emphasize or diminish; it can whisper or it can scream. It can move fast enough to barely suggest its message to the subconscious mind, or it can linger so long the entire effect is lost." He glanced at her with a smile. "Remember, it's the illusion, always the illusion. The weaving of dreams is a tricky business, and the director is the one who has ultimate power over it. He'll use his knowledge of people—both the viewer and the actor—to read them, manipulate them, motivate them, to get them to respond in exactly the way he wants them to. To get them to

believe exactly what he wants them to believe, and
to behave in exactly the manner he wants them to
behave. Being able to communicate on that unspoken level is only one of the skills you have to look
for in the man who's going to make sure the camera
records your fantasy."

Illusion, always the illusion.... Mallory had fallen under the spell of that illusion in the restaurant.
Colt had, without even meaning to, manipulated
her into feeling attraction for him and believing it
was mutual. All a trick, sleight of hand—an object
lesson. Mallory should have been warned for future
reference, but in fact she found it all quite im-
pressive. She smiled a little. "You sound as though
you really enjoy having all that power."

The quirk of Colt's eyebrow was self-effacing.
"That's the trouble with it...and the beauty of it.
The power disappears when the camera stops roll-
ing, like everything else in this business, I suppose.
We can never forget how fragile the fabric is upon
which we weave our dreams."

For not the first time that evening, Mallory wanted to ask him directly what had really happened in
the scandal that had ended his career. She knew he
would not have demurred from telling her, for the
one thing she had learned about him was that he
was unafraid of the truth. But somehow a discussion
of the subject seemed superfluous at the moment.
There were more important things she wanted to
learn about him.

"You *do* miss it," she observed with perception.

"It will always be a part of me. The one thing I do

better than anything else.... But the important thing is that I *can* do other things, just like you could if you had to."

Mallory shook her head in firm denial. "No, I'm not that flexible. I couldn't adjust the way you have. I couldn't simply move on to something else."

"You couldn't, huh?" His glance was amused. "What do you call what you're demanding now—participation in the production of your film? That sounds pretty flexible to me."

Mallory laughed. "Not flexible—just insecure. I'm so afraid someone else will take over and ruin the script that I have to have some control myself to make sure it's done right. It's really very neurotic."

"Maintain that control," Colt stated, but Mallory couldn't be entirely certain that the soberness in his voice was not gentle mockery.

"Right," she agreed brightly, and that was the first time she noticed that the route he was taking did not lead to her house. Mallory opened her mouth to protest, but some vague and rather confusing stirring within her prevented the words. She watched his strong profile in the flickering lights of passing traffic, and once again her throat grew dry. Colt was confident, at ease and in command, but those characteristics, instead of intimidating her, only inspired trust in her. All right, so he was taking her to his apartment. He had promised her books from his library, hadn't he? What better time to fulfill the promise than now? Mallory got a sudden flash of the highly erotic communication that had been taking place between them all night, and how it must have looked from his point of view. She wondered vaguely what other promises he might be thinking of fulfilling tonight.

But mostly Mallory was thinking how much she liked him, and how lucky she was to have met him and had the chance to spend this evening with him. Her face reflected nothing but gratitude and gentle puzzlement as she said, "Why are you being so helpful to me? I mean, you can't have any idea how worried I've been about this whole thing. I can't believe I even had the nerve to ask for so much say about the creation of this picture. I'm still not entirely certain it was the right thing to do, but after talking to you tonight it doesn't seem quite so impossible anymore. You've given me tricks of the trade it could have taken years to learn. I don't understand why," she admitted frankly.

Colt glanced at her. "It could be because I admire your work and I want to see this film be the best it can be. It could be because, as you said, once a director, always a director. I miss being able to tell other people what to do. And it could be—" his gaze traveled gradually from her eyes to the hollow of her throat, and then briefly back to her lips "—because I simply like you."

Mallory stubbornly refused to acknowledge that there might be other, more devious, motivations.

It was then that he turned off the road and into a quiet, nicely landscaped apartment complex. He did not offer any excuses, and if he was waiting for her to make some observation he was to be disappointed. *All right, Mallory, be cool,* she firmly commanded herself as he opened the door for her and she got out of the car. *You're both grown-up people here and just because you find yourself in a man's apartment doesn't mean that you have to head straight for the bedroom. . . .*

She took a quiet breath and forcefully relaxed as she felt Colt's hand lightly on her arm, guiding her up the steps. She could handle this. She liked him. She had enjoyed every minute of their evening together, and she would enjoy talking with him more once they were inside. She did not want to have sex with him. She wasn't ready for that. He would just have to understand.

He might not even try.

She smothered her slightly damp palms nervously and unobtrusively on her jeans as he inserted the key into the lock and swung open the door. "Welcome to my lair." He smiled, and Mallory stepped inside.

The apartment was small, neat and tasteful. The single lamp Colt had left burning emitted a golden shadowy light that was warm and inviting. The sofa was covered in a dark Indian print and stacked with comfortable cushions and flanked by a pair of low tables. Navy blue easy chairs were drawn up across from the sofa to form a comfortable conversation area. The one short wall opposite the door was occupied by a stereo set, encased in a glass cabinet, with two enormous speakers. The living area was enlarged by a small dining room with a round, dark wood table and a row of healthy hanging plants over the double glass door that opened onto the balcony. The walls were decorated with a few framed and

strikingly artistic movie posters. The entire effect
came together to produce an atmosphere of coziness
and comfort, closeness without clutter.

Colt turned almost immediately to the low, wood-
and-brick bookshelf that ran along one wall and retrieved an oversize, obviously well-read volume. "I
think you'll enjoy this. It has photographs of some actual out-takes from the first commercial films ever
made and interviews with the directors. Have a seat,"
he invited, gesturing to the sofa. "Would you like
some wine?"

Mallory almost said no. But she was already flip-
ping through the book and quickly becoming fascinated with the contents. She heard herself reply as
she sank to the sofa, "Thanks. I'd love some."

Colt disappeared around the corner. With her pe-
ripheral vision she saw a light go on in a color-toned
burnt orange kitchen and was aware of nothing else
until he pressed a cool glass of white wine into her
hand.

She looked up from the book with a laugh. "This is
incredible! Look—excerpts from old Charlie Chan
movies, with a running narrative from everyone on
the set!" She took a sip of the Chablis. "I had no idea
there was anything like this in print."

"There probably isn't anymore." Colt dropped to
the floor, leaning close to her as he turned a page.
"This is a collector's edition."

"Oh." His nearness, that faintly tantalizing scent
of his cologne, made Mallory feel a little unsteady,
and she carefully moved the wineglass away from the
book and onto the cocktail table before her. "I'll be
very careful."

He laughed. "No need. Books are meant to be read, not worshipped. This one has so many coffee and food stains on it that it's beginning to smell like a delicatessen."

Mallory laughed and began to relax again.

For a while he sat beside her, turning pages and reading along with her, pointing out sections of particular interest. But after a while he settled back on the floor again, letting her peruse the volume on her own, engaging in conversation only when she brought up some interesting point or directed a question to him. It was not that she was unaware of him, lounging before her with his weight on one elbow, sipping contentedly from his glass of wine, or that her immersion in the book in any way diluted her awareness of him. But she felt so comfortable, sitting there and drinking wine, lost in a book about her favorite subject, that she forgot to be nervous.

Mallory did not know how long she had been turning pages silently, or how long Colt had been patiently watching her. But at last she looked up guiltily and apologized. "You've found my secret passion, I'm afraid. I could do this all night."

"Could you?" His smile was slow and pleasurable, his eyes alive with a subtle inner light. What Colt saw in her face to put that look of deep contentment in his eyes Mallory could not imagine, but it made her stomach muscles clench and her pulse speed slightly.

He reached up and slowly took the book from her. "Come here," he commanded softly.

Part of Mallory was busily convinced that all he wanted to do was point out to her something of spe-

cial interest from the book, the other part was sternly deriding that rationale as idiotic. Still, her lips
curved in a gesture of consent, and she lowered herself onto her knees beside him.

In the same motion Colt's hand moved around
the back of her neck, and for a moment he simply
looked at her. *He's going to kiss me,* thought Mallory, and even before her pulse could begin to beat
its wild acceptance of the fact, a gentle pressure of
his hand brought her face to his.

This was no gently restrained, cautiously exploring first-date kiss. This was an explosion of passion
and desire, a communication of dominance and demand, a reflection of the man who mastered it.
Mallory was shocked and would have pulled away,
but the rush of response he generated in her was so
unexpected and swift that she didn't have a chance.
His mouth captured hers, his tongue invaded, and
everything within Mallory opened to him. Blood
drained from her veins and was replaced with a
gushing tide of adrenaline. It tingled through her
limbs and exploded in her head; it doubled her
heart rate and closed her throat. A rush of hor-
mones over which she had no control put her system
on overload, draining life from her body and dim-
ming her awareness of the outside world like a slowly fading light bulb. There was nothing, nothing,
but Colt's mouth on hers and the strong mating
rhythm of his tongue against hers, the muscled arms
that enfolded her and the searing heat that weak-
ened her. Dizziness and pulsating sensory awareness.
She couldn't stop it. There was nothing she could do.

Her head was resting in the crook of his arm, Colt's fingers threading through her hair. His lips were soft and his breath warm against her face. "You are a beautiful woman," he whispered huskily.

One hand rested weakly against his chest, as though in protest. Mallory could feel the strong beat of his heart, which was no match for the thunderous pounding of hers. She tried to open her eyes yet succeeded only partially. She had not been prepared for this. She thought she was, but she wasn't. Her hands were still shaking and her skin tingling. She made herself meet Colt's eyes, which were glowing and tender, almost blinding in their intensity. She whispered, as steadily as possible, "And a very vulnerable one."

As much as she tried to keep her voice firm and matter-of-fact, the words came out broken and breathless. She was trying to handle this, she was doing the best she could, but she was not a pro at this. Right now she felt like a very lost and very inexperienced little girl.

Mallory turned her head and closed her eyes against an unexpected wellspring of tears. She did not know why the tears were there, she did not know what caused the sudden indefinable ache deep in her solar plexus, but she seemed powerless to prevent that too.

Colt did not ignore her unspoken plea. He touched her cheek gently, smoothing back a strand of hair. "Mallory," he inquired softly, "what are you afraid of?"

She shook her head slowly. She knew if she opened

her mouth to speak the tears would win, and she refused to burst into sobs before him like a virgin with her first man. She would not give in to that humiliation.

"All right then." Colt's voice was soft. Very slowly, with ultimate care, he moved away from her. A final caress on her arm, and he released her. The absence of his touch, his warmth, left her bereft and confused. And still shaky.

She sat up, taking a deep breath, concentrating on restoring strength to her unsteady limbs. This was ridiculous. Colt had a right to expect more than this. No man could be prepared for a woman who went into hysterics over a single kiss.

Colt got to his feet and offered casually, "More wine?"

All right. She could handle this. Mallory smiled, although a little stiffly, and ran a damp-palmed hand over her hair, smoothing it. Her voice was hoarse but steady. "Sure."

Colt took the goblets to the kitchen to refill them, and Mallory sat on the sofa again. What she really wanted to do was curl up into a ball and bury her face in her knees, but she was not a child. So she used the time to compose herself, to regain whatever shreds of dignity she still had, to pretend to herself that she was a mature woman who could say to the man who was about to walk through that door, "Thanks, but I don't go to bed on the first date. Call me sometime."

Colt proffered the replenished wineglass, and she had to hold it with both hands. He sat beside her on the sofa—not too close—his arm resting casually across its back, his palm almost touching her shoulder. Almost, but not quite. The sudden need to move against him, to feel his touch, sneaked up on her. She took a long sip of her Chablis.

Colt's smile was relaxed and friendly. She wanted to touch those small lines around his eyes, to explore the ridges of his cheekbones and the softness of his lashes with her fingertips.

"So," Colt said easily. He was exceedingly aware of how carefully he must move with her, how easily she could be hurt. He did not want to hurt her. "Tell me why Mallory Evans, the woman with the golden touch, is having such a big crisis of confidence simply because she wants some control over a film she's proud of. It seems the most natural thing in the world to me, and you certainly have earned the right."

With no small difficulty, Mallory followed the shift of Colt's mood. And at the same time she felt a surge of gratitude. He knew. He understood. He was giving her space. "Do you think so?" she answered. Her smile was still a little shaky. She shrugged, glancing down at her glass. "I don't know, I have a crisis of confidence with everything, I suppose. I mean. . . ." And she looked at him, sincerity darkening her eyes, her brow furrowing with its familiar uncertainty. Why did she feel as though she could tell him anything, and he would understand? Why did she want to bare her soul to him? Was it just because he had kissed her, had stirred to life actions and reactions she didn't even know she was capable of? But no, she

had felt that way about him all evening. She had
shared more with him in three hours than she did
with most people in a lifetime. She didn't know why.
She just felt close. "I still can't believe all this has
happened to me," she confessed. "Success, money—"
Mallory cast a helpless glance around the room
"—that people actually want to produce what I
write. That actors get excited about the parts, that
cinematographers actually put film in cameras and
that people pay for tickets to see what *I* created...."
She shook her head a little. "I can't deal with it."
Again Mallory glanced down at her glass, unaware of
how her hands tightened slowly on the stem. "I've
paid my dues, I guess," she said slowly. "I've seen the
bad times. And it's like...all of this—" again she
gestured futilely "—is my reward. If I'm not very
careful, if I'm too greedy, or too careless, or if I get
too comfortable with it, it might all be taken away."
She smiled a little defensively, realizing how silly she
sounded. "Just like that." And just like that, she had
just opened up her largest vulnerability—her paranoia—to a virtual stranger.

But in Colt's eyes was no amusement; he did not
appear to think it was silly. "Mallory Evans," he said
soberly, "you are a very special woman. No one else
can do what you do. No one else can even come
close. You haven't even begun to explore what you
can be. Nobody can take that from you."

He said it with such tenderness, such confidence,
that for a moment Mallory believed it. Gratitude
brimmed in her eyes; she had to blink. It was impossible to prevent one hand from coming out to

gently stroke that forward-falling tousle of hair. It felt like silk against her unsteady fingers. She wanted more than anything in the world at the moment to be held by him. "You're a nice person," she said softly, letting her hand fall away. She laughed a little, shakily and self-derisively. The laugh broke off on a breath, and her eyes wandered briefly around the room before resting on his face again. "Not much of an evening for you, huh?" There was apology in her voice. "Stuck with a half-grown neurotic female...." Mallory placed her glass on the table and sat back, her hands clasped tightly around her knees. She couldn't look at him.

"Mallory." Colt's voice was quiet and commanding, his finger brushed with a feather touch across her cheekbone, forcing her to look at him. There was nothing but gentleness and understanding in his eyes. "I know how fragile you are, and, yes, how very vulnerable. I knew that from the moment I saw you standing in the foyer of Marcetti's. It fascinated me." His lips curved into a delicately teasing smile. "One of the most alluring legends in show business, the very epitome of success, standing in a crowded foyer with her watch tangled in her dress, looking like a lost child." That made Mallory smile a little, and she saw the deepening light in Colt's eyes in response. "I was drawn to you then," he said seriously, "and the more I learn about you, the more I'm drawn to you...the more fascinated I become." Colt's eyes moved slowly over her face, lifting and examining each weakness, each vulnerability that was written so clearly on her face...and returning them to her intact, without judgment. The stains of color that still lingered in Mallory's cheeks from his kiss grew more vibrant as his eyes moved downward to her throat. She wondered what it would be like to feel his lips there. And she felt his gaze upon her breasts, which were still heavy and straining against the flimsy silk. She felt the outline of her nipples begin to press anew against the material, and she made a self-conscious fluttering motion with her hand as she half turned from him, as though to hide. Colt caught her hand in midair.

"Yes, I want you," he admitted gently, and still he held her hand. Strength and protection were communicated through that clasp and the pleasure flowed through her, over and around her, a safe haven in a storm. "But I won't touch you again, if it frightens you that much. You're too important to me for that. I'll never hurt you, Mallory."

Chapter Eight

OH, WHAT BEAUTIFUL PROMISE IN THOSE WORDS. What tenderness, what caring. How badly she wanted to believe them. Slowly, she closed her eyes, while something within her just as slowly opened to a new awareness, like an exotic blossom unfolding petal by petal. He was so near, so warm. He made her feel so safe, so good. Though he didn't make a move, he drew her closer. She couldn't help it. She had to touch him.

Mallory's hand came out without her volition and brushed against the warm, coarse flesh of Colt's neck. Fingertips explored the feathery soft ends of his hair near the collar, moved beneath the material and discovered strong, masculine neck muscles. She felt his heat against her palm, she traced the outline of his collarbone with her fingers. Her heart was pounding, her skin on fire. And he just sat there, letting her touch him, only a slight tightening of his hand around hers giving any indication at all that he was aware of what she was doing. He hardly seemed to breathe.

Mallory's fingers moved around his neck, to the hollow of his throat. She opened her eyes to follow their path down the front of his open shirt, across his bare chest. "I'm sorry. . . ." Mallory clenched her hand against his chest and dropped her gaze. Her voice was high and a little tight. "I don't mean to be a tease. I just. . . wanted to touch you, and. . . be touched. . . ."

She was wrapped in Colt's arms, tightly, securely, lovingly. She never knew whether it was her move or his. She only knew that she wanted and needed the strength of a man's arms, the warmth and life of his body enfolding hers. She clung to him, moving ever closer, her fingers closing against the breadth of his shoulder muscles as her breasts pressed into his chest, her lips parting on one shuddering gulp of breath before she buried her face in his shirt. The embrace was hard and all-encompassing, desperate on her part, strongly protective on his. He held her. He cared for her. It was a miracle she hardly dared believe, the sensation of needing and being needed, the silent communication of one body to another. In that single gesture, barriers shattered and were blown away like dust in the wind, heavy shackles dropped to the ground around her, and a new woman stepped forth eagerly to grasp by greedy handfuls all she had been denied for so long.

Very lightly, Colt's lips moved against her face, kissing the corner of her eye, her temple, her cheekbone. "It's all right, love," he whispered. "Hold on to me. I'm here."

Mutely Mallory nodded against his chest and tightened her arms briefly. Yes, he was here. And she needed this very, very badly. Human warmth. Strength. The unexplained and unexpected closeness that had been developing between them all evening and was cemented in this one moment of touching and being touched. She felt Colt's hands moving soothingly over her hair, and her back, the movements punctuated every so often by the gentle, restrained pressure of his lips on her face. Mallory was drawn along in the sweeping tide of instinct, of demand and satisfaction, and the more she received the more she wanted. She turned her lips to Colt's neck and tasted the tangy hint of his cologne, the warm coarse skin beneath her tongue. Colt's hands tightened on her back even as there seemed to be a weakening of his muscles, and he leaned into the pressure of her mouth with an unexpected catch of breath. A surge of surprised power and wonder filled Mallory as she knew she was giving him pleasure. The need to taste and explore was released within her, exposing the woman who had been so long in hiding inside.

Colt's palms moved along Mallory's silk-covered back and then against her ribs, upward toward the hollows of her armpits where her arms stretched to encircle his neck. It was a gentle exploration at first, careful and restrained, but the pressure became more firm, the motions more urgent as Mallory's hungrily seeking lips moved across his face, touching, caressing. . . . And when Colt turned his head to cover her mouth with his, Mallory received it eagerly, drinking in the taste and the feel of him, letting the sensations carry her, desperately asking for more.

Colt's face was damp beneath her trembling

hands, wondering, delightedly discovering hands; his breathing was uneven. Their bodies were entwined as they lay together on the sofa, the heat from one inundating the other. Colt's lips traveled over her face, catching in the strands of hair that clung to the moisture there; his hand slipped inside her shirt to firmly clasp one breast. Mallory felt the hardness of his pelvis as he moved against her, her hips strained toward him instinctively. Her hands had loosened Colt's shirt from his slacks and were now beneath it, seeking the broad contours of his bare back, the smooth texture of skin, the heat that radiated from every muscle. Then his mouth nudged aside the thin covering of silk and closed over her breast, and with a gasp, Mallory gave herself to the swirling vortex of sensual pleasure.

Her body wanted Colt; her mind did not. Even as his hands loosened the buttons of her shirt and her own fingertips clutched at the bunched muscles of Colt's chest, a thin thread of reason prevailed. Yes, she needed him; her sexuality cried out for him, but that was all it was—sex. She was being foolish and destructive. How would she feel afterward? What would this do to her emotionally? For five years she had kept herself safe and secure, risking no exposure, no involvement.... Would she lose it all to one night of instinct, of mindless passion with no meaning or forethought? This was not her great romance. She had known the man less than six hours. She would probably never see him again. There was no love, no familiarity, no promise to give the act meaning. Mallory could not throw away her carefully built defenses for so irrational a reason. . . . She could not do this to herself.

Colt's lips were raining gentle nibbling kisses on her neck, her chest, her ribs, her stomach. Though with each touch of his lips or his tongue a renewed shiver of pleasure coursed through her, Mallory turned her head helplessly into the sofa, her fingers tightening on his shoulders in protest. It was a last desperate attempt to save her emotional equilibrium, and Colt responded to the signal.

His hands moved to gently cup her face. He rested his weight on his knees on either side of her. His skin was damp and pleasure-flushed, his breathing uneven. In his eyes Mallory saw the light of passion, but beyond it something else—a tenderness and a question, a hesitance. He would have stopped then if she had asked him to.

As his lips came down to clasp hers in gentleness and reassurance, an overwhelming emotion arose within Mallory again. It could have been need, it could have been gratitude for the caring she saw in his eyes. At that moment it felt like love. Her mouth opened beneath his, her fingers were no longer pushing against his bare shoulders but circling them, pulling him nearer. She felt the pressure of Colt's roughly textured chest against her swollen breasts, his hands tightening and tugging at her hair, a mixture of pain and pleasure that was symbolic of her desperate surrender. She could not stop him. She could not go back now. The situation was out of her control.

Mallory hardly felt his absence in the brief interlude Colt stood to discard his clothes, nor was she aware of the swift wrestling movements with which he flung aside her blouse and tugged her jeans from her hips. Their movements all flowed together in one unbroken moment of breathlessness and symbiotic heartbeats of need until she felt his lean bare legs nudging hers apart, the strength of him, the rough texture of his hair-covered thighs against the sensitive inner flesh of hers. Then there was a twinge of fear.

But even that vanished into the soul-swallowing depths of Colt's eyes, the rampant hunger of their merging mouths and the slow, deliberate entry of his body into hers. This was no delicate dance of sensory exploration, no gentle joining of tender lovers. A shuddering gasp was torn from Mallory as she arched herself into him; her nails dug into his back, her lips found his neck, his shoulders, his face. It was savage and unleashed, primal passion, a man and a woman reduced to their most primitive elements. Tongues sweeping and mating, hands grasping and seeking, ragged breath intermingling, they fought together the violent battle against a foe neither could name. Mallory used and she was used, she took and she gave, and endlessly, relentlessly, they surged onward toward the place where they became nothing more and nothing less than man and woman, needing each other. Their mating was not swift or easy but endless and desperate, bordering on brutal, requiring from them more than they thought they were capable of enduring, and Mallory was shaken to the very depths of her soul.

Her muscles were trembling with exhaustion and strain, perspiration dripped from her hair and shimmered on her lashes, melding their bodies together as they lay at last, weakly entwined on the sofa. Mallory felt drained, numb, completely spent. She could not think, or even feel anymore. Dimly she was aware of Colt's breathing, heavy and slow, but her own breath seemed to have evaporated somewhere between the thought and the deed. His hands caressed her shoulders as he held her. The murmur of his voice was soothing, but she did not hear the words.

Weakly, Mallory's fingertips brushed across the face of the man who had just made her whole. The texture was rough and prickly; she had not noticed that before. Colt's mouth caught her fingertips briefly as they trailed across his lips, kissing them, and then he tightened his hold on her for one swift moment, a last expenditure of energy, an expression of renewed ardor that lacked physical strength for its fulfillment. She could feel the muscles trembling in his arms. "Mallory," he whispered, "you are so beautiful."

Something within her reached toward him — a blossoming joy, a surge of need, an emotion so deep and so powerful it was unlike any she had ever experienced before. She was left helpless, shaken. It felt so much like love.

There was silence, long and steady, as warm as a down comforter. Colt's hand stroked her body from shoulder to hip over and over again; he could not stop touching her. Mallory's fingers were tracing small repetitive patterns on his chest, tugging weakly at the hairs, brushing the muscles, filling her senses with him. Filled with him, that's how she felt. A part of him. Exposed to him and blended with him, a new person.

Yet beneath the powerful afterglow of closeness they shared there was uncertainty. Neither of them had truly expected this to happen. Mallory knew it should never have happened. She had abandoned herself to instinct; she had chosen her heart over her head. She had forfeited control and opened herself for hurt and confusion. Oh yes, it had been totally transporting. Now, in the afterglow she could see the power, the magnificence, the awe. Magic hovered and wrapped them in its spell. They had come together in one rich moment and the world had changed. Only when the dust settled would she begin to see the destruction that lingered.

Colt, as sensitive after the fact as before, kissed her cheek lightly. His voice was husky. "Darling, are you all right?"

It was not a superficial question, not the polite remark that men seemed to be trained to provide on such occasions. The concern in his eyes was real. There was no denying it. Colt understood and he cared about what was happening to her now. He knew what this had meant to her. And he was afraid of what she would do with it.

There was no point in lying to him. No point at all. Mallory felt as though from this moment onward nothing about her would be secret from him. Colt had invaded her most cryptic places and made them a part of him. Her smile was a little weak, but that was more from the result of kiss-swollen lips and passion-grazed cheeks than emotional apathy. She dropped her gaze to follow the last trailing caress of her fingers along the bunched muscle of his forearm. "I don't know," she admitted softly. Her tone was a little strained. She guessed she wouldn't know for a long time. She didn't want to think about it now.

Colt hesitated, then lightly pushed her hair away from her face with both hands. His smile was gentle and encouraging. "I'll be back in a minute," he promised, and got to his feet. The separation of their perspiration-glued bodies was almost as painful as his initial withdrawal had been. Mallory's fingers clenched instinctively as though to hold him there. She had gotten accustomed to the feel of him close to her. Blending into her.

With vague, emotion-dazed eyes, she watched Colt walk nude from the room. He was lean and well formed, the picture of a man who valued himself and took care of his body. His muscles were not bulging or overdefined, but stripped and controlled. He was a beautiful male animal.

Mallory became aware that until this moment she had not seen Colt unclothed. In the blur of passion and urgency that had gone before, she had not looked at him. This was the man with whom she had just shared the most important experience of her life, and it was not until after the fact that she saw his body naked.

After a moment, Mallory made herself sit up. She

had to get herself together. The clock still ticked, the planet still revolved. Around the globe people were being born and dying, traffic lights flashed from red to green, milkmen were starting their routes in New York and offices were breaking for lunch in London. Wire services spewed forth ticker tape, and generals paced in war rooms, and all life on earth had not come to an abrupt stop because Mallory Evans had just made love with Colt Stanford.

She smoothed her hair and brought her hand away in slow surprise. It was not just damp. It was soaked. She squeezed the ends and droplets of moisture trickled down her wrist. She wanted to smile.

She reached for her panties and pulled them on with the slow, deliberate motions of a battle-weary soldier or an aging invalid. The air was warm with the scent of both their colognes and the secret intimacy of sexuality. The essence of animal savagery and the beauty of human compassion. Man and woman. Love and lust. For a moment Mallory paused, letting the aura seep through her pores. It was beautiful and poignant and somehow sad.

The silk blouse lay crumpled on the floor. Vaguely Mallory thought about the dry-cleaning bill. Colt and she had only engaged in sex after all. She had confronted an age-old conflict, succumbed to instincts as ancient as man and proved once again that human nature will, when given a choice, return to the cave rather than look to the stars. Logic has no chance against passion. There was nothing special about her; millions of men and women made the same discovery every day—were doing it at this moment.

But tonight Mallory felt as though she had touched the stars. Nothing would ever be the same again.

Something had happened, a bond had been formed. Mallory did not understand, but she knew that had happened. The physical act, an hour out of time, would not permanently change her life or affect the state of the world in any way. But what Colt had taken from her, and given to her, what they had discovered and become during that simple and very natural act would last forever.

She wondered what the statistics were for the proportion of the American population that had sex on the first date. She wondered if each and every one of them was moved as powerfully as she'd been. Probably not.

Colt returned with two filled glasses of wine and a towel flung over his shoulder. He set the goblets on the table and she smiled as he knelt on the floor near her and draped the towel over her hair, squeezing out the moisture. "Do you want to take a shower?"

All right, she could be sophisticated. After all, it happened every day. . . to other women, not to her. Mallory buttoned her blouse carefully over her bare breasts. "No, thanks. I'll wait until I get home."

She took the towel from him with a little grimace of disbelief at the state of her hair and began to slowly rub it dry. Colt sat back on his heels, completely unabashed about his nudity, and watched her. After what had just taken place between them, why should he be self-conscious?

His expression was sober. "How long has it been for you?" he asked quietly.

Mallory paused, but only for a moment. Secrets didn't matter anymore. She met his eyes. "Five years."

Momentary surprise crossed his eyes, shock, then a cautious skepticism as his gaze moved briefly over her half-dressed form. Would there be repulsion or derision in his eyes when they met hers again? Mallory did not want to know. She busied herself with the towel, shielding her face from his view. She felt the sofa shift as he sat down beside her with both feet firmly on the floor. She heard his long, slow release of breath. It was a sound mixed with wonder and despair. "Five years," he repeated, very softly.

Mallory ventured a glance at him then. His elbows were resting on his thighs, his hands lightly clasped between bare knees. His head was turned toward her, his hair damp and tangled across his forehead, giving him the endearing look of a puzzled little boy. She repressed an urge to smooth it back. "Why?" he asked simply. In his eyes was nothing but concern.

Mallory shrugged a little and, deciding her hair was a lost cause, discarded the towel. "I don't have time for relationships," she said, reaching for her jeans, "or even dating. My life is so full there simply isn't room for anyone else." She disentangled her panty hose from the inside of her jeans and stuffed them into her purse. That simple action made her feel like a wanton. As though she did it every day.

"But. . . five years." The concept seemed to baffle Colt. And she was touched because the look she saw in his eyes appeared to reveal more than simple curiosity; his concern was personal and directed at her. Having known her, Colt cared about her. And caring about her, he wanted to know more about her. He shook his head in slow wonder. "That's a long time to go without another human touch. A long time to live inside your head."

Mallory paused in the process of drawing the jeans over her ankles. It was surprising how easy it was to talk to him. This subject, so deep and painful to her, was no different than any other they had discussed tonight. What was even more surprising was how steady her voice was. Everything else was still quivering inside. "I suppose I put a lot of subliminal energy into my work," she admitted. "And yes—" here her voice dropped "—I missed being touched."

Quickly Mallory stood up to pull her jeans over her hips, and she swayed a little on her feet. She felt Colt's light supporting hand on her waist and was briefly grateful. Again that surge of something. . . reaching, needing, perhaps just affection, pure and simple. It felt good.

She fastened her jeans and reached for her purse. Colt handed it to her, and while she futilely searched the contents for a hairbrush he stood and pulled on his own slacks. The purse was small and Mallory didn't have a brush or a comb. Why should she? She had not expected her hair to even get tousled, much less. . . .

"There's a hairbrush in the bathroom," Colt offered. "First door on the right."

Mallory smiled her thanks and somewhat hesitantly followed his directions. With the door locked on the neat beige-and-white room, she was for the first time alone with her thoughts.

Except there was nothing to think. She had done it. She had impulsively discarded five years of rules to live by. She had made herself vulnerable to the first man who came along, but other than that nothing had basically changed. Mallory knew she would not be very proud of herself in the morning. She had thought she had more character and strength of will than this. But regret would not change the events of the past few hours. She was not entirely sure she would want to change them.

The fluorescent lights were not kind. Her hair was plastered darkly to her head in ropy strands and clinging to her neck. Mallory picked up the hairbrush on the vanity and started to make whatever repairs she could, but hesitated. Then she smiled at her own reluctance. Colt had just engaged with her in the most intimate act that was possible between two human beings; why should he care if she used his brush?

She managed to release most of the tangles and swept her hair behind her ears in a style that was neat, if not very attractive. But there was not much to be done about her face. Her eyes were rimmed with dark raccoonlike mascara circles, her lips swollen and cherry red, her fair skin chafed and raw. Her eyes were luminous and looked enormous in an unfamiliar face. The cold water she splashed on her face did nothing to lessen the vibrant—if somewhat alarming—color in her cheeks. How could she look so happy when everything within her was in turmoil?

She took a damp tissue and wiped away the worst of the mascara stains, then carefully reapplied lip gloss. The muscles in her arms were still quivering, her fingers tingling. Then she went back to the living room.

"This place has a bedroom, you know." Colt smiled, handing her a wineglass. "You're more than welcome to spend the night."

Oh, no. She had done enough to complicate her life for one evening. Mallory shook her head as she sank down beside him on the sofa, not meeting his eyes. "I'd better not. Tomorrow is a working day."

Colt's lips tightened briefly in a near grimace. "Why was I so sure you'd say that?" he murmured. Then he settled back against the sofa cushions, long legs stretched before him, hands cradling the glass lightly. His gaze was steady and even. "Talk to me, Mallory." His voice was almost casual. "Tell me how you feel about what just happened."

Once again, he made evasion superfluous, if not impossible. She shrugged somewhat uncomfortably, but she told him the truth. "Confused. A little upset. I don't know what to think of myself anymore. I wish it hadn't happened."

Colt lifted his eyebrows somewhat skeptically, and she met the gesture with an unflinching gaze. "Does it matter so much what you think of yourself?"

She nodded firmly. "I'm all I have to rely on. I have to keep my head straight."

Colt watched her for a moment, digesting that, examining her face and appearing to read more between the lines than she had even intended to reveal. He sipped from his glass and met her eyes again. When he spoke she was struck once again by how mesmerizing and sensuous his voice was. "Mallory, at the risk of sounding crude—" he paused, eyes gentling to reach her, preparing her for a truth she probably did not want to face "—you needed what happened tonight and wanted it, probably more than I did. I knew you were having trouble—I didn't know why, but I knew you were having some trauma. I meant it when I said I wouldn't touch you." She knew that was true. "I wanted you, but I wouldn't risk hurting you over.... But, darling, you wouldn't stop. You wouldn't let me back away. You needed a man tonight, very badly." And he paused, watching her. "I think it's important you understand that."

Mallory took a deep breath, her hands tightening ever so slightly on the glass. All right. She could deal with that. "Look," she said evenly, "I'm not blaming you, if that's what—"

Colt made an impatient sound and an abrupt movement at the same moment. Mallory's tightly drawn nerves jumped, and as she watched him cautiously, the frustration that tightened his face quickly faded. "Blame is not an appropriate word. That's exactly what I was afraid you would do— take tonight and twist it into a guilt trip. You have a tendency to do that, don't you?"

The brief hint of a teasing smile flashed in Colt's

eyes, urging her to stop taking herself so seriously. Of course he was right. It was no big deal. It happened every day. And Mallory did not have time to undergo a long drawn-out trauma over the events of one short evening. Nothing had changed.

She released another breath, forcing the tension to drain from her body. She even managed to smile at herself and her foolishness. "All right. I'm a grown-up woman, and I can take responsibility for my own actions. No guilt trip."

Colt may not have entirely believed her, but his smile did not show it. His fingertips lightly trailed over her forearm, and Mallory was surprised at the renewed response of electricity he was capable of generating. Colt touched her, and every cell in her body opened to him. His gaze followed the movement of his fingers until they rested lightly atop her hand, then he looked at her. His eyes, she noticed, were so brown. Like cocoa-colored velvet. They touched her even when his hands did not. The sensation was like the brush of a rich fabric; it soothed and mesmerized her senses.

"You told me before you were a cynic," he said, and the faint smile he gave her might have been the amusement directed at himself, or anticipation of her reaction. "Well, guess what? I'm a diehard romantic." He dropped his gaze briefly, and when he looked at her again he was serious. Gentle, but serious. "What happened between us tonight was very special, Mallory. I wasn't expecting it. I didn't plan it any more than you did. But we can't ignore it. We can't forget it. There's a bond there that I can see

already you're going to do your best to try to break.
That would be a mistake, Mallory."

"I think," she said softly, and she was not even
aware of the thought until she had said the words,
"it might have been better if we had known each
other longer."

Colt smiled. The gesture was indulgent and
knowing, but not condescending. "Time is an illusion, Mallory, especially when applied to relationships. We may not have known each other very
long, but we know each other better than most people do when they first make love. . . and if that feeling ends tomorrow nothing will take away what we
shared tonight. Can you understand that?"

Mallory cast her eyes down quickly, she could feel
the tension creeping up her arms and her legs again.
What was the matter with her? Those were exactly
the words any woman would want to hear in her
situation. Why did they frighten her so badly?
"Look, Colt," she said carefully. Her eyes were unflinching and added strength to her words. "We're
both adults. Let's not make more of this than there
has to be. I don't have time for involvements. You
know that already. You're right, I didn't expect
this, and I'm still a little confused, but we don't
have to—"

Colt's low chuckle interrupted her, he shook his
head in slow wonder. The amusement in his eyes as
he looked at her was easy and friendly. He relaxed
her even as he confused her further. "You're incredible, you know that?" he demanded, and lightly
he brushed his knuckles along the side of her face.

His eyes softened. "That little piece of twisted logic that just bubbled forth from your lips is only one of the reasons you fascinate me, I suppose."

She glanced at her glass, giving over to the irrational thrill of pleasure that coursed through her with his touch, his words. "Do I fascinate you?" she murmured.

"You know you do. You, as a person, as a professional. . . as a woman," Colt emphasized. "I want to know you." His voice was sincere. "I want to discover you. That's what this evening was all about."

Mallory shook her head in an almost imperceptible gesture of incredulity, her eyes studying the clear Chablis. Two people who are fascinated with each other, who laugh together, who share a common professional interest and stimulating conversation, who discover as a bonus the magic of earth-shaking passion. . . . It sounded so simple. Why was she so uneasy?

Because the whole situation was too good to be true, that was why.

She knew she did not want to pursue this subject, and she looked up at him, hoping he wouldn't press her. Colt was watching her. "You were an abused wife, weren't you?"

Something caught in her throat; quickly she lowered her eyes. That had come from nowhere, totally unexpected. Abused? Was there any way, she wondered, that one could love and not be abused? Dimly, almost as though the memory belonged to someone else, she remembered anger and desperation and violence directed at her, but mostly she remembered helplessness. . . the crush of arms that wouldn't let her go, the rain of blows when she tried to escape, the sobs of regret afterward, fingers digging into her arms so desperately they left bruises. Mallory remembered that quite clearly. For almost two years she had constantly gone around with the blue-black imprints of three fingers on her upper arm, a symbol of need turned into desperation, promises into power, love into sickness. Physical abuse was such a small part.

The memory hit her like a pail of cold water and jolted her back into the world where there were real troubles, real traumas, real problems to be dealt with. Mallory ventured a glance at Colt, and if the expression in her eyes reminded him of a trapped rabbit, he gave no indication. She took a sip of her wine in what she hoped was a casual gesture. When she spoke her voice was a little tight, but revealed no other sign of distress. "What makes you think that?"

There was nothing in Colt's tone but a mild statement of fact, mere observation. "At dinner, I made a sudden movement with my hands, and you flinched. You did it again a few minutes ago. That's usually a sign that a woman has been physically hurt or traumatized in some way."

Mallory sipped more wine and said nothing, not meeting his eyes. Then she felt the caress of Colt's fingertips across her cheek, forcing her to look at him.

"Mallory," he said very seriously, "you know I would never hurt you, don't you? Not physically, not emotionally. You are too valuable to me for that."

She could not maintain the gaze that communicated so openly Colt's sincerity and her need to believe it. Oh, yes, he was an exceptional man. Far too exceptional. And he made her believe him far too easily. Illusion, always the illusion.... Half the magic is giving the people what they want to see.

Mallory knew she had to be very careful.

She finished her wine in two quick gulps and set the glass on the table. Her smile was composed and easy, a gentle suggestion. "It's really very late."

Colt hesitated, and in his eyes Mallory saw words begin to form. Her stomach tightened, ready to defend herself against whatever further stripping truth he had to offer, but then he appeared to change his mind. He smiled at her, a slow and easy reassurance, then he stood up and began to pull on his shirt and shoes.

The twenty-minute drive to her house was mostly silence against the soft soothing background of FM radio. The digital clock on the dash announced it was a quarter to three. Mallory was exhausted.

Colt held her hand warmly against his thigh as he drove. That was the gentle communication she needed and wanted, the natural communion of two people who had shared a deeply moving intimacy. He was right—something special had happened. There was a bond. But she did not think she would ever see him again.

When they arrived, she opened the car door before he could make a move to get out. Colt noticed the gesture and his eyes acknowledged the reason for it. Mallory turned to him with a smile that was both falsely bright and drained, uncertain and hopeful. What could she say? What was she supposed to say?

He said it for her. Very lightly, his knuckles stroked her temple. His eyes, for the moment he looked at her, were so deep and full of unreadable emotions that Mallory shivered. Then he placed a single tender kiss upon her cheek. "Sometimes," he said softly, "we live so long in our dreams we can't recognize what's real. I don't want that to happen to you, Mallory."

The touch of his mouth was soft, warm and filled with gentleness and meaning she did not want to decipher, as were his words. She bit her lip against a new surge of confusing emotions. She could not take any more now. Not now.

"Good night, Mallory."

No promises. Just good night. She liked that.

Colt waited in the car as she walked up the short drive and searched for her key. She had of course forgotten to leave the porch light on, and it took a while to get the key in the lock. She so rarely went out at night. But at last the door opened and the headlights of his car swung over her as he backed down the driveway. Mallory did not turn around.

Chapter Nine

THE RINGING OF THE TELEPHONE awakened Mallory the next morning. Through the fuzzy web of sleep she was aware of anticipation forming. Her voice was husky with the warmth of a leftover dream when she answered.

"How did it go?" Jeannine demanded.

It took a moment for Mallory's befuddled mind to recognize the caller. Was she disappointed not to hear a male voice on the other end of the line? If so, the letdown barely had time to register on her as a sleepy smile filtered into Mallory's voice. Perhaps part of her was still dreaming. "Oh. . . it was nice. Real nice."

"Well, tell me about it." There was impatience and excitement in Jeannine's voice. "Where did you go? What did you talk about?"

Absently, Mallory drew a strand of her hair across her face and inhaled the scent of a man's cologne. The memories evoked were pleasure-clouded. She almost felt she was still a part of him, and the night lingered on. "Oh. . . we had dinner. Steak and lobster. We talked about the business and he gave me lots of good pointers." But she was waking up. She struggled to sit up, squinting in the hazy white light toward the clock. "What time is it?"

Jeannine laughed. "What time did you get in?"

"About three." And then she found the clock. Ten-thirty. Mallory suppressed a groan as her eyes widened in amazement. The day was half over. She never slept this late.

"Well, I guess you *did* have a good time. Did you like him?"

Mallory did not have to give that much thought. The answer was instinctual, born of emotions she had no intention of analyzing in her sleep-hazed state. "He is the most charming man I have ever met. I've never known anyone else like him." For it was true that if she had to take such a dramatic step in her life she could not have chosen a better partner. Yes, she liked him. Too much, perhaps, to have given herself to him so wantonly. Maybe that was why, as she pushed her hair away from her face and remembered his similar gesture, Mallory felt a little sad.

"I'm glad." There was a note of uncommon seriousness in Jeannine's voice. "I've got to tell you, Mal, I was a little worried about you last night."

Mallory's laugh was both surprised and a little dry. So now her best friend worried about her... now, when it was too late. "Why?" she demanded.

"Well, you've got to admit, kid, you've been out of touch for quite a while. You're not exactly a pro at this, and you're pretty vulnerable right now."

A slightly wry smile lingered on Mallory's lips as she nodded her head in slow agreement. Oh yes, she was very vulnerable. She had not forgotten that for a moment.

"And a man like Colt Stanford. . . well, I don't know the fellow, but surely anyone who got as far as he did in show business must be pretty good at getting what he wants. Don't be offended, Mal, but it seemed a pretty big coincidence, his coming into your life just when you were looking for a director. . . ."

Mallory was not offended. Maybe it was a coincidence, but not a threatening one. She knew that Colt Stanford was a determined professional. That was one of the things she most admired about him. And maybe she admired him now more than ever. Colt had manipulated her even when she knew what he was capable of, and she didn't even mind.

"Do you think you'll see him again?"

Mallory's reaction to that was powerfully clear. Why had her heart speeded for a moment when she answered the phone? Colt was the most interesting man she had ever met; she felt honored to have spent even one night in his company. They had developed something very close to a friendship even before they returned to his apartment, and it was a friendship she would have liked to have continued, but. . . . "I don't think so." Mallory's response was easy and nonchalant, effectively disguising from her friend her true emotions. That made Mallory uneasy. She had always been able to speak honestly to Jeannine about anything and everything. Why was this such a strong exception? "I don't really have time for this dating thing. Last night showed me that. I mean, here it is almost noon and I'm not even out of bed yet. I can't afford to be so lazy." But she was thinking about the passion that had flared between Colt and her so quickly and so dangerously, feelings that overcame reason and made her lose control. No, she couldn't afford that. Not at any price.

Jeannine chuckled. "Same old Mal, I see. Nothing gets past your precious insecurity, does it?"

Mallory swallowed hard and did not answer. No, nothing. . . .

"All right, kid, hit the typewriter. I've got another important phone call to make." A note of secret excitement crept into Jeannine's voice that Mallory had never heard before. She sounded almost girlish, and that tone, coming from her jaded and worldly-wise friend, was enough to prick Mallory's curiosity. "Do you remember that man who came into the shop yesterday?"

She did not, but Jeannine was apparently eager to talk about him, so Mallory listened attentively. "Well, his name is Byron Warnham. Can you believe that? *Byron.* Just like out of a book. He looks like he belongs on the cover of a book too—tall, dark, and beautiful. And get this, Mal—he's *very British.*" Jeannine rolled the words in an imitation of the accent, forcing Mallory to grin at her friend's enthusiasm. "I mean, not the Mick Jagger kind of British, but *old* British, cultured, distinguished."

Mallory could not help laughing. It was good to hear Jeannine so excited, even if it was about her favorite subject—a man. And today Mallory could relate exactly to what Jeannine was feeling. "He doesn't sound like your type at all!" Mallory had to point out.

Surprisingly, Jeannine grew serious. "Maybe," she suggested thoughtfully, "I never knew what my type is. Maybe it's about time I started thinking about real men and real relationships, instead of just playing at love." Mallory's attention quickened, but Jeannine, as though embarrassed at having been caught daydreaming out loud, went on brightly, "If a woman *were* thinking about old-fashioned love and marriage, what better man to do it with than someone named *Byron Warnham?* Anyway, I've got to call him this morning... I don't want to take a chance on his getting away!"

Mallory laughed and wished Jeannine good luck. She really wished the best for her friend in her new romance, hoping that maybe this time she had found the real thing... and she wished the best for herself too.

Mallory did not linger in bed, as much as she would have liked to lie there, staring at the ceiling and trying to sort out her thoughts. She went into the bathroom to shower, determined to get a firm, if somewhat belated, start on her day.

Her face in the mirror did not look changed. Her eyes were slightly puffy and dark circled from too much wine and the late hours, and maybe her lips were still a little swollen, but there was no other sign that this was a woman who had just undergone one of the most important experiences of her life. Same old Mallory. The changes were all on the inside.

But she refused to spend valuable working time wondering what they were. She showered and shampooed her hair, then briskly toweled herself dry. Her skin smelled of nothing but soap, her hair nothing but orange-blossom shampoo. She slipped on white shorts and a top and wrapped her hair in a towel. She did not have time to blow it dry this morning.

When she started to make the bed, the familiar scent of a man's cologne drifted up to her from the folds of the sheets. It made her smile softly to herself as her fingertips smoothed a pillowcase. Silly Mallory. Maybe there was more of a romantic streak in her than she imagined. She decided not to change the sheets, hoping the fragrance would still be there to haunt her when she went to bed tonight.

Mallory worked in a restless rhythm that day, strangely filled with energy but given to long periods of reflective staring into space. The ticking of the clocks seemed almost oppressive, and her airy sunfilled house not so far from a prison after all. She was restless, on edge, eager for something she could not define.

Why did she feel as though she had opened herself to a whole new world? How could she have taken such a dramatic step so impulsively? Everything looked different today, exciting and filled with promise. She had done something courageous and daring: she had actually let herself get close to another human being, if even for only one evening. It had scared her a little, but had done no lasting damage. Her mind's eye kept wandering to a vision of Colt's face, the warmth in his eyes, the tousled dark hair, the intimate curve of his lips. It was a sweet memory. And with renewed flushes of pleasure, she reviewed the details of their conversation, wondering how easily their minds had blended. He had learned things about her she would have never dreamed of willingly telling a stranger. He read even the unspoken signals with authority and ease, and though that should have frightened Mallory, she only felt confident. With him, exposure had felt good. She could handle it. And he had been right. Last night was exactly what she needed.

She thought about what Jeannine had said. She had to remember nothing was what it seemed. How well did Mallory really know Colt Stanford? He had, after all, made a point of tracing her down. . .*after* he had heard there was a possibility she would be choosing the film's director. Was anybody in this business ever motivated by anything other than ambition?

She thought about it, but it was hard to believe Colt Stanford had any ulterior motives at all regarding her. She might not have known him long, but she knew him well, and *devious* was not a word she could ever apply to him. So what if he was hoping she would consider him as a candidate for her film? Could she ever hope to find anyone better qualified? Not that she even had the right to make that decision yet anyway. The entire matter was academic. She decided not to worry about it.

Sometimes, she thought, life hands you tests as well as bonuses—progress reports to measure your growth by. She had taken a risk last night, she had faced the challenge, and she had learned something very important. She wasn't frightened any longer. It had been a positive experience, and she was proud of herself. Now she felt as though she could do anything, and that was exactly what she needed at this point in her life.

While in that frame of mind she received a phone call from Evelyn Bouchard. Mallory's first reaction was one of mild distress. Since when had her highly protected unlisted phone number become public property? Twice in two days it had fallen into unexpected hands....

But she successfully hid her irritation, and after the amenities had been exchanged she merely inquired, "How did you get my telephone number, Miss Bouchard? It's unlisted."

"Is it?" The surprise in Evelyn's voice sounded very genuine of course. "Why, the studio gave it to me. The public-relations department, to be exact."

Mallory demanded, a little too sharply, "Which studio?"

Evelyn laughed lightly. "Rowntree, of course. They thought it might be a good idea to go ahead and start building up publicity for your new film. Naturally I'm happy to oblige.... Am I calling at a bad time?"

Mallory's mind was racing. New film...did that mean Jake had sold her counteroffer? Who would know before anyone else but Evelyn Bouchard? Her heart started thumping and her mouth went dry. Could he possibly have done it so fast? Would they

have been that eager to buy the script that they
would take it at any price? Then it hit her with
renewed clarity: if they had accepted the script on
her terms, it meant the film would be in her hands.
She was going to have her chance.

"Mallory?"

"Oh. . . I'm sorry." Mallory pushed her hair away
from her face and tried to calm her scrambled
mind. "I guess you did catch me at a rather bad
time." She kept her tone professional, but much less
cool than it had been at first. Part of her was leaping with joy, the other part desperately searching
for the catch. Why hadn't Jake told her? He could
have at least called. But then, he had hardly expected Mallory to be in touch with anyone from the
studio today, certainly not the gossip that traveled
faster than the speed of light. Jake was never in
a hurry about anything. He probably knew she
wouldn't be expecting results this soon. He figured
he could take his own sweet time about letting her
know the most important news of her life. Sometimes Mallory was so frustrated with him she could
scream.

"Well, I won't keep you more than a minute,"
Evelyn was saying. "All I wanted to do was see if we
couldn't set up some time for that interview. Shall
we do it over lunch one day?"

"Lunch," Mallory said. She was hardly even listening. "Sounds fine."

"Terrific. How about Friday?"

Absently Mallory flipped over the pages on her
calendar. Because of her newfound confidence, she

simply did not think to be wary. She had to start facing the world on her own terms, and last night had not been a bad beginning. "That's good for me."

"Shall we say Marcetti's at noon?"

Mallory jotted a note on her calendar. "See you then."

"Right." There was, for just a moment, a note in Bouchard's voice that made Mallory think of a cat with canary feathers sticking out of its mouth, but she did not take the trouble to analyze it. She quickly disconnected and dialed Jake's number.

He wasn't in. Mallory glanced at her watch in annoyance. It was two-thirty. Long lunches were a trademark of the profession, but Jake should certainly be in within the next few minutes. She left a message and hung up.

Then she sat at her desk and laughed out loud. Sometimes everything just happened at once, and it all seemed to have begun with her making the decision to engage in an innocent flirtation with a waiter...to let go and relax a little. With that act she had let down the barriers keeping all the good things out of her life, and now treasures were spilling through. Life had never looked better and all she had needed was a little self-confidence.

Within the next half hour the phone rang twice, and she leaped for it both times. One call was from her dentist's office, reminding her of an upcoming appointment. The second was a wrong number. By three-thirty Mallory was pacing the floor and glaring at the phone as though it were itself treacherous.

1. How do you rate _____ ?
   (Please print book TITLE)

   1.6 ☐ excellent   .4 ☐ good   .2 ☐ not so good
   .5 ☐ very good   .3 ☐ fair   .1 ☐ poor

2. How likely are you to purchase another book in this series?
   2.1 ☐ definitely would purchase   .3 ☐ probably would not purchase
   .2 ☐ probably would purchase   .4 ☐ definitely would not purchase

3. How do you compare this book with similar books you usually read?
   3.1 ☐ far better than others   .4 ☐ not as good   ℞
   .2 ☐ better than others   .5 ☐ definitely not as good
   .3 ☐ about the same

4. Have you any additional comments about this book?
   _____ (4)
   _____ (6)

5. How did you *first* become aware of this book?
   8. ☐ read other books in series   11. ☐ friend's recommendation
   9. ☐ in-store display   12. ☐ ad inside other books
   10. ☐ TV, radio or magazine ad   13. ☐ other _____
                                                  (please specify)

6. What *most* prompted you to buy this book?
   14. ☐ read other books in series   17. ☐ title   20. ☐ story outline on back
   15. ☐ friend's recommendation   18. ☐ author   21. ☐ read a few pages
   16. ☐ picture on cover   19. ☐ advertising 22. ☐ other _____
                                                                   (please specify)

7. What type(s) of paperback fiction have you purchased in the past
   3 months? Approximately how many?

	No. purchased		No. purchased
☐ contemporary romance	(23) _____	☐ espionage	(37) _____
☐ historical romance	(25) _____	☐ western	(39) _____
☐ gothic romance	(27) _____	☐ contemporary novels	(41) _____
☐ romantic suspense	(29) _____	☐ historical novels	(43) _____
☐ mystery	(31) _____	☐ science fiction/fantasy	(45) _____
☐ private eye	(33) _____	☐ occult	(47) _____
☐ action/adventure	(35) _____	☐ other	(49) _____

8. Have you purchased any books from any of these Harlequin Series in the past
   3 months? Approximately how many?

	No. Purchased		No. Purchased
☐ Romance	(51) _____	☐ Superromance	(57) _____
☐ Presents	(53) _____	☐ Temptation	(59) _____
☐ American Romance	(55) _____		

9. On which date was this book purchased? (61) _____

10. Please indicate your age group and sex.
    63.1 ☐ Male   64.1 ☐ under 15   .3 ☐ 25-34   .5 ☐ 50-64
    .2 ☐ Female   .2 ☐ 15-24   .4 ☐ 35-49   .6 ☐ 65 or older

Thank you for completing and returning this questionnaire.

NAME _____

ADDRESS _____

(Please Print)

CITY _____

ZIP CODE _____

POSTAGE WILL BE PAID BY ADDRESSEE

BUSINESS REPLY MAIL

FIRST CLASS   PERMIT NO. 70   TEMPE, AZ.

NATIONAL READER SURVEYS

2504 West Southern Avenue

Tempe, AZ   85282

NO POSTAGE
STAMP
NECESSARY
IF MAILED
IN THE
UNITED STATES

Abruptly she sat down and dialed Jake's number again. He still hadn't returned. She did not know how much longer she could take the suspense. "Do you know when to expect him?"

"No, Miss Evans. I'm not even sure he planned to come back to the office this afternoon. I'll give him your message first thing in the morning though."

Mallory sighed. That was another one of Jake's irritating habits. He hated the confines of an office and avoided it as much as possible. "No, that's all right. I'll try him at home tonight." Then she added hopefully, "Miss Blackwell. . . he didn't say anything to you about the deal he was working on for me, did he? I mean, has he heard anything?"

"I'm sorry, Miss Evans," the secretary replied regretfully, "I really don't know. There haven't been any messages relating to you today." There was a smile in her voice as she added, "I loved the script. I know it's going to be your biggest hit yet."

Mallory suppressed another sigh. "Thank you. I hope so."

So, there was nothing to do but sit and stare at the phone and wait. Jake might not even be home that evening. He had day deals and night deals, always moving along in his slow but thorough way. He would let her know about the negotiations for her in his own good time.

The doorbell rang suddenly and she ran to answer it. It could be Jake. . . .

Mallory flung open the door, breathless and a little flushed from racing, wispy tendrils of her hair catching on her cheeks. It was not Jake. The lean form of Colt Stanford lounged against the frame.

He was wearing white tennis shorts and a red jersey, running shoes and no socks. The golden brown skin of his muscled thighs and forearms was vivid against the bright colors. The smile in his eyes took her breath away—or perhaps just the shock of seeing him had that effect on her. Perhaps it was his mere presence, so unexpected, on her doorstep that caused the slow stain of color to creep into her cheeks and the rapid lurching rhythm of her heart. Perhaps it was the sight of those strong brown thighs, lightly furred with golden hair...perhaps his smile.

Colt lifted amused eyebrows at her silent reaction. "I could say I was in the neighborhood and thought I'd drop in," he volunteered, answering a question he must have known she had no intention of asking. "Or I could say I just stopped by to see if you'd like to join me in a game of tennis. But the truth is—" the slow twist of his lips was self-mocking and unbearably endearing "—after my big speech last night about you giving in to a guilt trip, I'm the one who's got it, I'm afraid." Behind the smile in his eyes there was seriousness. "I had to know how you were."

The state of Mallory's stomach was like fluttering butterflies. He could not have said anything more pointedly designed to fluster her further. But she should have known by now that Colt Stanford was nothing if he was not direct.

Nervously her hand touched the base of her

throat as she moved away from the door, and Colt's eyes followed the motion. She wondered what that meant in body language and forcefully returned her hand to her side. "Come in," she invited.

Colt stepped into the foyer, and she closed the door behind him, taking that moment away from direct eye contact to compose herself. Was it embarrassment for the memories of last night that burned in her cheeks and turned her limbs to jumping nerve bundles, or was it excitement? She didn't know. She only knew that he was here, he had come here to see her, he was concerned about her. . . and beneath the confusion there was pleasure. Yes, definitely pleasure.

When she turned that pleasure must have shown in her eyes, because his own eyes softened in response. That was the first time she realized he was holding a book. "I also wanted to bring this by," Colt told her, handing it over. "You forgot it last night."

It was the same volume Mallory had been reading last evening. She took it with a thrill of gratitude and surprise. "Oh, Colt. . . thank you! May I keep this for a few weeks?" She glanced up at him hopefully. "I'll take very good care of it, I promise."

Colt smiled, his gaze moving over her face in slow absorption, as though he found something of infinite wonder there. Mallory responded to that gaze as vividly as if it were a caress. It stopped her breath; it sent a tingling sensation down her arms to her fingertips. He said casually, "Don't worry. Keep it as long as you like."

Mallory's expression was a little uncertain, and she held the volume close to her breast. "Come sit down," she invited. "Can I get you something to drink?"

Colt shook his head and followed her deeper into the house. "No, I don't want anything but a little bit of your time."

Mallory's living room was large, multiwindowed and bright, like the rest of her home. The carpet was white, the sofa fabric sprayed with peach flowers. The delicate chairs and cushiony ottomans were in shades of peach and green, the end tables chrome and glass. It was definitely a woman's room.

Colt smiled as he looked around. "You do like your space, don't you?" he observed. "A person could get the urge to fly in a room like this."

Mallory did not deny it. "I don't like the feeling of being closed in," she answered, placing the book on the bottom tier of the glass coffee table.

Colt lifted one expressive eyebrow, but made no further comment. As he sat beside her on the sofa the scent of his cologne drifted toward her, familiar, tantalizing, lovely. The ticking of the clocks was a soothing background sound, the sunny room a bright refuge from the doubts and worries that might have assailed her elsewhere. Earlier uncertainties about his motives seemed ridiculous and irrelevant, and she spared them not another thought. Mallory felt herself sinking into the warmth of his presence even though a good two feet separated them. Tingles of excitement began in the tips of her toes and the sensation coiled around her body, as though she were being subjected to the force of an extraordinarily powerful magnet. She shouldn't be reacting to him like this. She still liked him and she would be honored to have his friendship. She was pleased to have him there...but they had shared only a one-night stand—just two people together under the forces of natural and unrestrained passion....

"You didn't expect to see me again, did you?"

Mallory felt no compulsion to avoid his eyes. "No," she admitted frankly. "I didn't."

Tender amusement played in Colt's eyes. "Why not?"

He certainly did have a way of getting to the heart of the matter, cutting through defenses and evasions, allowing no shadows she could hide in. Why should she find that characteristic so attractive? It should have terrified her.

This time Mallory turned the tables on him. Her smile was quick and shrewd, and she could have had no idea how it lit up her face, making her appear both girlish and seductive woman, both direct and coy. Colt drank it in like a soothing draft. "Why are you here?" she demanded.

Colt let his eyes move from the enticing curve of her lips, over her pink-and-ivory cheeks, to eyes that sparkled with life and challenge. And he felt everything that he was reaching out to her, wanting to enfold her in his embrace.

"Because," he answered soberly, and his hand moved forward to lightly capture hers, "neither one of us is the type to play the games that seem to be in-

herent in the Hollywood life-style—the one-night
stands, the brief encounters, the take-it-while-you-
can philosophy. Because you're unique, and there's
something in me that wants to be responsible for
you. Last night...." Colt dropped his eyes very
briefly. "I was the first for you in a long time," he
said simply. "Whether you want to admit it or not,
that makes me special. And gives me a special responsibility."

A sense of wonder and undefined affection spread
slowly through Mallory. A man of honor, in this day
and age? Oh yes, he was special. She wondered if he
even knew. "And," she supplied for him with a gentle note of teasing, "you want to handle the situation
with dignity and grace."

Colt grinned. In a flash of understanding both of
them acknowledged the inadequacy of that description. "Something like that," he admitted.

Mallory got up and walked a few steps away,
choosing her words carefully. "Colt," she said, not
quite ready to turn and face him, "that...means a
lot to me. It's quite wonderful of you, really.
But...." Then she turned, looking at him with
large and truthful hazel eyes, underscoring a gentle
message that asked merely for his understanding.
"It's not necessary. I don't want a relationship with
you. I don't have the time or the emotional energy. I
thought I made that clear last night. I like my life
the way it is."

Colt simply watched her—the interlaced hands,
the controlled pacing, the nervous licking of her
lips—and once again he was seeing more than she

wanted to reveal. This time, his perceptiveness made her even more nervous. "Come sit down."

Like a child, Mallory obeyed.

Colt took her tightly clasped hands in one of his, and with the other he deliberately began to pry the fingers apart. "Don't do that," he said quietly. "That's all I ask of you—don't close yourself off from me."

"Colt, you don't understand—"

Their eyes met and held. The message was as clear and as certain as if the words had been spoken out loud. Mallory's hands lay open and quiescent inside his. Colt was going to kiss her. He was going to kiss her because at that moment that was what she wanted more than anything else in the world.

Colt's lips fell gently upon hers, just a brush of his tongue at first, a provocative taste that swept across her lips and drew her to meet him. Everything within her tightened and stilled, then rushed into dizzying life as his lips clasped hers more firmly. The magic descended. That glorious sensation was not just a figment of her imagination, nor had it been created merely by last night's desperate passion. It was real, and still there.

Mallory's mouth opened beneath his, admitting the warm presence of his tongue. Her hand fluttered up to cup his strong neck and his curved around her waist. Her heart was tripping in her chest and her skin prickled; her senses were filled with him. What she experienced was sweet, tender, and even more intense than the blinding passion that had exploded between them last night. She was left resting weakly against Colt's chest, trying to calm the runaway beating of her heart. Her fingers entwined in the bunched-up material of his jersey. She wanted never to leave the safety of his arms.

"Ah, Mallory," Colt sighed, and brushed his lips against her hair. His fingertips gently rubbed the back of her neck; she responded by nestling her head against the solid security of his chest. "I don't think it's going to be that easy, walking away from each other. . . ."

Mallory's finger tightened slightly on the soft material of his shirt, then relaxed again. No, there would be nothing easy about that. How could she have ever imagined she would be able to leave him after a one-night stand? She moved slowly away from him, her mind frantically working to provide excuses, answers, strength from logic. "Colt," she said carefully, not looking at him, "you've got to understand. I didn't plan this. I just don't have the time, or the energy—"

"Don't you know I would never do anything to interfere with your life—or your work or your time?" Colt interrupted her patiently. "I admire you and what you've done too much to ever ask you to make those kinds of sacrifices." He bent down and touched her chin with his forefinger, raising her eyes to meet his. Behind the smile she saw there his expression was unrelentingly serious. "You do know that, don't you?"

Then what does he want? The brief and ugly suspicion came out of nowhere, and Mallory dismissed it quickly. Paranoia again.

She hesitated only a moment, then nodded.

Colt's smile broadened in acknowledgment. "I realize that you need your space—" his eyes wandered briefly and meaningfully around the room "—and I'm not going to infringe on that. So—" his gaze rested on hers again, a quiet demand "—what is it about relationships that scares you so much?"

Mallory moved restlessly in his arms. Colt's embrace tightened imperceptibly, and she was glad. She did not really want to move away. "Men . . ." she said, and then stopped. She could not look at him. Her voice was so low he had to strain to make out the words. "Men have a tendency to fall in love with me," she said simply.

Colt stroked her hair soothingly. He gave no sign of a reaction. "And that's bad?"

She was hit suddenly by a memory as intense as it was unexpected. . . . Larry, sobbing at her feet, holding her ankles, his words repeated over and over again until they became unintelligible, "I love you, Mal. Don't leave me—I can't make it without you. I only did it because I love you and you make me so mad. Don't go, Mallory, I love you." The repulsion and the pity she felt, the slow sick turning in her stomach and the desperation that fought within her like a trapped bird beating its wings against the bars of a cage. She couldn't get away. Day after day the wings beat until the small fragile creature that was her spark for freedom exhausted itself and sat numbly in a corner, staring with dull unblinking eyes through the bars. She could not get away. He loved her, and there was nothing she could do.

"Yes, it's bad," she said hoarsely.

Colt felt the tension and his face bent to her hair, his hands began mesmerizing stroking motions across her shoulders. "All right," he whispered. "All right." Then his fingers slipped beneath hers. Until that moment Mallory had not realized she was clutching her upper arms in a tight protective gesture. "Darling," he said in soft alarm, carefully prying her fingers loose. "Look what you're doing."

Slowly, Mallory looked down at her arms where he indicated. The dull red imprints of three fingers on each arm were visible. Later there would be bruises on her upper arms just like. . . .

Mallory forcefully relaxed her hands and took a deep breath, pushing herself with all her might away from the past, away from the memories. Even her own subconscious betrayed her, dragging her back no matter how much she fought. Would she ever be free?

It was a long time before Colt felt the tightness gradually fade from her back and shoulders, and a long time after that before he spoke. Then he bent down, making her look at him again. "Are you afraid I'm going to fall in love with you?" he inquired gently.

It was an honest question that deserved an answer. Once again Mallory had to lower her eyes. "I don't know," she admitted. Then she looked at him. "I know I don't want you to."

Colt smiled, and if there was a trace of indulgence in that smile she did not mind. "Fair enough," he said, and Mallory did not realize until much later that that really was no agreement at all.

Lightly Colt stroked her cheek, and the concern she saw in his eyes kindled a new surge of sensation within Mallory, pulling her, drawing her, making her want to be close to him. She wanted to be free, to step out of the prison of her own fears and into the sunshine of a new life, and all she had to do was try. . . .

She cupped his rugged face with her hands, letting this new and blindly wonderful emotion carry her away, letting all her joy and her need shine in her eyes. The moment of communication was pure and electric, anticipation building with the slow darkening of intensity. Their lips met, tenderly at first, then with increasing demand. Pleasure flowed through her, nerve endings responded to the overwhelming sensory input. Yearning tightened in Mallory's stomach and coiled in her toes, quickening her heartbeat and robbing her of breath. He made her tremble. No man had ever made her tremble before.

Colt lifted his face slightly, leaving her mouth tingling and swollen from the hungry pressure of his, her hands still tightly clutching his shoulders, her need reaching out to him with an almost tangible force. No, she could not easily walk away from this — not at all.

His eyes scanned her face; his breath, warm and a little unsteady, brushed across her cheek. "Mallory," he whispered, "do you want me to go?"

For just a moment she hesitated. Was this what she wanted? Last night's moment of unexpected passion could be overlooked. She had been caught off guard. Today, if she made a conscious decision to become more involved. . . .

But as always Colt demanded honesty from her. And as always she was unable to refuse. Slowly, she shook her head. "No," she whispered. She did not want him to leave.

The tenderness of his smile engulfed her as he bent again to lightly kiss her lips. "Then, does this place have a bedroom?"

She took his hand very slowly and led him out of the room. Mallory was aware with every step that she was moving toward something from which it would be increasingly hard to escape. If she turned back now, last night could be no more than a poignant memory, and she could go on with her life. She did not have time for a love affair. . . .

Chapter Ten

MALLORY STOOD IN THE CENTER of the bedroom, her eyes upon the wide, sun-splashed bed. Her room. Her bed. Colt stood close behind her, not touching her, waiting.

Was this what she wanted?

Mallory could feel the pounding of her heart. The warmth of his presence engulfed her. She took three steps to the window. There she hesitated one last time. Then she deliberately drew the curtains and turned to him.

Colt wrapped her within his arms. "Mallory," he whispered, his lips against her neck. "Dear, sweet Mallory. . . you are so delicate. Thank you for coming to me."

Last night's fulfillment had been filled with hunger and raw need. Today's was slow and sweet, sprinkled with golden sunlight and dancing sparks. Last night had been a violent battle. Today was an innocent sharing. Last night they had used and taken from each other with all the intensity of their souls. Today they learned how to make love.

With his eyes and his lips and the brush of his fingertips, Colt touched her, he gentled her. Wordlessly he taught her the tender communication of bodies, he revealed to her secrets she had never known she possessed. She wanted to give to him, to share with him. She wanted to be the best she could be for him. She wanted to be part of him.

Mallory had never imagined anything could be so sweet, so beautiful as their lovemaking was on that soft spring afternoon. She had never conceived of such closeness, or such need for closeness. When they lay sated and dreamily entwined in each other's arms, she knew for certain that something had changed. She did not want to believe it, but the discovery that had begun last night had only been confirmed this afternoon. She would never again be the same woman she had been before Colt Stanford had come into her life.

They lay in the center of her huge bed in the midst of a tangle of cologne-scented daisy sheets. His fingers caressed her ribs; her hand made repetitive, adoring strokes across his chest. She was content. Only. . . .

Colt immediately sensed her disturbance, though whether it was some sound or move she made or simply his innate sensitivity that alerted him, she did not know. He looked down at her inquiringly. "Mallory?"

She smiled a little, shifting in his arms to lie on her back, looking up at the ceiling. She should have known it was impossible to keep a secret from him. "I was just thinking how sad it will be. . . when it's over," she said softly.

Colt's smile was understanding, if a little weary. "Always the optimist, aren't you?" he murmured.

Then he propped himself on one elbow to look down at her, his hand resting warm and flat on her chest, his eyes thoughtful and sincere. "I don't know how long we'll last," he admitted. "A relationship isn't defined by time. Sometimes it's only for a day, a week, a few months." He smiled at her, lightly tracing her lips with his forefinger. "Sometimes it's forever. We can't make promises about the future; we can only do the best we can, and. . .just wait and see."

Mallory tried to disguise her sigh by turning her head toward the window. Forever. What a risky word, a hedge against uncertainty, a trust in things beyond human control. She did not want that. She could not even say exactly what she did want, but she knew by name the things she could not afford to want.

Colt felt her stiffening, and demanded immediately, "What?"

Last night had been sudden and unexpected, and Mallory had been brought to depths of intimacy she had never imagined before. By the very nature of the word, *intimacy* implied closeness, involvement, much more than she had bargained for. She shook her head helplessly, torn.

"Mallory. . ." Colt insisted.

"Don't you see?" she pleaded. "I don't want. . .a love affair and all that implies. I can't afford it. I. . .don't want to become dependent on you, and I don't want to be responsible for meeting your needs. I don't—" her hands tightened at her sides "—I don't want to *care*."

Mallory heard his sigh, felt his hands move lightly to stroke her arms. She knew, with a sense of tightening desperation in her, that Colt was going to get up and walk away from her in defeat. Why should that make her so depressed? It was what she wanted, wasn't it?

Instead he leaned forward and lightly touched his lips to her face. She arched instinctively to the movement. "Ah, Mallory," he said softly. "You do have so much to learn. It doesn't have to be that way. Dependency, need. . . those are words of a sickness not a love affair. I don't want that any more than you do. We're both intelligent enough to get what we want." Colt's smile was both rueful and a little sad as he bent to kiss her hair. "I wonder whether you're more afraid that I'll fall in love with you. . . or that you'll fall in love with me."

Mallory turned her head to look at him. His face was so close she had to touch it. Her eyes were very serious. "No, Colt. Don't expect that from me. I can't love you." She turned her head away and looked again at the ceiling. Honesty. She would never be less than honest with him. That was the best she could offer him. "I'm too selfish to love anyone. I don't want to share my life with anyone. I don't want to divide my attention or curtail my freedom. I just don't want to get involved. And I won't make promises I can't keep."

Colt did not appear to be in the least offended. "Fair enough," he agreed. "No promises, no demands. The very essence of a modern relationship."

Mallory looked at him suspiciously. His expression was quite serious, but was there a spark of mischief in his eyes?

"Relationship?" she repeated darkly.

"Ah, I beg your pardon." Colt laid a thoughtful finger across his lips, and she broke into a grin. Just as she had suspected, he was teasing her. "Another one of those taboo words. Now let's see, how many are there? *Love, involvement, commitment, promises.* . . ." He began counting on his fingers, and she struck him over the head with a pillow.

Laughingly he gathered her to him, wrapping her in the warmth of afternoon sunshine and sweet familiarity. For a while they simply held each other, then he murmured lazily into her hair, "Well, my dear, I don't know quite how to break it to you, but we do appear to be involved in some sort of relationship."

She lifted her eyes to his inquiringly.

"And worse yet, people have a very nasty name for it." Colt looked at her soberly. "They call it being lovers."

Mallory smiled and snuggled closer to him. Lovers. It had a nice sound. "I think I can live with that," she murmured and closed her eyes. The tick of the clock faded to a drone in her ears, and she tried not to think about how soon this lovely feeling of contentment from being in his arms must end.

JEANNINE RARELY USED THE YACHT. In fact, she hardly ever even remembered she owned one. It had been a present from her father on her last birthday, and it had spent most of the time since then securely

moored at the marina. Now, however, it was anchored in a private little cove off Catalina Island,
and Jeannine was extraordinarily glad she had remembered it.

She heard Byron's footsteps behind her as she was
placing a match to the second of the glass-globed
candles that decorated the table. The sweet scent of
gardenia and hyacinth that completed the centerpiece filled her nostrils.

"Why do I get the feeling I've been kidnapped?"
Byron inquired smoothly behind her.

Jeannine shook the match gracefully and turned,
a secret, delighted smile flirting with her lips.
"Why, sir," she protested, "that you could even suggest such a thing!"

Byron's eyes widened with pleasure as they took
in her appearance in the moonlight. Her hair tonight was pulled back from her face with two shimmering ivory combs, spreading over her shoulders
in a cascade of curls too magnificent to be real.
The pale blue silk sarong she wore was tugged and
flattened to her body by the ocean breeze, and he
suspected she wore nothing beneath it. The arch beneath her eyebrows was swept with silvery shadow,
and her lips were as brilliant and moist as fresh
cherries.

Byron took both her hands in his and inclined his
head a little as he brought them to his lips. "My
dear, being with you is a constant adventure," he
declared. "May it never end."

Reluctantly Jeannine withdrew her hands and
turned to pour the champagne. Her fingers still felt
the electricity from the touch of his lips.

This was their third "date," and that casual caress was the most intimate thing they had yet shared. That fact confused Jeannine.

She had spent one whole day driving him around Los Angeles—instinctively Jeannine knew this was a man with whom she would have to move slowly, and following up on her offer as a tour guide had seemed a safe beginning.

They had had a wonderfully intimate lunch in a charming little café in old Santa Barbara. They had discussed history and real-estate values and poked through dusty antique shops. He had told her about his country estate outside London and about his childhood, his prep school and Oxford education and his eventual career as an investment broker with a prestigious international firm.

Jeannine hung on every word. Usually she found listening to men talk about themselves an inconvenient and boring prelude to more vital things, but every sentence Byron uttered fascinated her. Perhaps it was his accent. Or perhaps it was the man himself. She had never met anyone before about whom she wanted to know absolutely everything. She could not get enough.

And when she delivered him to the door of his rented Malibu cottage he did not invite her in.

But the next day he sent her long-stemmed pink roses. Jeannine was completely captivated. The last time she had gotten roses was from her father on her sixteenth birthday. No one sent flowers anymore. At least, not anybody Jeannine knew. For the first time in her life, she was beginning to understand the meaning of the term "romance."

Jeannine called him; she invited him to dinner at her place. He suggested instead a private dinner club to which he had entrée, and there followed one of the most memorable evenings of Jeannine's life. She was wined and dined by a man of style, breeding and Continental flair. He ordered the best wines and menu selections with authority and ease. He parried Jeannine's brilliant chatter with a dry wit. When they danced they seemed to be floating on a cloud, and Jeannine could not help imagining how beautifully he could orchestrate more intimate communication. Imagining kept her color high and her pulse fast all evening.

But when he took her home and she asked him in for a nightcap, Byron politely declined.

In the past year Jeannine had been involved with a madcap rock star, a promiscuous director, a manic-depressive writer and an actor on the verge of becoming famous. All of them were urbane, attractive and very good in bed, and she had never regretted a moment of the experiences. . . until now.

Jeannine was not aware that something was missing from her life. She did sometimes succumb to wistful yearnings for something more permanent in her life—a man who loved her as much as he loved himself, a single face to wake up to every morning, marriage, children—the whole works. She had simply never believed such a thing was possible. Until now.

Byron was real, solid and genuine. With his old-world heritage, his quiet values and simple purpose, he was a world apart from this land of fad diets and trendy issues, plastic glitter and make-believe. He rose above all that like a mountain in the desert, granite towering over the shimmer of a mirage. Jeannine could not help reaching for him.

Jeannine turned and handed his champagne glass to him. She lifted her own in a toast. "To the continuing adventure."

He smiled and touched his drink to hers. "And its lovely creator."

He was always saying things like that. Just the right thing, at just the right moment, with just the right touch.

Jeannine was an expert in fakery and phony charm; she knew how to emulate it, she knew how to recognize it; born and bred to huge wealth, she had been practically raised on insincerity. But looking into Byron's eyes, she believed every word he said.

Of course that was the ultimate puzzle. He was attracted to her; she saw that in every move he made, every word he uttered, every small, echoing smile. She had not lived to be a very sophisticated thirty-one-year-old without being able to recognize a man's desire.

But he persisted in keeping her at arm's distance. She had given him open invitations, both verbal and nonverbal; he acknowledged them and politely refused them. She had never met a man like that before. His behavior made absolutely no sense.

Her first and most natural conclusion was, with a startling shot of disappointment, that he did not like women. And being Jeannine, she had to ask him directly.

He had laughed so hard she had grown annoyed and had been half afraid he wouldn't be able to contain himself long enough to answer. Finally, however, with great amusement still snapping in his eyes, he replied, "Just when I think I've grown used to you and your incredibly uncontrollable tongue, you always come up with something else to put me in my place!"

Jeannine scowled, and he took her hands in his. "No, my dear," he assured her a bit more seriously, "I am not hiding a secret predilection for young boys or muscle-bound football players behind this disarmingly suave exterior. If I had not already discovered the boundless delights of bed partners of the opposite sex, you, I do assure you, would have reformed me."

There remained a vague possibility—improbable as it was to imagine—that he held some old-fashioned ideas about fidelity to the woman he was supposedly engaged to. Jeannine did not believe in engagements—she barely believed in marriage—so she felt no twinge of conscience about tempting him away from the straight-and-narrow if that's what she was doing. Not that he had needed a great deal of tempting. No one had forced him at gunpoint to spend a day touring Los Angeles with her, or made him send her roses or coerced him into taking her to dinner and dancing. No one wrung those beautiful phrases from his lips or painted the desire-sparks in his eyes when he looked at her. And she hadn't really kidnapped him. It was really quite simple: if he was not interested in her, why was he spending so much time with her?

That was exactly what Jeannine intended to find out tonight. She was beginning to be a little afraid of the answer.

She had not told Byron where they were sailing, just that she felt obligated to return his hospitality for last night's dinner. If he was surprised to find himself on a yacht anchored in the Pacific, he did not show it. In fact, the entire situation seemed to agree with him.

The table was set on deck, complete with white linen, crystal, Dom Perignon and the chef's most elaborate concoctions in silver-covered platters, still warm from the galley. The captain and crew made themselves invisible. The moon rippled like spilled milk across the shimmering dark water. Shadowed candlelight played on their faces. The only sounds were the gentle lapping of the water against the hull and the whisper of a tart ocean breeze. The sweet scent of the cut flowers in the centerpiece perfumed the air — that, and the almost intoxicating quality of Byron's presence.

Never before had Jeannine had to seduce a man, and perhaps far back in her mind was some vague recollection that such things were greatly enhanced by candlelit dinners. In the kind of life Jeannine was used to, however, things were generally much more uncomplicated. When a man and a woman met, the first and foremost decision to be made was whether or not they were going to have sex. Usually the answer was yes. It was that simple. While Jeannine was willing to concede the candlelit dinner to the cause of seduction, she really did not have the temperament or the stamina to play games much further. She had to have an answer. Tonight.

The nouvelle cuisine fare was light and succulent—melon, broccoli soup, cold asparagus tips with raspberry sauce, smoked salmon. For a time Jeannine did nothing but nibble at the dishes before her, watch the play of candlelight on his face, the way the breeze lifted thick dark locks of his hair, and meet the tender smile in his eyes when he looked at her. Midway through the salmon she said, "Why don't you want me?"

For that was her greatest fear—that he, after all, did not want her. Jeannine was not accustomed to being denied anything. That her first experience with rejection should be with the only truly valuable thing she had ever desired was almost too much to comprehend.

Byron touched his napkin to his lips; he sat back and lifted his champagne glass. His eyes were watchful and in the flickering candlelight, seemingly enigmatic. Jeannine's heart began to speed nervously.

He responded simply, "Why do you want me?"

A dimpling smile hid her uncertainty, and she lifted an asparagus tip with her fingers, biting off its crisp head. "Because you have the most gorgeous body I've ever seen."

A slight indentation appeared at the edge of his mouth as he brought the champagne glass to his lips. "The feeling is mutual," he returned.

"And," she added thoughtfully, "because you're mysterious. Because I don't understand you. Because you're so totally unlike anyone I've met before." *Because,* she added silently, *I look at you and I see something that could last forever, and it's something I've never seen before. . . .* "Because you don't belong here."

"A little mystery always adds excitement to the pursuit," he observed. Then, sipping from the glass, watching her steadily, he said, "You are accustomed to getting everything you want, aren't you, Jeannine?"

"As a matter of fact, yes."

"Then, perhaps you only want me because I'm the first person who's ever said no to you," he suggested.

Jeannine got up and walked away from the table, not wanting him to see exactly how much that observation had disturbed her. Jeannine wasn't stupid. She had thought of that. It was the spoiled-little-rich-kid syndrome, and though she thought she had outgrown it, maybe he was right. She did not want to believe it. What she was beginning to feel for him, much to her surprise and dismay, was genuine. It had potential. She did not want to believe that this, like so much else in her life, would turn out to be nothing more than illusion once she had a firmer grasp of it.

She leaned against the rail, folding her arms over the polished surface, and looked out over the ocean. She said quietly, without turning, "Byron, I'm thirty-one years old. I've spent my life going from one fantasy to the next, and I'm tired. Maybe you're right. Maybe the trouble with always getting everything you want is that pretty soon you don't want it anymore." She shrugged, her eyes fixed on the winking lights of Catalina, and she realized she had never spoken these words to anyone before. She had never even admitted them to herself. "All I know is that the only sad thing about living in Disneyland is that sooner or later you outgrow it." She smiled a little, though she could not make herself turn to look at him. "Maybe it was just your bad luck that you happened to come along when I was ready to grow up. I saw you, and all of a sudden I started thinking about vine-covered cottages and the sound of little feet . . . a real life, in the real world. . . ." Embarrassed, she let her voice trail off. She had never meant to say such things to him. Not to anyone, but most certainly not to him. He didn't want her. He wasn't interested in soulful confessions or unfulfilled yearnings. He didn't want her. She had no right to make him listen.

She heard Byron leave the table, and she heard the soft fall of his footsteps as he came up behind her. His palm touched her shoulder, lightly, and its warmth spread through her. His fragrance, clean and old-world, drifted around her like a promise. She tightened her hands on the railing.

"Jeannine," he said softly. "My sweet, lovely, wonderful girl . . . you are the most delightful thing that has ever happened to me. Everything about you charms me, fascinates me, keeps me ever waiting for your next surprise. You have come into my life and turned it completely upside down. But I'm a very old-fashioned man, I'm afraid." Jeannine held her breath, knowing that this was what she had been expecting, what she had been afraid of . . . the final rejection. She was almost relieved to have him put it into words.

And then she felt his breath upon the side of her neck, his lips touching her skin, his smile curving against her. "I like to do the pursuing," he said simply.

Then, before she could take her next breath, she was turned into his arms, his lips upon hers, his hands embracing and caressing her, and though Jeannine had thought she had known the magic in every possible form and variation, she was to learn that night that it was only beginning.

"I want to be real for you, Jeannine," he said softly. His eyes, deep and starlit, searched hers. His hand came up and gently loosened the shoulder tie of her sarong. "Let me be part of your life. . . ."

The material loosened and fell, exposing her nakedness to the moon and the ocean and to him. His rapt eyes absorbed every detail about her, and she trembled with the power of his gaze. Then, wordlessly, he bent and scooped her into his arms and carried her below.

A LONG TIME LATER Jeannine curled into the curve of his body, the moonlight streaming over their bed, the musky scent of love cradling them in its embrace. Jeannine reached up her hand and lightly stroked the thick, glossy hair away from his forehead. She had never thought of sex and love in the same context before. She had never really even thought about love. But she knew what it meant now, and it was a scary feeling. Scary, confusing, exhilarating. . . .

Byron smiled at her. "See how much fun it can be when the man takes the lead?"

She returned his smile a little tremulously. So many emotions were bubbling and straining inside her that she felt she might burst with the effort to control them. She did not understand any of them, she did not know where they had come from, she could not imagine how this had happened to her.

Byron sighed and closed his eyes, pulling her more comfortably into the curve of his shoulder. "I have just made a decision," he murmured drowsily. "Tomorrow I will buy the first suitable piece of property the real-estate agent recommends. I have a feeling I'm going to be spending a great deal of time in Los Angeles."

Jeannine smiled and closed her eyes, and she was surprised to feel behind her lids the tingle of happy tears.

Chapter Eleven

"FOR GOODNESS' SAKE, JAKE, it's been almost a week!" Mallory paced tensely back and forth to the extension of the telephone cord. "Where have you been?"

"Workin', peaches," he drawled. She heard the squeak of his chair as he assumed his customary position at his desk — booted ankles crossed on the desk top, hat tipped back, chair leaning backward at a dangerously uncertain angle. "Just like you pay me to. What's been up with you?"

What had been up with her? She could not tell even Jake that. There had been days wrapped in gold and sparkling with silver, two days of endless discovery and flaring excitement, two days of magic that never waned but only increased with every passing hour. Every morning for almost a week she had awakened in Colt's arms, heard his voice on the telephone at lunch and class breaks, spent the afternoons and the evenings and into the far hours of the night talking to him, sharing with him, discovering him and never tiring of the endless fascination of the adventure. Still her heart leaped at the sound of his voice, still her breath quickened when she looked at him, still everything within her coiled in anticipation of his touch. Should she tell Jake that Colt Stan-

ford was reading her script? No one besides Jake and
the necessary producers had ever been allowed to
read Mallory's scripts before; she was superstitious.
Jake would be shocked. But Mallory was under the
sparkling influence of a spell called romance, and
she was no longer the woman Jake had once known.

Of course Mallory was constantly behind schedule,
preparing for a date with Colt or recovering from
one. She hardly worked anymore, and she couldn't
concentrate on anything while away from Colt. But
she justified all to herself with the assurance that it
wouldn't last, the magic was self-limiting, the love
affair would end and everything would return to normal. . . .

The smile that had momentarily softened Mallory's features faded with this thought, which had
come to disturb her more and more lately. She impatiently directed her attention back to Jake.
"Never mind that," she said shortly. "Tell me about
the deal. What did the studio say?"

"Well, little darlin', you know how these folks
are. They're still ruminating on it. It's a big step for
them—gonna take some time. Put it out of your
head for a week or so. Let me do the worrying."

Mallory took a moment to absorb what he was
saying, and a longer time to realize what he meant.
"Do you mean," she inquired at last, carefully, "you
haven't even gotten a decision from them yet?"

"Why so surprised, peaches? You should be a pro
at this waiting game by now. Delicate negotiations
like this have to be handled with kid gloves. I'm not
about to rush in there with both guns blazing and

blow the whole thing sky high. You never expected me to." Jake sounded slightly insulted, as though she were questioning his judgment.

"But—" she drove a hand slowly through her hair, frowning, trying to sort out her thoughts "—but Evelyn Bouchard called me the other day and said the deal was all set. She said the studio had put her in touch with me to start preproduction publicity."

Even before she heard Jake's long, carefully restrained sigh, Mallory knew the truth of it. "Little darlin'," he explained to her regretfully, "I'm afraid you've been conned. The woman was fishing, no more, and you took the bait. She couldn't possibly have known anything about the deal because no deal has been made, and that's the long and the short of it. I'm sorry, sweetheart."

Mallory slowly closed her eyes, forcefully subduing the ugly bubbles of fury that churned in her stomach. "All right, Jake," she said in a moment, very calmly. "Thanks. You just let me know as soon as you hear anything."

"That I can do. You take it easy now, you hear?"

"You bet I will," Mallory muttered as she flipped through the telephone directory for Evelyn Bouchard's number. Her instincts were to kill.

She found the number, dialed, got the correct extension and asked calmly for Miss Bouchard. All the while her hand was clenching into a fist around the telephone receiver; she was imagining that impersonal instrument was the woman's neck.

A cheerful voice answered, "Evelyn Bouchard."

The cool pleasantness in Mallory's voice came

through gritted teeth. "This is Mallory Evans, Miss Bouchard, calling to cancel our luncheon appointment."

"Oh...dear." This disappointment was, of course, genuine, but not deeply felt. "Well, let's see, what day would be better for you?"

"I said *cancel*, not postpone," Mallory enunciated clearly. "I very much regret that lies and manipulations have always had an adverse effect on my appetite."

There was a brief and stunned silence, yet nothing but puzzlement in the woman's tone when she spoke. "I'm afraid I don't understand."

Mallory was growing impatient with this whole business. She did not know how much longer she could even be civil. "I don't know how you got my phone number, Miss Bouchard," she said curtly, "but I do know it wasn't through official channels at Rowntree. I'll thank you to stop harassing me, because the fact is I have no intention of giving you an interview now or ever."

The silence on the other end was brief and electric. But Evelyn Bouchard's voice was as smooth as honey. "I am terribly sorry to hear that. You see, I've been getting quite a lot of pressure from my paper. You're *such* a phenomenon, you know, and we've been embarrassingly lax about fulfilling our readers' need to know about you." She laughed lightly. "I'm really afraid what it boils down to, Mallory, is that I'm going to have to write *something* about you...whether it's what you would like to see in print or not. I was hoping we could work together and come up with something mutually agreeable, but if not. . . ."

Mallory was seething. She could feel the vein of her temple throbbing, and when she closed her eyes briefly to try to regain some control of her temper, she saw red. "Fine," she bit out. "You write whatever you damn well please. But don't ever harass me again, Miss Bouchard, because if you do I swear to you I'll press charges." And she slammed down the phone.

She was shaking.

MALLORY TOLD COLT about the conversation that night over dinner. Strange that in less than a week she had grown so used to telling him everything and that the telling itself seemed to be a halfing of the burden or a doubling of the joy. Wasn't that why relationships—partnerships—were so highly lauded? Wasn't this the way it was supposed to be? She had never known what she was missing. This was wonderful.

Colt's smile was a little dry as he tipped his glass toward the candle flame, examining the play of colors in the rich burgundy. "That's the first rule of survival in this business. Stay away from the vultures. Take it from the expert."

"Vultures," Mallory repeated thoughtfully, liking that word. It had never applied more aptly than to Evelyn Bouchard.

Colt grinned as he lifted his glass. "Sure. You know the poster print with the mean-looking bird glaring down at the ground and the slogan that says, 'Patience, hell! I'm going to kill something.' Miss Bouchard, I salute you."

Mallory laughed and clinked her glass to his. In just a few short moments he had taken all the horror out of the episode. Everything was better when shared with him. Everything.

She became serious as she sipped from her glass. "Is that what happened to you, Colt?" she inquired curiously, albeit a little cautiously. She was always hesitant to broach the subject of Colt's lost career to him. She could not believe it was not still painful.

But whatever bitter or regretful emotions there might have been were no longer evident. His eyes were frank, his expression blandly reflective. "The media certainly made an international event out of something that deserved about half the attention it got. There were an awful lot of reporters," he added with a grimace, "who were more than happy for the opportunity to cut my throat — I had never been one of their favorite people.

"But mostly," he told her easily, "I made the mistake of ignoring the corporate politics going on around me and concentrating instead on just making a good film. There was a lot of controversy about who they were going to hire in the first place — the next runner-up being, of course, the fellow who eventually took over the film. I had made some pretty powerful enemies over the years, as you probably know, mostly because I wouldn't bow down to the powers that be and play their games. The fact that I always did things my way *and* was successful was too much for the game

players to swallow. Most people can forgive you anything but being right.

"So when I agreed to do the film I was totally unaware that I was being set up. I was promised that I
would have complete directorial control and one of
the biggest budgets in history. In return I promised
them a film that would be both Oscar material and
a commercial success."

He shrugged as though the rest of the story hardly
bore telling. "Of course, all it was from the beginning was a power play. They were determined to
put Colt Stanford in his place once and for all. The
budget was cut. Deadlines were moved up. That
didn't bother me, I'd worked under pressure before.
But then they started interfering in the film, cutting
key scenes, replacing actors. When the final show-
down came, I was told they weren't interested in a
quality production, only a money-making one. I
could either do it their way or not at all."

The wry twist of his lips was not so much resentful
as self-mocking. "I suppose integrity has always
been one of my weaknesses—not so much my own
personal honor, but the integrity of a quality product. I couldn't take a beautiful script and shred it
like that. I couldn't take a potentially powerful film
and turn it into garbage...I just couldn't," he said
simply, and Mallory understood.

"So," he concluded, "I resigned from the project,
just as they expected me to. The contract had already been broken on their part, and I suppose I
could have made a fuss about that if I'd wanted to,
but there hardly seemed to be any point by then. I

still didn't realize what they were planning. There was factionalization within the company to begin with, and I was the pawn. No matter which side won, I would have been the scapegoat. If the film had been a success, it would have been in spite of me. . . if it had been a bomb, as it was, it was because of me. And because the studio went to such great lengths to make sure I was credited with ruining the film—or rather, walking out in the middle of it—the rest of the industry was afraid to touch me. So—" again he shrugged "—I realized I'd better get into another line of work."

Mallory watched him as he sipped his wine and was amazed by his apparent lack of concern. How strange to hear firsthand the story she had tried to put forth in her script, to see for herself an example of one man's courageous fight for honor in an industry in which such a concept often seemed virtually nonexistent. She had given Colt her script to read three days ago, and she wondered if he had recognized elements of his own story in it.

She wondered how Colt would feel about directing a film whose subject matter he was so intimately familiar with.

"Colt, do you think you'll ever be able to work in filmmaking again? How long can they hold this against you?"

"As long as they like, I suppose. What you've got to understand, Mallory, is that when the megabucks necessary to make a film today are involved, people tend to get very protective. There aren't many risk takers left anymore. No studio in its right mind would take me on, and even if they did the film would be under such close scrutiny it would be nothing but a hassle from day one. Most producers don't feel it's worth the chance."

Mallory nodded, not really understanding, and thoughtfully resumed her meal. That was another odd thing—for the first time in her life she had undergone a crisis without resorting to compulsive consumption of food as a panacea. She always seemed to be too excited—and too happy—to eat. She smiled a little to herself as she lifted her fork to her lips. Wouldn't Jeannine laugh if she could hear that?

Mallory knew she was under a spell and that the enchantment was illusory. This wonderful intensity of discovery wouldn't last, the newness and excitement would fade away, the glitter would wear off and reveal nothing more than a cardboard stage prop, but right now the experience was beautiful. Right now she was enjoying every moment.

"Why haven't you ever married?" she asked, putting down her fork. She would much rather talk to Colt than eat.

His eyebrows moved upward to express no more than curiosity about where the question came from. He touched his napkin to his lips and answered, "But I was."

That was a shock. Was Mallory's disappointment generated by the fact that there had once been a woman in Colt's life whom he'd cared enough for to marry, or simply that she—who thought she knew him so well—had not been privy to this one very important fact? She sipped her wine and kept her tone casual. "I didn't know that. What happened?"

For the first time, she saw she had touched a

nerve of the controlled and unflappable Colt Stanford. For a moment she thought he wouldn't answer. Then he dropped his eyes, absently fingering his wineglass. "She left. About the same time my career started to go on the rocks. Deserted a sinking ship, you might say, which was probably the smartest thing she could have done." He met Mallory's eyes then, and though there were remnants of regret, there was no sign of bitterness. "Whether she couldn't take the stress or she couldn't handle the failure, I don't know."

"I'm sorry," Mallory said softly and sincerely.

Again there was that familiar wry twist of his lips, the little quirk of his brow. He lifted his glass in a casual gesture toward her. "That's the nice thing about life, Mallory. Nothing lasts forever—not even the pain."

She looked down. Was there still pain for her? The worst was gone, she supposed, but the scars. . . .

As always, Colt read her too easily. "When are you going to tell me about your marriage?" he inquired gently.

Mallory's hands tightened in her lap, but if she thought the tablecloth would hide the movement from him she was mistaken. Purposefully she unfolded her hands in response to his meaningful look. "I don't know, Colt," she answered honestly. "I'm . . . not sure I can. Not now anyway." She did not understand that part of herself, or pretend to. She could tell Jake, and Jeannine . . . but not Colt. Perhaps because their relationship seemed so fragile and illusionary, a fantasy film in soft focus. Such harsh realities did not belong here.

He nodded quiet acceptance, and her heart went out to him. To receive unquestioned understanding from another human being was a wondrous thing.

They were dining in a small tourist-trap Chinese restaurant — the kind of place everyone went, except movie stars and celebrities. That was another thing Mallory liked about Colt. He never went out of his way to cater to her status. When she was with him she felt special because she was with him, not because her name was on the screen of movie theaters across the country; he took away some of the burden of success. Being with him had become comfortable in its familiarity; yet each time she saw him she seemed to discover him for the first time. Even as she looked at him now across the dimly lit table, the light and shadow highlighting the clean planes of his face, the tightly fitting blue turtleneck he wore softening his features yet accentuating his strength, she felt a renewed thrill of pleasure merely by being with him. This wonderful state of existence had possessed her since Colt Stanford had walked into her life. She wondered why no one had ever told her about such rapture before.

Colt was smiling at her, watching her, receiving joy from the thoughts she communicated unconsciously. Mallory had even become used to that; she was no longer startled that he could read her so well. "You didn't expect us to last this long, did you?" he asked unexpectedly.

She laughed. "Less than a week? That's hardly a world record." Then she sipped her wine and admitted, "No. No I didn't." She hadn't expected it to last past the first night.

He gently swirled the wine in his glass, eyes revealing secret amusement. "How long do you give us then?"

She pretended thoughtfulness that was only a disguise for the real seriousness of her words. She knew everything had limits. By Colt's own admission, the only time people got into trouble was when they started to believe in the permanency of circumstances they could not control. What she and Colt had right now was beautiful, stimulating, almost surreal in its perfection. But she knew their relationship was no more than the mysterious alchemy of life—a stretch of good luck she had been fortunate enough to stumble into. Success, money, her career on the upswing, and now the perfect lover—everything could disappear as quickly as it had come, to be no more than scraps of memories on the cutting-room floor. She was prepared for that. She had to be.

"Generously," she decided at last, "six weeks. More likely a month. You'll become bored with me by then."

He lifted his eyebrows. "Glad you told me—now I can arrange my schedule. We have an awful lot to do in six weeks."

Her eyes widened and caught the spark of amusement in his. "Like what?"

"Oh," he replied nonchalantly, "loving, fighting, making up, growing, comforting each other, strengthening each other...all those mundane things that relationships are made of."

"Colt..." she began uncomfortably, and he lifted a finger to silence her. His tone was still light, but there was sincerity in his eyes.

"Sorry, Mallory, you're probably right—avoid long-term hassle and set a deadline now. It's so much neater. I mean, consider what we'd have to look forward to—all those necessary growing and stretching stages that make life so dull." Was that a flicker of irritation she saw in his eyes? "Nobody likes to watch the romance fade away, but it will. There'll come a time when we won't want to make love every night and our blood pressures won't skyrocket everytime we touch . . . we'll become comfortable together. We'll start to take each other for granted, even. We'll run out of things to say and sometimes we'll be bored with each other. We'll have crises and major problems and we may or may not weather the storms . . . depending on when we decide to give up. Six weeks is an optional limit." He shrugged. "But it will do as well as anything else. There will be plenty of time before or after then to throw in the towel, if we miss that deadline."

She did not flinch from his gentle mockery. "Are you saying that I'm lazy?" she inquired evenly.

Colt glanced briefly at his plate. "Not lazy, necessarily. A little cowardly."

Mallory focused momentarily on a point just beyond his right shoulder, giving the muscles in her throat a chance to relax. She did not want him to be angry with her. "Sometimes cowardice is a virtue," she said quietly. "And sometimes it's just another word for control."

Colt's smile was a little sad. "Ah, Mallory. You make things sound so simple."

Her returned smile was weak. "I think you've already discovered I'm not very adventurous. I don't like risks."

Now Colt laughed, softly and in genuine amuse-ment. His brown eyes sparkled. "The hell you're not! You make your living in a business where careers are made and broken in a single day, where more ant-acid tablets are consumed per capita in one hour than in an entire week on Wall Street, where the sui-cide rate is higher than any industry in the world. You built your house on top of a fault line that could open up at any minute and swallow you whole. You marched out here five years ago with no more cre-dentials than what came out of your typewriter and took the most dangerous business in the world by storm. Darling, you're a born risk taker. It's in your blood. And the only reason you pretend otherwise is so that you'll have a built-in excuse for failure. Your lack of confidence is nothing more than a self-protective device. Set your standards low enough and you're bound to meet them, thus forever avoiding disappointment. Very neat, clear-cut. . . and the classic portrait of an underachiever."

Underachiever. No one had ever called her that before. If anything, Mallory had always thought of herself as an overachiever, always expecting more from herself than she would from anyone else, push-ing herself to the limits in everything she did. But could Colt be right? Could her insistence on setting a time limit for the duration of this relationship be only a built-in excuse for failure? Was that the only reason she guarded herself so carefully against be-coming too involved with him? A lighthearted love affair she could handle. A commitment of caring implied entirely too much risk.

Mallory was mostly silent on the drive home, absorbing and digesting the new way he made her look at herself. She was not sure she would ever be entirely comfortable with it.

Once inside her house Mallory decided to put the brooding thoughts behind her and take advantage of the time they still had together. That was, after all, the joy in an uncommitted relationship—every moment must be savored to the fullest. She turned to him with a bright smile, and Colt surprised her by presenting her with a vinyl-bound folder. His expression was unreadable.

"Oh," she said, taking it from him. "My script. You finished it." Mallory felt anxiety tensing in her chest, but she tried to keep it from showing on her face. She ventured a glance at him, not wanting him to know how very much his opinion mattered to her. Then she realized how silly that was. Colt Stanford was one of the most brilliant directors alive; his opinion would matter a great deal to any screenwriter. But she'd sought more than just his professional approval, Mallory admitted to herself reluctantly. She wanted him to like her script because it was her creation. She wanted Colt to respond the same as any woman seeks approval from her man. Which, of course was ridiculous.

Why didn't Colt say something? Why did he just keep looking at her with carefully shuttered features as though he could not bear to tell her how much he had hated it? That was it. The script was terrible. He should know—he had examined hundreds of them and he knew quality. She had been wrong,

Jake had been wrong, even the producers at Rowntree had been wrong; that's why they were taking so long to make up their minds on the new contract — they were reexamining the script.

"Well," Mallory said nervously, when she simply couldn't stand it any longer, "what did you think?"

He looked at her somberly. "Mallory Evans, there are many things I'm learning to love about you." Seeing the flutter of panic in her eyes he repeated sternly, "Yes, though I use the word advisedly, I said *love* — and this — " Colt touched the blue folder that she held protectively against her chest " — is one of them. It is magnificent."

Mallory took approximately thirty seconds to convince herself that what she had heard him say was not, "It's the worse thing I've ever seen in print." When the truth finally dawned on her, she began to glow, slowly and radiantly. "Is it?" she ventured. "I mean, I thought so, but — "

"It's the finest thing you've ever done," Colt assured her, and he grinned. "Who else but you could write such a thoroughly convincing, terrifyingly pessimistic view of fantasy land?"

He grew serious as he slipped his arm around her shoulders and began leading her toward the sofa. His head was bent close to hers; the intensity with which he spoke vibrated between them like a physical thing. "Darling, there's potential in that script to make the film a classic, but you were right about insisting on control." They sat together on the sofa, the script on her lap between them, their knees lightly brushing and Colt's hand barely touching hers to give emphasis to his words. Mallory's face was lit with the sincerity of the mood that engulfed him, her eyes avidly scanning his and drawing from them an excitement that refueled her own.

"There are so many subtleties that can be interpreted so many ways. That's the beauty of a script like this. Your final statement is going to depend entirely on the director. There's a hidden wonder in these pages that the camera will try to elude, but if you know what you're going for, if you can advise on setting up the camera shots and controlling the actors. . . . Here, let me show you what I mean."

Colt reached for the script and Mallory felt a surge of contentment that suggested perfect happiness. She snuggled next to him as he opened the folder between them. Her smile was a reflection of the melding of minds and the effortless communication of spirits that was so rare she simply had to stop and savor it.

That night, watching his eyes glow and his face come alive as the swift sparks of communication and exchange flowed back and forth between them, Colt had never seemed more magnificent to her. His face and his form were so familiar they were almost a reflection of herself, but every time Mallory glanced at him she was flooded by new sensations of wonder and delight. Everything about him thrilled her. He was to her security and affection, stimulation and warmth; he made her mind work and he filled her heart. He shared her secrets; he made her feel important. He admired her accomplishments and spurred her on to new ones. He made her feel as though there was nothing she couldn't do, and when she had doubts he showed her how to triumph. A genius in his own right, Colt honored her by teaching her to excel. He was strength and inspiration and confidence.

Mallory knew right then that Colt Stanford was the only possible choice to direct this film. Of course it was not, as of this moment, her decision to make, but even if she had had the right to ask him, Mallory was not entirely sure she was ready to. She was not even sure whether if she did ask him he would accept. She was more afraid he would refuse. So much depended on this film, and it was very dangerous to let her personal feelings cloud her professional judgment.

But she was having increasing difficulty heeding the warning that this wonder couldn't last. Every time Mallory was with Colt she had to fight to remind herself not to become too happy, not to get too involved. . . .

The tick of the living-room clock was relentless and steady, and tonight, while the wonder that felt so very much like being in love filled her, she was even more afraid it was already too late.

Chapter Twelve

MALLORY SAT PERFECTLY STILL, silently scanning the newspaper Jeannine had put in her hand.

> Seen about Town: Mallory Evans, elusive lady of mystery and creator of the Oscar-winning *Nestar* trilogy, with director Colt Stanford, who achieved notoriety in the *Adam's Choice* scandal that rocked Hollywood two years ago. Could the two of them be planning their own intergalactic love story? There certainly are enough stars in their eyes these days. Or could it be Miss Evans is merely interviewing directors for her new screenplay, *Day of the Last*, which has already gone to Rowntree for a whopping $250,000.... Careful, Mallory, Stanford has the touch of death, and business and pleasure mix best *outside* the bedroom....

Mallory folded the paper with two slow, deliberate movements and did not say a word.

"It could have been worse," Jeannine volunteered helpfully.

Mallory was trying very hard to quell the nausea

churning in the pit of her stomach. As a result, her voice sounded rather flat. "Oh, yeah? How?"

"Well...." Jeannine's face brightened. "She could have given a play-by-play description of what she'd seen with a telescopic lens through your bedroom window, including illegal positions, which we've all been guilty of at one time or another."

When Mallory glared at her, she sighed helplessly and patted her friend's knee with a multiringed hand. "I'm sorry, hon. I know this kind of thing upsets you—I don't know why, but I'll sympathize anyway. After all, the slogan of this business is 'as long as they spell your name right....'"

"That's for people who *want* publicity," Mallory snapped, and got to her feet. "I don't! I only want to be left alone." Nervously, she hugged her arms, already regretting using such a short tone with her friend but unable to find the mental energy to apologize. Those hateful words kept echoing through her brain... "business and pleasure...outside the bedroom...." It was ugly, spiteful. She felt as though the words themselves had turned into little black-and-white poison daggers that leaped off the newsprint at her, pursuing her around the room no matter how hard she tried to duck them.

"I'm nobody," she said tightly, pacing away from Jeannine. Her hands were clutching her upper arms so tightly that the circulation was almost inhibited. "I'm not on camera. I'm not onstage. I don't handle the money or make the decisions...I'm just the person who puts the words on paper, and I don't affect anybody's life but my own. I don't bother anyone, I don't ask for anything. Why does she want to do this to me?"

"She's not doing anything to you personally," Jeannine explained patiently, but her worried gaze followed Mallory's restless path around the room. "Gossip is her business and your name is hot right now. Nobody's out to get you."

But Mallory felt stripped naked and laid forth for all the world to gape at. Her private life was no longer hers but had become public property. What she felt was akin to the insecurity of having all the locks removed from the doors and windows. Now she could do nothing but wait for someone—or everyone—to walk in and take what they liked. That terrified her.

Jeannine smiled, fingering the folded newspaper unhappily. "I feel responsible. I'm the one who kept nagging you to get out and enjoy yourself. . . and look what happens. But—" she looked up at Mallory hopefully "—you've been so happy these past few weeks. You *have* been enjoying yourself, haven't you?"

Mallory couldn't help but soften upon hearing the almost childlike note of pleading in her friend's voice. But her smile was a little weak. "Yes, I have," she admitted. Yet she had known from the beginning nothing came without a price tag.

"Darling, you're taking this whole thing entirely too seriously," Jeannine tried to convince her.

Mallory closed her eyes, and forced a radical readjustment of attitude. "I guess you're right."

Jeannine sighed. In her own life things had never

looked brighter, more promising or filled with hope. Byron was all she had expected him to be and more...more than she had ever asked for. For the first time, she was feeling her life beginning to take on shape and meaning, for the first time she knew the tremendous rewards of caring for another human being. She could see a future with purpose and it was exhilarating. She wanted everything to be perfect for Mallory too, and she was saddened that it was not.

Jeannine's smile was kind and perceptive. "I do understand why. But, Mallory, you've got to stop letting your past haunt you like this," she insisted, her eyes growing dark with the seriousness of her voice. "You're afraid of things that don't exist anymore and that fear will ruin your life. You're on a leash that's anchored to a Mississippi town five years ago. It will stretch just so far. Every time you start to make a real step to assert yourself, you're jerked back. It's time to slip the noose, Mal," she advised soberly.

After a while Mallory sat down in the green-sprigged sling chair across from Jeannine, leaned her head back against the cushion and wearily closed her eyes. "I know," she admitted. "I know you're right. Getting over those fears is just a lot easier said than done."

Jeannine hesitated. Her expression showed that she knew exactly to what limits she was pushing her rights as a friend. But typically, the intrepid streak in her nature won out, and she said firmly, "I really don't understand you, you know that? What you're most frightened of with all of this publicity business is that someone somehow will uncover something about your past, and *that*'s what's got you all tied up in knots. But it doesn't make any sense. No one imagines that you sprang full grown onto the Hollywood scene five years ago or that you hatched from an egg or dropped in from outer space or anything. Your past is no more terrible than anyone else's."

"But why should anyone care?" protested Mallory. Her hands were slowly tightening into fists in her lap. "It's nobody's business as long as I do my job—"

"That's exactly the point," interrupted Jeannine firmly. "Nobody *does* care about a screenwriter who had the bad judgment to marry one certified crazy and get her picture on the front pages of local papers. Hell, honey, there's better stuff than that going on in this town every day! It might be a matter of passing interest, but nobody *truly cares*. Why should you?"

Mallory sighed. Everything that was logical within her knew Jeannine was right, but her fears came from a totally illogical source. Jeannine knew the facts that had resulted in Mallory's appearance on the front page of a newspaper, but she did not know the emotions that accompanied it. No one could know that horror unless they had gone through the experience. Hadn't Mallory a right to be a little phobic? It was more than simply being terrified that the scandal from the past would be dragged up again, although God knew that was enough. Maybe it was simply that *she* wanted to pretend she had sprung full grown onto the Holly-wood scene a few years ago. She wanted to forget Larry and everything connected with him. She wanted to keep herself to herself, to be secure and unexposed, not to be reminded of failures every time she looked into the eyes of a stranger on the street.

Perhaps it was merely simpler to maintain the illusion when no one was aware of the truth but herself.

"Well," Mallory said with sudden resolution, getting to her feet, "worrying never solved anything. In fact, I know only one solution to a crisis as big as this."

Greatly cheered by her friend's sudden change of mood, Jeannine demanded, "What?"

Mallory turned with a knowing wink and a smile that was totally false and said, "I have an entire half a cherry pie in the refrigerator. Care to help me eat myself into oblivion?"

MALLORY KEPT UP THE PRETENSE of being cheerful until Jeannine left to open the shop. Then Mallory was alone with her real doubts, her real fears.

Colt. That was one part of the entire episode she had not mentioned to Jeannine. Her deepest concern Mallory had not even fully admitted to herself, but now, alone with her thoughts, she had to face it. Colt was involved too. His becoming part of her life had resurrected old scandals, old pains. How was he feeling right now? Had some well-meaning friend or neighbor eagerly brought him the morning paper and with malicious delight pointed out the article on page five? "Colt Stanford, who achieved notoriety in the *Adam's Choice* scandal. . . ." Five years had passed and he had almost erased that stigma. He had put the painful experience behind him and started a new life. How would he feel to see it all dredged up now? Was he hurting? Was he reliving the nightmare that had cost him his career, his wife, his life's ambition? Was he feeling bitter, was he blaming Mallory? Why didn't he call?

And why should she care?

Was she interviewing directors? Hadn't that been in the back of her mind all along? Hadn't Colt's skill as a director been one of the main things that had attracted her to him? Everyone was so worried that Colt might be using her, but was Colt thinking now that she had been using him?

He had never said a word to her about directing her film. But then she wasn't in a position to negotiate yet.

Now she wondered if, despite what was best for the film, she had the courage to ask Colt to direct it. Could she stand the notoriety? Could she take the risk that the studio might not back her decision, thus putting the whole project in jeopardy?

Could she live with her own doubts about whether or not the film was all Colt had ever wanted from her?

Mallory paced the floor between the telephone in the office and the telephone in the living room, making an occasional foray to the telephone in the kitchen, where once she actually put her hand on the receiver, ready to dial his number. Was he angry? Did he ever have fears as desperate as hers? Did he ever feel relentlessly pursued by the past?

She shouldn't care. She had enough problems of her own without worrying about him.

Why didn't he call?

When the phone rang, she jumped for it.

"Mallory, are you all right?"

She closed her eyes against the sweet comfort that flowed through her with the concern in his voice. Not anger. Not pain. She did not deserve a friend as wonderful as he.

"Colt," she said softly. "I'm glad you called. You. . . ." She almost subdued the catch in her voice, but not quite. "You saw the paper?"

"Just now." His voice was grim. "I'm sorry, Mallory." His tone softened with sincerity, his understanding reached out to embrace her. "I know how you hate exposure."

Yes, Colt knew. Jeannine didn't know, Jake didn't know, even Mallory couldn't completely explain it to herself. But Colt understood that the bottom line to this entire episode was vulnerability. She let the gratitude fill her, wishing she could touch him, show him how much he meant to her. "Yes." She took a deep breath as her hand restlessly played with the coiled loop of the telephone wire. Her fingers moved over the plastic-coated surface as though they were caressing the face of her lover. "Well, I guess I should have expected it when I refused to give her the interview."

"I'm sorry," he said again, his tone filled with

simple regret. "I know it can't do you any good to have your name linked with mine. I wish there was something I could do."

Immediately her head came up; she shook it violently in denial. "No, Colt, that's not—" Mallory took another breath, not knowing how to put into words emotions she had never planned to feel, things she had never expected to say. "I was worried about you." Why should that be so hard to admit? It felt so good to say. "I was upset because it might be painful for you to be reminded of your last picture. She said some ugly things."

"But true," he reminded Mallory, and in a moment she could sense the smile beginning to form on his lips. "You're a pretty terrific lady—you know that, don't you?"

She tried to laugh. "If you say so."

"You can handle this, can't you?"

Now she could. "Yes." The brightness she forced into her voice made it sound strained. "Sure. I'm fine."

"Do you want me to come over?"

Again Mallory forced cheerfulness into her tone, and her false smile pulled at the muscles of her face. She was lying to him, and she had never done that before. That's what happened when people started getting too close—the gentle lies, the kind deceptions.... Yes, she needed him but she would not give in to that weakness. She had to be more careful. "Don't be silly, Colt, you don't have to babysit me. I was upset for a while but it's not a big deal, right? As a matter of fact, I think I'll just turn in

early tonight and get a fresh start on the morning."
She lied far more easily than she had ever expected
she could.

"All right." Was that doubt she heard in his
voice, or disappointment? He hesitated, and Mallory's hand tightened on the receiver. The concern
in his tone reached out to her like a caress, and was
almost her undoing. "I just wanted you to know that
I cared."

Her throat tightened and her eyes closed over a
blur of tears. This was too much for him to ask her
to take. "I — I know," she whispered.

And that was really the worst part about the
whole episode. She cared about him too — much
more than she deserved to, more than she had ever
intended to and far, far more than she should.

That was why she decided to sleep alone tonight.

LIKE ANY CAREFULLY WRITTEN and well-produced
drama, life unfolds with a flair and pace designed to
build suspense and have the most powerful impact
on an unsuspecting audience. Nothing ever happens
randomly or without reason. It's all part of the act.

Early the next morning Jake appeared on her
doorstep. No warning phone call, no hint as to what
might have developed — nothing, in fact, had been
heard from him at all in over a week. He tipped his
hat to her, strolled inside and drawled, "Mornin',
peaches. Coffee on?"

Mallory leaned against the door to close it, arms
akimbo, gazing after him with a mixture of amusement and caution. He did make quite a spectacle at

eight o'clock in the morning in his battered denims, Western-cut plaid shirt and Stetson, scuffed cowboy boots—and a shiny alligator briefcase that could have been as old as he was, but was used so rarely that it had never lost its expensive department-store newness. Mallory did up the top button of her robe, smoothed her tousled blond hair and replied with a muffled yawn, "Not unless little elves came in while I was sleeping and made it for me. What on earth are you doing here at this time of day?"

He half turned to her with a look of reproof. "It's a working day, little darlin', or are we on different calendars? Why aren't you in there pounding away at the typewriter, making me another million?"

"Knock it off, Jake, I had a rough night." She dragged her fingers through her hair again, with more force this time. She never should have let Jeannine talk her into that expensive stylist. She was much happier with her hair in a ragged topknot, her wardrobe out of last year's Sears catalog, her life in a predictable routine. . . and her privacy intact.

Jake was familiar enough with Mallory's moods to leave her to her silence as she led the way to the kitchen. He did not like the way she looked this morning, worn and tired. A lot of her distress had to do with yesterday's Bouchard column, Jake knew, but he also suspected it ran deeper than that. . . .

He knew, of course, about Colt Stanford. He had not interfered, he had not voiced an opinion. He knew Mallory could not be closed in, even by the best of loving attentions, and he would always give her the freedom to make her own mistakes. Soon she would realize that Stanford was one of those mistakes, and Jake would be there, ready to comfort her. But he did not like to think about the pain she would have to endure in the meantime. Nor did he think he could remain completely silent any longer.

Mallory went through the motions of making coffee, trying not to notice the look Jake fastened on her. She *had* had a restless night, filled with doubts and confusion, wondering how her life had ever gotten so entangled. She was lonely and a little frightened, lying there in the dark in the oversize bed thinking about the vicious work of a spiteful woman. Mallory had tried to convince herself it was one of the prices of fame she would have to get used to. Reliving the past few weeks, she'd wondered how so much could have changed in so little time. Occasionally she would doze off, and when she awoke her hand would be reaching out for someone but would only be grasping bedclothes. That was both embarrassing and unsettling. Colt even invaded her dreams now. So much of her life had become wrapped around him that one night apart from him gave her nightmares.

She was beginning to depend on him, and that was dangerous.

Last evening she'd spent hours questioning if there was any way she could draw her life back into the safe little cocoon that had shielded her a month ago, and wondering if she really wanted to. With Colt, she had sought something she had no right to want, and now she would spend the rest of her life afraid of losing it. For her attachment to Colt had grown too strong for her to back away now. She felt alive only when she was with him; when they were apart she spent the time wishing he was there. She was even starting to think as he did. Colt had invaded every part of her and if he should disappear off the face of the earth, she would never be the same again for having known him.

No, there was no way she could go back to the secure, introverted, screamingly dull life she had lived before meeting Colt Stanford. He had shown her a taste of the magic and made her greedy for more.

Still, once in a while she wished she had never known what she was missing. Then she wouldn't have so much to lose now.

Jake settled himself in a chair, tilted it back on two legs, pulled his hat down over his eyes and proceeded to ignore Mallory while she made the coffee. Mallory thought she knew why he was there. As unconcerned as he carefully made himself appear to be about the workings of the outside world, Jake Farrow never missed a single detail about what went on in his clients' lives. He had read the article in the paper yesterday, and he wanted to find out how much was true. But Mallory simply did not want to go into it with him today. Or ever.

She brought two cups of coffee and set them down on the table—one, her morning fortification, so heavily laced with cream and sugar the coffee was almost an afterthought, the other, for Jake, so black and thick a spoon might be able to stand straight up in it. Then she took the chair opposite him and silently began to sip her breakfast. If Jake expected her to open up the subject, he would be waiting for a long, long time.

"Well, well, well," Jake decided at last, regarding her over the rim of his cup. "It does look to me like I might have caught you at a bad time. Maybe I should just write you a letter."

Mallory glanced at him with heavily lidded, sleep-swollen eyes. "About what?"

Jake did not trouble to meet her gaze. "My news."

Mallory's befuddled mind was a little slow in accepting the fact that he might have come for reasons other than she suspected. "What news?"

"Well, little peaches—" he slowly set his cup down and reached for his briefcase "—there is, as they say in the business, good news and bad news. Which do you want first?"

This was entirely too much; one crisis on top of another. She blinked rapidly, trying to get her mind to focus. Her limbs were already tensing for the worst. Automatically, she said, "Bad news."

Jake grinned as he placed his briefcase on the table and snapped open the catch. "The bad news is, it was too damn easy. The good news is, you got your contract, at your price, on your terms."

Mallory stared at him. It took forever for his statements to sink in. After all this time, waiting and watching and almost giving up hope, walking around on pins and needles waiting for the verdict and mentally preparing herself for disappointment, hardly daring to look into the future.... Just like that. "It was too damn easy." She simply stared at him.

"Careful of the flies, peaches," Jake said dryly. Mallory closed her mouth with a snap as he drew out a sheaf of legal documents from his briefcase. "Sign on the dotted line."

Very carefully, trying not to spill the contents, Mallory lowered her coffee cup to the table. She tried to make her mind work logically, but it was leaping ahead in cartwheels of joy and starbursts of amazement. Colt. She must tell Colt. "Wait a minute," she said, trying not to let herself get too excited. "Do you mean...are you sure...? They're giving me final cut *and* my choice of director?"

"They think it's a lovely idea, sweetheart. They were beside themselves."

Mallory gave him a long, skeptical look, and he relented with a grin. "All right, so they didn't exactly declare a national holiday, but we've got it in writing, and you've got your chance."

Mallory took the contract from him, handling it as though it were a holy relic. She wanted to read every word.

"What they've done is given you final approval of the choice of director. Of course they'll be parading a whole batallion of possibles before you. You may as well be prepared for the fact that they'll try to push you into what they want, but nothing goes until you give the okay. Actually, that was the easy part. Final cut took a bit more work. By the way, I've wangled you a nice little sum for your services on the set too. I don't think you'll be disappointed."

Mallory laughed, shaking her head in wonder as she let the words before her fade into an abstract tangle of meaningless characters. "You mean they're going to pay me for overseeing my own film? I would have paid them!"

"That's what you have an agent for, peaches." He pulled a pen from his shirt pocket and handed it to her with a flourish, obviously very pleased with himself. "Now, if you'll just affix your John Hancock...."

Mallory paused with the pen over the paper, the familiar pucker of doubt creasing her forehead as she glanced up. "This is it then? Nothing can go wrong?"

A slow smile of resigned frustration crossed Jake's rugged face. He released a patient sigh. "Darlin', anything from earthquake to flood to fire to an invasion from outer space can go wrong. But we gotta play the odds. You know this business as well as I do, no contract is ironclad. The studio always has an out. But as long as you do your job and don't screw up too bad I think we can count on meeting the release date. So how about it? Are you going to sign?"

Mallory took a breath and carefully wrote her name on the line at the bottom of the last page. She could hardly believe that her entire destiny was wrapped up in those few pages.

The ceremony was completed with the signing of three more copies, initialing each page, with Jake witnessing. He gathered up the copies and replaced them neatly in their proper folders, leaving Mallory feeling somewhat dazed. It was done. All she had had to do was take a chance, to assert herself, to ask for what she wanted... and it had materialized.

Jake settled back, fixing her with an all-too-knowing look. "Any ideas on who you want to direct?"

Mallory avoided his eyes quickly. So he had read the Bouchard column. "No," she said, a little too adamantly. "Of course not. I haven't even thought much about it. How could I, when I wasn't sure the studio would take my deal?"

He seemed to accept her answer, but Mallory should have known better. "So tell me, little one." Jake returned the folders to his briefcase, not looking up or in any way giving her any indication that what he was about to say carried any particular import. "Any truth to these rumors about you and Stanford? Or did you just rub Madame Buzzard's feathers the wrong way?"

He spoke so matter-of-factly that Mallory needed a moment to register the words. Even then she was in such a state of dazzled euphoria that she forgot to be defensive. She laughed. "Both. I refused to give her an interview so she wrote what she wanted, exactly as she threatened to do." How strange that half an hour ago that column by a scandalmonger had been the most significant thing in Mallory's life. Now it hardly seemed worth talking about.

"Well, a little romance is a healthy thing, I always say." Jake snapped the briefcase shut and leaned back in his chair again, sipping his coffee. "Course, that's providing romance is what both parties have in mind."

Until that point Mallory had been barely paying attention. Something in his manner, his tone or perhaps the words themselves, stiffened a warning inside her. Her fingers curled cautiously around her coffee cup. "What do you mean?"

His gaze was steady. "I imagine Mr. Stanford has lots of good advice to give you about how to direct this film."

Mallory did not want to believe what she thought he was implying. She did not want to fight with Jake. "Some," she admitted, still very carefully. Her eyes and her voice were cool. "I could hardly do better. He's only one of the accepted experts in the field."

Jake nodded, once, and almost imperceptibly. "He's also a guaranteed panic button for any production company in the business. I'd be careful if I were you, peaches."

Mallory wanted to let his advice pass, but she couldn't. Not this time. She met Jake's eyes unflinchingly, and there were flecks of stone in hers. "What are you implying?" she demanded coldly.

Jake had never been intimidated by her yet, and this was not to be the first time. He calmly finished his coffee, tilted his hat back and got to his feet. "You know perfectly well what I'm implying," he said smoothly. "You don't take anybody at face value in this town, and a person in your position has to sleep with one eye open and your finger on the trigger. You just watch yourself." He picked up his briefcase and was at the back door before Mallory could utter the first stuttering words of furious protest. "Catch you later, peaches. Keep cool."

Jake could not have said or done anything more

effectively designed to take the joy out of Mallory's victory. She alternated between fury with Jake and fury with herself for letting him upset her as she paced the floor, wishing Colt were here. Jake did not even know the man. He had no right to make such despicable suggestions. Colt had been nothing but generous with her. She had not *asked* him for advice, he had given it to her, freely and without coercion. He *enjoyed* helping her. His only reason for being with her was not just because she was involved in a high-budget film. . . . She *knew* Colt, for goodness' sake. He was one of the most honorable, straightforward, unpretentious men she had ever met and Jake had no right. . . . But eventually anger gave way to doubt, Mallory's greatest weakness. She did know Colt. She knew him to be a master manipulator. He knew how to control people. He knew how to control his environment. He had the ability to take any set of circumstances and turn them to his advantage. Those very abilities were what had made him a legend in the show business world. That same ingenuity and adaptability had enabled him to survive the collapse of his empire in a way very few men would have been able to. Could there possibly be some truth in what Jake said?

After all, Colt had come to Mallory at a highly vulnerable time. He was her first lover in five years. For that very reason, he had more significance in her life than any other man, at any other time, had ever had. He gave her confidence. He made her feel wanted. He showed her things about herself she had never thought existed. He affected her life in so many ways; he brought so many changes. . . . He was making her dependent on him.

He could, right now, have anything he wanted from her.

But something deep within Mallory refused to accept that. Her logical, cynical mind told her to expect the worst, but this one time, in this one case, she refused to listen.

She was going to ask Colt to direct her film.

Chapter Thirteen

"CONGRATULATIONS!" Colt Stanford lifted his champagne glass in salute. "To the most talented screenwriter and the most deserving aspiring young industry giant in the business today."

They were having dinner on the patio beside Mallory's pool, because this was a private triumph that she wanted to share with only one other person. He alone knew how much this really meant to her, could identify with what lay ahead of her, understood that she was almost as afraid of success as she was of failure. She needed Colt tonight, and he was there for her.

Mallory laughed a little nervously as she accepted the toast. The warm June breeze tickled a strand of blond hair across her cheek and fluttered the hem of her crepe caftan around her ankles. Starlight turned the night into a misty blue veil and softened the glow of the single candle on the table before them. The lazy lapping sounds of the pool water a few feet away could have been a mountain lake or a forest stream or a distant, deserted beach. She and Colt were together, and they had created a world of their own.

If only Jake's ugly remarks from the afternoon would stop intruding on the mood.

"Deserving? Aspiring?" Mallory sipped from he
glass. "I'm not entirely sure I deserve all those adje
tives!"

"I noticed you didn't object to talented," Co
teased, and Mallory demurred gracefully.

She was radiant tonight, but Colt could not b
entirely sure whether that was from excitement (
nervousness. Her eyes were a luminous hazel, he
skin looked almost transparent in the golden re
candlelight. She smiled a lot and her hands were i
almost constant motion, punctuating her sentence
But her eye movements were evasive in a way sh
could not possibly be aware of, and there were tim
she fell into brief and strangely reflective silence
Colt knew Mallory well enough to know now th
she had gotten what she wanted, she was bound t
be scared. But was that all it was? Something wa
bothering her, and Colt wished she trusted hir
enough to tell him what it was.

Mallory was frightened, but she could not confic
in Colt. Her doubts of the afternoon had left he
feeling guilty and tainted all day, yet her steadfa
belief in Colt made her feel foolish and uneasy. Ho
had she let herself get so involved with the mar
How could she, Mallory Evans, avowed cynic an
nobody's fool, be so desperately torn between har
facts and what she knew to be illusion?

Looking now into the soft brown of Colt's eye
she could not believe that his motives had ever bee
anything but pure. No, Colt would not lie; he wou
not deceive her. But he was only human. He wou
not be averse to taking advantage of an opportun

ty. Hadn't she offered him the perfect opportunity already? Unofficially and vicariously, he had already begun to direct this film. She knew he wanted it. And she would benefit from his expertise. It could be nothing but a mutually satisfactory alliance. Then why did it make her so unhappy to imagine that might be the only reason he continued to see her?

Because it was an unworthy suspicion, that was why, one that degraded both of them. She should have learned how to better combat her old paranoia by now. Mallory suppressed a sigh as she looked at Colt and smiled. He looked so beautiful sitting there with the swaying shadows from the candlelight playing on his face, the breeze catching and rearranging the wayward locks of dark hair across his forehead. He was leaning back in the wrought-iron chair, one elbow propped on the arm as his forefinger rested against his temple, the glass of champagne held casually in the other hand. His expression, as he studied her, was thoughtful and tender, his eyes alert. He was composed, relaxed and in control—all the things Mallory was not and never could be. She felt a physical tightening of need in her chest as she looked at him. How important this man had become to her. How very much she had come to depend upon him.

The more attached she became to him, the greater chance there was of losing him. And the more afraid she became.

"There are going to be some big changes in your life now, Mallory," Colt observed. His smile softened a pronouncement that, in other circumstances, would have been ominous.

She smiled quickly, maybe a little too brightly. "Good ones, let's hope."

A swift and subtle light kindled in Colt's eyes as they flickered over her face, touching her eyes, her nose, her lips, her chin, brushing the shadow of her collarbone and the outline of her breasts. It was a familiar look, not a sexually threatening one but filled with appreciation for what he knew of her. Mallory felt as if she was coming home to a warm embrace. As long as she could continue to look up and see that reassurance in Colt's eyes she knew all the changes would be good ones.

"That depends on you, doesn't it?" he said. Though the low and mesmerizing tone of his voice drew a shiver of yearning from her, she had to listen to the words.

Yes, it all depended on her. She mustn't forget that. The new direction Mallory's career was taking would be a high-risk, all-involving venture. She had fought hard to get to this point; she had invested a lot. She had to believe she could see it through.

And where did Colt Stanford fit into her new life? Could she afford to make a place for him?

Could she afford not to?

She crumpled her napkin on the table with another quick smile and stood. "Ready for dessert?" she inquired brightly.

But he caught her hand as she turned to go. His expression was deep, and everything within Mallory stilled in anticipation as he slowly pulled her down into his lap. "Mallory," he said softly, and his hand lightly caressed her arm. His eyes were gentle and filled with concern. "I can't play the guessing game any longer. You've been fluttering around all night like a nun with a guilty secret. Something is bothering you, and I can't figure out what it is. Tell me, love," he persuaded gently. "Tell me what you want."

Mallory closed her eyes, and the whisper of breath that escaped her parted lips was like the weary raising of the flag of surrender. Her throat was tight and her chest ached with a yearning she could not define and was no longer willing to fight. "You, Colt," she whispered, and her hand curled against his chest with the effort it took to admit that. "Just you...."

His hands came up to cup the back of her head, fingers threading through her hair. His eyes were somber, yet within them was a gentle consent that radiated promise. He was hers, he had always been, and whatever she needed from him was hers for the asking.

Colt's fingers danced very lightly on the back of her neck, generating waves of pleasurable anticipation through her nervous system. Quietly and firmly his eyes spoke to her of a need as great as her own. His motions were slow and deliberate, infinitely provocative, and the silence was tension packed—a scene from an old movie, in which the characters made love with their eyes and not their bodies. His head was tilted as though in question as he held Mallory's face cupped in his hands, and the answer to that question throbbed in her chest. She could sense the promise in Colt's eyes as his fingers brushed across her cheeks and blended into her hair. An electric touch that traced across her face and made her want to press her cheek into his palm, but a soothing motion that left her paralyzed with anticipation. Over and over again, his fingertips played a feather dance across the sensitive skin and into her hair, hypnotizing with promise, burning with need.

His fingers stopped with a rippling, massaging motion on Mallory's jawline just underneath her ears. A slow, sure pressure, so light it was more of a suggestion than a deed, moved her face fractionally closer to his. Colt's expression told her worlds of time stretched before them. And his eyes. . . what was she seeing in his eyes? Emotions so deep they drowned her own weakly struggling feelings, honesty so pure it opened everything within her to him. There was no need for words between them. Everything was spoken with bodies, with eyes, with touch and response. . . . They stepped onto another plane when they were together.

Mallory's breath was suspended, her lips parted and aching for his kiss as they moved ever so slowly together, just like the first time. Every time was a first time for Mallory in the endless discovery of this man. The magic did not fade.

With only a fraction of an inch separating their faces, Colt stopped. He looked at her, deeply and endlessly, caressing her with his gaze. The message she saw there stopped the beat of her heart and then it pounded wildly as she felt the flicker of his tongue lightly, ever so lightly, across her lips. The circular movements of his fingers on the back of her head were a sensual counterpoint to the quick delicate brush of his tongue over her lips. Her breathing was light and shallow as he brought his fingers to her face, caressing her cheeks in slow, sweeping motions that matched the rhythm of his kisses. His tongue met the tip of hers and the dance they created together was brief, delicate, tantalizing.

Colt's hands moved under her arms, making her skin prickle with his long sweeping strokes up and down her spine. His touch was so light that his fingertips barely brushed across the material of her dress, never pressing the flesh beneath but promising more, so much more. Her open mouth caressed his, their tongues met and parted and lightly met again as she was held beneath his spell of building sensuality and growing desire—a communication of minds, not bodies, an opening of hearts and a connecting of souls.

Colt lifted his face, his gaze holding her. Mallory could feel his need, see it in his face, read it in his eyes. Hers was the same. She let him command her. She was completely his, as he was hers.

Colt took her palms and placed them gently along the sides of his face. Her eyes closed with the pure sensuous pleasure of his flesh beneath her fingertips, the coarse heated texture, the planes, the curves, the angles and ridges. His hand moved lightly along her leg from hip to knee, exploring, caressing, awakening nerves and filling her with pleasure. Her fingers traced the outline of his collarbone and felt the soft texture of hair upon his chest. Pushing aside material, Mallory flattened her palms against his hard muscles and wonder shivered through her as he enfolded her within his embrace. Her arms circled his chest beneath his shirt, hands pressing into the taut structure of his back, delighting in the feel of smooth bare skin. She felt his lips against her neck, just beneath her ear, the quick warm flicker of his tongue that started a tight sensation in the muscles of her stomach; she caught her breath. Then his arms slipped beneath her thighs, he lifted her with him as he stood, and she buried her face in the masculine fragrance of his chest as he carried her inside.

With dazed, desire-brightened eyes she lay upon the bed and watched him undress in sure, unhurried motions. The revelation of his body in the yellow glow of the bedside lamp was beautiful to her—strong, lean and masculine. The muscles of his chest, the dipping pattern of hair. The prominent vein in his upper arm that roped well-formed biceps, the strength of his bronzed wrists. The stripe of white skin low on his abdomen that his swimsuit had covered, the unashamed power of his sexuality. The hard thighs, the lightly furred legs. Her eyes could not get enough of him.

Colt came toward her slowly, and she felt her breathing change as muscles clenched in anticipation. In one smooth motion he bent over her and slipped the caftan over her head, letting it cascade to the floor. Then he carefully lowered himself on top of her, flesh against flesh, touching at all points.

His kiss was deep and powerful, promising fulfillment and gently withdrawing. He shifted his weight, pulling her with him onto her side. Their legs entwined and his open mouth covered hers. She gasped as she felt the pressure of his knee between her legs and his hands touching her breasts, inflaming her. Her body arched to him as liquid bolts of fire filled her veins and then calmed to showers of sensation as his palms opened over her breasts, tenderly massaging, and his knee lightly stroked the inside of her thigh. Softly yet deliberately he kissed her, his tongue tracing the outline of her lips, then traveling slowly, worshipfully over her face.

Suspended in pleasure, Mallory let her fingertips move in a path of discovery over his body as his lips moved with slow and maddeningly sensual exploration over hers. Every part of him was beautiful to her, and she memorized with her fingers each plane and angle, each curve and indentation, as though she were exploring for the first time. The breadth of his shoulders and the ridges of his spine, the smoothness of his waist and the hardness of his buttocks. The small rounded points of his hipbones, the flat, muscular abdomen, and lower, brushing across the rigid evidence of his arousal and drawing a gasp from him.

She trembled from the circular motions of his tongue around her nipples, overly sensitized nerves reacted as he swept down the center of her abdomen and made a swift probing exploration of her navel. Gently nibbling and licking, he covered the soft flesh of her stomach and the points of her hips, traced a pattern on the inside of her thigh and tickled the back of her knee. Again and again, with no more than the caress of his lips and his tongue he brought her to the peak of arousal and backed away again, calming her, making her wait, stretching out the experience. The deep ache built within her womb for him, her skin tingled and burned for him, every cell of her body pleaded for him. Colt's uneven breathing matched hers; within his eyes was the same raw passion that darkened and deepened hers. His eyes closed languidly as he turned his head to her tremulous touching of his face, capturing one of her fingers and drawing it inside his mouth, releasing it slowly. His hands cupped her breasts and applied a steadily increasing pressure until she gasped and squirmed beneath him, wanting him, yearning for him so badly it hurt. Then his mouth covered hers and he moved between her legs.

Never had there been such openness, such sharing, such depth of feeling between them. There had been passion, there had been tenderness, there had been a discovery of sexual limits. There had been teaching and learning, giving and taking. Tonight, together, they surpassed the limits and crossed the borders that confined them. Tonight they touched the very edges of each other's souls. They said with their bodies things they would not say in words, and though Mallory did not fully understand the message, something deep within her acknowledged it, responded to it, shared it. Tonight she knew that she wanted him forever. And in his arms she forgot that was not possible.

Mallory wrapped her arms and her legs around his body, unable to get close enough to him, unwilling to let him go. She felt the strength of his returned embrace, his hands pressing into her back, his breath warm and steady against her neck. She was protected, secure, shielded from all danger in this snug cocoon where nothing but joy could enter. As long as she held on to him, as long as Colt's arms enfolded her, they were immortal.

Mallory could not remember what she had been afraid of. She could not remember what doubts had assailed her. How could it be that each time they made love it was better? How could the physical act of touching, caressing, exploring intimacy leave her so moved, so changed in every way? Perhaps it was because he taught her with her body to reach for heights her emotions dared not explore. . . .

"Oh, Colt." Her arms tightened briefly around him before her hand moved to stroke the adored face above her. "When I'm with you everything seems to be all right. Why do you make me so happy?"

He turned to push her hair away from her face with both hands. His eyes were deep and soft and full of meaning. They touched her soul and seemed to draw her heart outward. "Possibly. . ." he said, and there was a moment as swift as a breath in which she should have known. She should have known what was coming. "Because I love you," he said simply.

Mallory let the words sink in slowly, trying not to reject them, trying, in fact, to pretend she had not heard them. But like little spears of ice they penetrated her fragile defenses, ripping at the very fabric of her security, letting all of the world that was hard and true come rushing in.

Nothing lasts forever, and the veil of trust that had bound them together was dissolving like cellophane before a flame. Colt had fallen into that fatal trap, and nothing would ever be the same again.

Mallory sat up slowly, and Colt let her go, watching her closely. He had known what to expect. He knew exactly what effect those words would have on her. He knew the risk he was taking when he uttered them. Then why, oh why, couldn't he leave well enough alone?

I love you. The three words that every woman wanted to hear. Any woman would want to hear them from a man like Colt Stanford. Mallory should have been happy. She should have been ecstatic. But this was not what she wanted. He *knew* this was not what she wanted.

She turned away from him, the sheet drawn up to cover her breasts, her head lowered so that her hair swung forward to cover her face. "You don't have to say that," she said.

Colt sat up cautiously behind her, very close, not touching her. He replied just as carefully, "I do if it's true."

Mallory tilted her head back; she inhaled a long tight breath through her teeth. Her hands clenched in her lap. "No, Colt." She was trying very hard to keep her voice even, her tone reasonable. "It's not true. You don't even know what it means."

She missed the flinch of pain that crossed his face, the momentary flash of vulnerability in his eyes before the armor of control came up again. His voice too was very calm. "All right then. You tell me what it means."

Mallory swept her hair behind one ear in a restrained gesture that nonetheless signified helplessness. "Commitment," she said shortly. "Promises. Caring, involvement... I don't want those things from you, Colt!" she cried, turning to him. "All I wanted was what we had—the friendship, the companionship...."

The sound of impatience he made was totally unlike Colt. "Darling, we haven't been 'friends' since about forty-five minutes after the first time you walked into my apartment."

Mallory shook her head violently, indicating both denial of what he said and a plea for him to understand. "Colt, we had an agreement. None of the false romance that turns into ugliness—a relationship without bitterness."

The lines of Colt's face were very tight, his eyes dark. "Damn it, Mallory, how can you take something so natural and so beautiful and twist it into another doomsday plot? I've been trying to find a way to tell you I love you since about three days after we met, and I've done it in every way I know how without saying those words that I knew would scare you to death. Well, I'm tired of playing games. I do love you," he said, and his hands closed around her arms. He held them firm even when she tried to pull away. "I *am* involved with you and I *do* care about you. There's nothing you can do or say that will change that now. I love your brilliance and your beauty, and I want nothing more in the world than to watch you become the best you can be. I love your fragility. I want to protect you. I love all the tender womanly things about you and the greatest joy in my life has been in watching your own discovery of them...watching you blossom from a shy little girl to a mature woman who takes what she wants and isn't afraid to give. And yes, I even love your courage—the courage it takes to face your fears and live with them and even move beyond them. I want to be there to inspire you and cheer you on. I want to make a commitment to you. I want to make promises to you. Why does that terrify you so much?"

Mallory could no longer look at him, no longer listen to the tender pleading in his voice. Her eyes stung and blurred and her throat knotted with the force of tears she would not release. She pulled her arms away and turned to fumble for the robe that lay across the dressing bench at the foot of the bed. "Promises were meant to be broken," she said hoarsely, drawing on the robe. "I'd rather not hear them at all."

Mallory stood and belted the robe. Walking away from him, she could hear the slow release of his breath mingled with the shifting of the bedsprings and the rustling of the sheets as Colt too got up and pulled on his slacks. She was afraid to look at him, to meet the hurt and disappointment in his eyes. What a lonely sound, the sound of dressing, signifying an end to intimacy, a drawing of borders, a closing of doors.

But then she heard him sit down on the bed again, and she turned. He was shirtless, his hair was still tousled from their passion, his face tired and lined. He had never looked so vulnerable. She wanted to go to him, to smooth back his dark hair, to put her arms around him. To hold him and be held by him. But she did not move.

"Mallory," he said quietly, "I understand your insecurity. I know it's hard for you to believe in winning because you're so afraid of losing. And yes, I knew I was taking a chance of frightening you away when I told you I loved you. The only way you allowed me into your life was on your terms—no commitment, no involvement. What can I do, Mallory, to make you believe in me?" Colt pleaded softly. "How can I convince you that all promises don't end in disillusionment? What are you so afraid of, my love?"

Very slowly, she walked over to the closet, opened the doors and stood on tiptoe to reach for a shoebox at the very back. She'd needed that moment to give her the resolve to share with Colt something he should have known long ago—her last secret, her last gift to him. But the gift was not a symbol to enrich their relationship, rather to end it.

For a moment Mallory held the box in her hands, and a scent drifted up to her like the dust of moldy funeral flowers. Then she walked over to Colt and sat on the dressing bench. She put the box in his hands.

Inside was a collection of mementos, faded snapshots, crumbling corsages, a yellowed wedding garter—a witch's bag of dark potions that wove the spell of a murky past. On top of the stack was a newspaper clipping, newer than the rest, and it was this he picked up first. The headline read, "Woman held hostage for thirty-six hours." And underneath: "Husband holds off police at gunpoint."

Mallory told her story in a flat, unemotional voice. "We were married in college. We were so much in love." A smile, sadly reflective, drifted like a shadow across her face, and her hand reached involuntarily for a dried flower at the top of the pile before falling away without touching it. "He used to bring me a yellow rose every night and I'd put it on the packing crate we were using for a dining-room table until we could afford to buy 'good' furniture. We had this tacky little apartment. You know, like everyone does when they're first starting out. . . ." She shrugged. "And like everyone else, we found the lean years were the best. We both worked. I was teaching school and he was climbing the corporate ladder. We started building a home together, just the way we wanted it. We bought our dream house, we furnished it, we each had a car—the American Dream. Then the corporation came under new management. There was a reorganization. A lot of people were fired, and Larry was one of them." Mallory paused only briefly, but long enough for Colt to see the painful memories flash across the screen of her eyes. "He never recovered from that," she continued in the same flat tone. "Jobs were hard to find, it's true, but whenever he did get one he couldn't hold it for more than a few weeks. He started drinking, which didn't help. And. . . he started taking his frustration out on me. The worst part was, of course, that I let him." Now there was just the faintest hint of a wry twist to her lips, a shadow of bitterness in her eyes. "I let him," she said softly, "because I *loved* him. I thought it would get better. But it got worse." Her voice had become hard, controlled and matter-of-fact. "The last two years were a nightmare. I saw him turn into a monster. I went to bed in fear and I woke up in fear. We never had any money, and that only made him worse. I had to start hiding my purse from him so I could pay the bills, and then he'd get angry and. . . hit me. . . until I gave him whatever cash I had. . . . One day I came home to find he had sold all the furniture. I never knew what happened to that money. I had to scour my friends' attics and basements for a bed and a few chairs. He wrecked his car. Then he sold mine.

"I used to write a check for the mortgage payment every month and leave them on my desk for him to take to the mailbox. Eventually I found out he'd been taking those checks out of the envelopes and cashing them by some illegal means and we were about to lose the house. Finally one day I came home from school and he was sitting with a gun pointed at the door. I was too scared to run. Maybe I thought I could reason with him." Her voice was growing tired. "Before I knew it, it was too late to run or to reason." Then, for barely a moment, Mallory let herself slide back, deep into that shadowy tunnel that opened onto an airless room and the pressure of a gun against her flesh and the smell of

sweat and whiskey.... "Thirty-six hours," she said
Her voice was hoarse and came from far away. He
lips hardly moved and her face registered no emo
tion, as though she were not even aware she wa
speaking out loud. "A day and a half.... There wa
a clock on the mantel. I just kept watching th
clock, watching the hands move, because I kne
it couldn't go on forever.... It was as though a
long as I could hear the clock ticking, I could tak
it, I could hold on. It was my way of staying sane,
guess...only...." Her breath caught with
dragged-in sound, the gasp of a diver trying to su
face. The grimace that twisted her lips might hav
been a weak attempt to smile as she slowly made h
way back to the present. "It was only a twenty-fou
hour clock and eventually—" all traces of a smil
vanished, and her voice was not much more than
whisper "—it stopped ticking." *It stopped ticking.*
stopped ticking and all that was left for Mallory wa
emptiness and uncertainty and perhaps the rest
her life would resound with the silence of an unpr
dictable future. The promise of order, of tim
marching relentlessly forth, of one minute followin
another was all she had had to hold on to, and whe
that was gone there was no longer any hope. On
chaos.

Colt carefully replaced the clipping in the bo
He did not look at her. "What happened to him?"

"They took him to jail." Still a methodical a
counting of the facts. "He hanged himself in his ce
twelve hours later. And you know what?" Mallo
looked at Colt, and now there was in her eyes all th

anger, all the hatred and all the despair that had been so carefully missing from the rest of her speech. Colt saw in that moment the raw depths of human anguish, the suffering that would never be erased, the scars that would never fade. It tore at his soul. "I didn't care," she said deliberately. "I once loved the man more than I loved life itself, and then he was dead and I *didn't care*." She got up abruptly and walked away from Colt. Her shoulders were stiff and her hands clasped rigidly before her; she was staring fixedly at the opposite wall. "I never, ever," she said slowly, "felt anything at all. Not sadness, not happiness, not sorrow or regret for the man I loved...just relief that he was gone. He would never bother me again and I was glad."

There was an endless silence while Colt saw her draw further and further into her protective shield of suffering and self-disgust and he knew he could not reach her. The bleak chasm that separated them grew with every minute, but there was nothing he could do.

Then Mallory forcibly relaxed the muscles that had held her body taut. She said simply, "You wanted to know what I thought about love. That says it as well as anything, I suppose. Love starts out with all good intentions and promises meant to be kept and ends up as only another illusion that dissolves just when you need it most. I thought it was forever too...once upon a time."

Colt sat looking at the box in his hands. Somehow he found even its presence repulsive, as though it could alone and in itself conjure up evil...the evil

that dwelt within the twisted mind of a man who
had all but destroyed the woman Colt loved. "So,"
he said quietly, "you wove a dreamworld around
yourself, where the bad guys are easily identifiable
by their Lycra monster suits and the good guy
always gets the girl and love conquers all. You put
your demons on the screen and zap them one by one
with your laser pistol, and nobody has to worry
about anything as long as *you* are in control."

Mallory looked at him, her face carefully revealing nothing. She let his words bounce off her like
raindrops off an umbrella. He could not hurt her
now.

Colt's sudden movement startled her as he suddenly got to his feet and strode past her to the
French doors opening off the bedroom. Mallory
watched him cross the terrace in the glow of the
security lighting. She heard the rattle of a trash-can
lid. When he returned, his hands were empty. Colt
was once more in command.

"That should have been done a long time ago,"
he said firmly. "The past has too much hold over
you already. You don't need reminders dragging
you down."

Mallory's smile was a little weak. "You can
destroy the evidence, but you can't erase the
crime—as everyone from Billy the Kid to Richard
Nixon has found out."

But her attempt at lightness had no effect on
Colt. "I won't be condemned for another man's
sins," he told her.

He reached for her but Mallory stepped away

Her nerves were tight bundles of distress. Didn't he realize what it had cost her to tell him the truth? Couldn't he see why she could not give him what he needed from her? Mallory did not know how much more she could take tonight.

Colt caught her arm; he made her look at him. "I'm sorry, Mallory. This is not another script. You can't write a neat and poignant ending to this one, and I'm not a paper character trained to speak your dialogue." He sighed. With his eyes softening, he brought his hand up as though to touch her face, but she quickly and somewhat desperately tilted her chin. Her throat was tightening, the scalding tears were building again.

"No, Colt." Her voice sounded high and unnatural even to her ears. Her eyes pleaded with him not to push her too far. "I don't want to hear it. You . . . you've directed this entire relationship like a film from the beginning. *You* called the shots, you were the voice on the set. And you did it beautifully, perfectly. You gave the people what they wanted. . . ." Her voice was starting to break; she strengthened it determinedly. "But you're right. This isn't a movie. You're not in charge anymore, and you can't make me listen to your promises."

The swift expression of pain and helplessness that crossed his face tore at Mallory's heart. His grasp tightened on her arms. "Darling, I wish I could make it easy for you," he whispered. "Just because your dreams died once you won't believe anymore. I wish I could snap my fingers and make it different. I know that sometimes terrible things happen that we

can't control. . . . I wish I could offer you something
besides promises, but, darling, promises are all
have. I can't see into the future. I don't know what'
going to happen to us. I only know that I love you
and if we work on forever one day at a time, even
tually we'll look up and. . .it will be forever. That'
what loving is all about, Mallory."

Oh God, if he could only know how much she
wanted to believe him. If he only knew how hearing
those words sliced at her soul. But long-ingrained
self-protective instincts were taking over; Mallory
Evans knew when she was in over her head. And she
knew when to draw her last weapon.

Mallory's chin lifted; she met his eyes. The threat
of tears evaporated into coolness and she said, "Is it
Is it really, Colt? Or maybe for you and me it'
about a film with a multimillion-dollar budget that
needs a director. Maybe forever ends with the fina
cut." Why was she saying that? She had never in
tended to say that. . . . But in growing horror she
heard her words echo and she could not erase them.

Her dagger hit him. She saw the unmasking, the
startled shaft of pain in his eyes, the tightening o
his jaw and the stiffening of his lips. And within hi
pain she saw a reflection of her own; the part of her
heart that belonged to him broke that moment too.

Colt murmured, "You didn't mean that."

No, no she didn't mean it. . . . But her hand
clenched at her sides, her lips pressed tightl
together and she said nothing.

Colt turned slowly and walked over to the bed. He
sat down and pulled on his shoes. He stood and pu

on his shirt. Her heartbeat counted each movement of his fingers as he fastened the buttons one by one, yet she did not move.

"Well," he said at last, very quietly. "I guess you did get to write the last line after all."

She saw him standing in the center of the room, looking at her. Waiting for her. She knew all she had to do was open her arms and her life would be changed forever. Mallory remained motionless.

She heard his footsteps crossing the room. She sensed him stop, change direction and walk very close to her. Then, with the last remaining courage in her soul, she turned to look at him.

In Colt's face was nothing but sorrow, in his eyes, nothing but love. Then he reached out and lightly brushed her cheek with his fingertips. "This time," he said softly, "it was real."

MALLORY DID NOT CRY THAT NIGHT. She had sealed all her emotions away and she was numb.

That night she lay in her cool bed with the scent of him tangled in her hair and on her skin, and she thought about how much she hated to sleep alone.

And the clock ticked on.

Chapter Fourteen

THE LONG SILVER LIMOUSINE glided through the gates of the grand Brentwood estate. Color splashed through the early twilight like an aurora borealis. The sweeping lawns were dotted with striped canopies and bathed in blue spotlights, and in and out of those lights wandered the most glittering of all of Hollywood's famous faces.

Liveried attendants escorted first Mallory, then Jake, out of the limousine when it stopped at the front entrance to the mansion. Mallory had to pause for a moment, standing at the bottom of the red-carpeted steps, drawing a deep breath and trying to fortify herself for what lay ahead.

She could not tell whether the cacophony of gaiety was spilling from the outside of the mansion to the lawn, or whether all the sounds were coming from the crowd on the lawn, but at any rate there seemed to be no refuge for a woman who wanted to remain as unobtrusive as possible. The steps provided a view of a steady influx and exodus of bizarrely dressed, bejeweled people, all with bright and fatuous smiles, lilting voices and ringing laughter.

Mallory had not wanted to come. For the past two

weeks all she had been able to do was drag herself out of bed in the morning and force herself into some semblance of a routine. A party was the last thing she needed. But this particular affair was being given by her producer, and she was more or less obligated to attend. And Jake had insisted on escorting her. Life, after all, did go on.

It was late in the morning after that final, fatal scene with Colt when the consequences really hit her. Until that point she had been fine. She had convinced herself she had really lost nothing; theirs hadn't been intended to be a long-term relationship and how much better that it end now of her own choice rather than later when she was not prepared. She had known all along that she did not have room for a man in her life. She did not need the emotional turmoil, the distraction, especially not when her career was undergoing such exciting changes and she had so much in her life that needed her full concentration.

Probably the only thing Colt had ever wanted from her was a chance at a comeback. That was only logical. He needed a job, she had a job. She couldn't blame him for trying.

But she did not need Colt Stanford, not as a director or as a lover. She didn't need the distraction he had brought into her life, the constant feeling of living on the edge, the terror of losing him even when she had known that eventually she would. And she certainly did not need him as a director. He might have been the best in the business, but he was entirely too risky. She couldn't chance the success of her film on him. She must have been crazy even to have considered it.

Then suddenly, just as she was settling down with her second cup of coffee, tears flooded down her face without check no matter how hard she tried to stop them. A twisting pain formed deep in the pit of her stomach and spread slow aching poison to every muscle in her body. A flashback of every scene in last evening's nightmare passed in slow motion and freeze-frame—the gentle love in Colt's eyes, the need and the vulnerability; the strength and the plea as he tried to persuade her to believe him; the pain that hardened his face as she flung her last hateful words at him. He was gone. He had left hurting, just as she was hurting now, and there was nothing she could do to bring him back.

Mallory could not remember the last time she had cried. Early in the nightmare of her marriage she had learned that tears were a waste of energy; they solved nothing and only made her weaker. So she sealed off the part of her that could be touched and made to suffer and gradually over the years had convinced herself that stoicism was a display of strength. She had lived from moment to moment with disaster her only future and she had not cried. She had heard that the man she once had loved to the exclusion of all else was dead and she had not cried. But Colt was gone, and now she cried all the tears for all the anguish and all the terror that had gone before. She had lost him and she cried for the end of hope.

She had gotten what she wanted. She had maintained that precious control and forecast her own future. She had let her fear of losing deprive her of the greatest prize of her life.

She thought she would recover. She had survived much worse than this, hadn't she? She had watched her life dissolve around her like ashes in the wind, she had walked a broken woman from the smoking ruins; she had squared her shoulders and begun to build again—bigger and better than ever before. She would survive.

But hers was not to be an easy task. Everywhere Mallory looked there were signs of what she had so willfully tossed away. The scent of Colt's cologne in her sheets. A song on the radio they had heard together. The view of the pool they had shared on quiet mornings. A certain billboard on the highway they both had laughed at. How much of her life had been occupied with him . . . and what a vast, aching space his absence left.

For days afterward, she found herself collapsing under the weight of sobs at unexpected moments. Just when she thought she was finally learning to cope, the ache would sneak up on her again and she couldn't prevent it. No, she was not handling this well, not well at all.

Jeannine, who dispensed hard advice and little white pills in lieu of tea and sympathy, said at last, "Well, that's the pity, isn't it? You know, you're like people who don't take the time to value their property until after the burglary, then they're astounded at how much they've lost. You thought this was a simple love affair, easy come easy go, but after it's gone you find out it was the real thing."

Of course, that was the worst part. For as much as Mallory had fought it, as hard as she had played the word games and refused to admit it, she loved Colt. And love was not something that disappeared just because she decided to toss it out the window. The remnants of it existed in every corner, the memory of it lingered in the evening shadows, the essence of it would stay to haunt her the rest of her life.

If it ends tomorrow, nothing will change what we've shared tonight. . . .

Some things did last forever. And loving Colt was one of them.

In the beginning she had wondered if she would ever be able to get on with her life. Sometimes the pain was so excruciating it was crippling. At other times it was merely a throbbing ache far in the background of her mind, a shroud of sorrow she simply could not cast off. She tried to comfort herself with what she still had—her work, her success, her name. Mallory Evans, a hot commodity. The woman who took Hollywood by storm. The woman the most powerful men in the business would go to war for. Mallory Evans, whose imagination had become a part of the lives of every man, woman and child in America. She walked through the airy, spacious rooms of her own house, touching the possessions she had acquired, trying to summon some pride in her success. She had worked so hard for this. She had come so far. She had done well. But the big rooms seemed to echo emptiness. The carefully chosen expensive furnishings were, after all, no more than props. Why had she ever thought any of this was important?

She did not want to be Mallory Evans, superstar. She only wanted to be the woman Colt Stanford loved.

STANDING IN THE MIDST of all the glitter and glamour that teemed around her, Mallory was once again reminded of how shallow and transparent it all was. *Is this what I've given the past five years of my life to. . . what I've just sacrificed the man I love for,* she thought dully.

A notorious film star passed by on the arm of his latest wife. He did not know Mallory, but he craned his neck to look at her, his gaze sweeping her appreciatively up and down, and when his wife paused to speak to someone else, he winked at Mallory and made a step as though to come over to her. Mallory quickly averted her eyes, knowing that would not discourage him. Then she felt Jake's possessive hand on her elbow.

"Not to worry, peaches," he said smoothly. "You're safe with me."

"I don't know if I can do this," Mallory said, and everything within her rebelled at setting her foot on the first step. She did not want to be there. She wanted to be safe within the walls of her own home, away from the sparkle and the noise and the blur of famous faces and false laughter.

But somehow she was guided up the steps and into the spacious, glass-enclosed atrium. Delicate silver and gold slippers moved and danced across

imported Italian marble floors. In the center of the
room a champagne fountain splashed over a magnificent ice sculpture of a castle, and the entire structure was backlit with colored bulbs. Champagne
gurgled perhaps three feet into the air. Along two
walls were buffet tables piled high with red and
black caviar, flaming chafing dishes and canapes
shaped like everything from guitars to cameras. A
live rock band was playing somewhere, and the
noise was deafening.

Almost immediately Mallory spotted the actress
who had just written a titillating account of her life,
complete with famous-name bedmates and suicide
attempts. She was in conversation with another
actress-turned-exercise-guru. Both were well on
their way to being drunk.

The legendary star of the great Western and war
movies of the fifties was with the ex-wife of one of
the hottest comedians in the business. The comedian himself, whose off-color Las Vegas show netted
him over ten thousand a night and whose drug habit
was notorious, had pinned a not-quite-unwilling
young lady against the wall and was laughingly exploring the intricate ties of her top.

A rock star, dressed in tight leather pants and vest
with many chain belts and no shirt, had his arm
around the waist of a beautiful young man in a voile
shirt and was whispering something in his ear.
Whatever he'd suggested the other man apparently
found agreeable, because they left soon after, arms
entwined.

There were pills and booze in abundance, and

everyone was getting high on something—even if it was no more than their own reflections in the strategically placed mirrors that lined every hallway. There were feathers and lace, fringed suede and worn denim; there were designer gowns in silk and satin and lots of jewels. It didn't matter that most of the jewels were not real—the emphasis here was on quantity, not quality. The sparkle counted, not the value. And there was plenty of sparkle.

When Jake left her to find more champagne, Mallory became easily swallowed by the crowd. In her simple white crepe Grecian-style gown, with its single band of clear stones decorating the neck from shoulder strap to bodice, she was no competition for the clash of color and brilliance that surrounded her. Many faces she recognized, but no one recognized her. Which was just as well, because the only face she wanted to see right now was Colt's, and Colt would never be found at a party like this. He did not belong here any more than she did.

Jake pressed a glass of champagne into her hand and slipped a casual arm around her shoulders. The slight pressure of his fingers was bracing, but his expression was relaxed, unconcerned and deceptively mild. "Well now, peaches," he said, and beneath the broad brim of his tan dress Stetson busy eyes assessed and cataloged every face, every word, every nuance of expression that went on around him. "You can either stand here all night looking like a piece of the statuary, or you can mingle like a good little girl and let me get on with some business."

Mallory sipped the champagne. For such a fine

vintage, it did not go down quite as smoothly as it should have.

She knew Jake was right. She could not stand there all evening looking as though she had suddenly awakened to find herself in someone else's nightmare, even if that was exactly how she felt. And Jake was also right in insisting that she be present tonight. Her absence from her own producer's party would have been far too much fuel to add to Evelyn Bouchard's fire. Mallory had no right to ask Jake to babysit her through this. This was her world, the one she had chosen, and she had better get used to living in it.

Mallory lifted her head. With a small, tight smile that was far less convincing than it should have been, she said, "You go ahead. Do your business. I'll be fine."

Jake touched her chin with his forefinger, making her look at him. The deep concern in those pale blue eyes touched Mallory. "You sure?" he inquired gently, and Mallory knew that if she had asked him, he would have stayed by her side all evening, protecting her, coddling her, taking care of her just as he always did. But he wanted her to learn to start standing on her own, and he was right. It was way past time.

Her smile softened, and this time she sounded more genuine. "I'm sure." She gave his arm an encouraging squeeze. "Go on."

The last caress of Jake's fingers imparted strength, and she watched his strong broad form merge with the crowd and finally disappear.

Fortifying herself with another sip of champagne, Mallory squared her shoulders and began to move through the room. She could at least appear as though she were trying to be a good guest.

There was a swimming party in progress across the lawn and something very erotic was taking place in the hot tub on the terrace. Mallory turned away from the picture window. The entire scene belonged in a surrealist painting that could be entitled *Decadence*. Bodies of satyrs and nymphs should be painted with the leering faces of Hollywood personalities. Fire and brimstone should be pouring down from the heavens.

Mallory smiled a little at the puritan image, and when she turned she collided with the only friendly face she had seen tonight... and the last one she had expected.

"Jeannine!" she exclaimed. "What are you doing here?"

Jeannine grinned, very pleased with herself. "I thought that was you over here trying to hide behind the curtains! Some shindig, huh?" She peered at Mallory curiously. "How did they drag you out of hermitage?" But without giving Mallory a chance to reply, she leaned back a little, brought her finger to her chin thoughtfully and scrutinized her friend from head to toe. "Really, Mal," she reproved. "You should have let me fix you up at the shop. You look so... classy." She said it as though it were a dirty word.

Mallory laughed. Jeannine herself was dressed in what appeared to be no more than a collection of layer upon layer of scarves—gold and silver ones wrapped turban style around her upswept curls, a paisley print tied into a bandeau top and covered with a metallic-splashed knit shawl worn diagonally, African prints wound low on her hips to form a skirt that fell to her ankle on one side and barely to the middle of the thigh on the other. The finishing touches were a wide leather belt and a collection of chain belts draped across her hips, gold fringe earrings that dangled to her collarbone, and a collection of studded leather ankle and wrist bracelets. Jeannine's look was definitely not "classy," but it was very Hollywood.

"You may have just saved my evening," Mallory told her, and she felt the tension leave her body for the first time that night. Her eyes actually took on the faint hint of a sparkle. "But you didn't answer my question. What *are* you doing here?"

"I thought you could use a little moral support," Jeannine replied, then relented with a grin, excitement dancing in her eyes. "I came with Byron," she confessed. "Would you believe it? Who would have thought such an upright, straitlaced loyal subject of the Queen would have friends like these?" She wrinkled her nose a little, imitating his accent. "Only he calls them 'business acquaintances.'" She laughed again, clearly pleased with herself. "He didn't even tell me about it until this afternoon, so I thought I'd surprise you."

Then Jeannine's expression softened, and she squeezed Mallory's arm. "I *am* glad you came, Mal. No man's worth what you've put yourself through these past weeks. You have to get out and join the living, you know."

Mallory's wan smile turned into a grimace as her arm was jostled by a balding television comedian and a bikini-clad starlet who were doing a melo-dramatic tango across the room to the beat of a top hit from the forties. Mallory quickly held her glass away from her body, and champagne splashed on the floor rather than her dress. It might not have been one of Jeannine's designer originals, but she did not want to stain it.

On second thought, she realized a stained dress might be a good excuse to go home.

Mallory looked at Jeannine again. "I know," she ad-mitted. A sigh escaped her as she glanced around the room. "It's just that I still find it hard to think of all this as 'living.'" Her slight smile didn't quite reach her eyes. "This looks like a scene from my film."

"So what's wrong with that?" challenged Jean-nine. "It's life, right?"

Heartbreak, corruption, back-stabbing and double-crossing, viciousness, immoral and illegal acts. . . all going on right before her eyes. Careers would be made tonight, lives would be broken, promises given and turned into threats, ambitions would be arbitrarily crushed and hope destroyed. Yes, this was real life, the truth behind the glitter that Mallory had written about, the darker side of the dream that Colt had turned his back on. She had never wanted to be part of this world; she had only wanted to write about it. She wondered what Colt would say if he could see her now.

"No," Mallory said quietly, lowering her eyes briefly to her glass. "It's not real life. It's just some perverted kind of make-believe."

But Jeannine wasn't listening. Her attention had strayed to a point over Mallory's shoulder, her eyes narrowed ominously, and with a murmured, "Uh-oh" under her breath, she grabbed Mallory's arm to steer her the other way.

But it was too late. "Mallory," rang out Evelyn Bouchard's venomously sweet tones close to her ear. "How lovely to see you."

Mallory took a breath, squared her shoulders and turned. She shouldn't have been surprised. At any moment in time where more than two Hollywood names were gathered Evelyn Bouchard was bound to be lurking in the shadows. Mallory should have been prepared.

Evelyn was dressed tonight in an incongruously innocent gown of white taffeta with a high, lace-trimmed neck and winged sleeves that came to a point almost eighteen inches straight out from her shoulders. The dirndl skirt with its modest pink sash and lace trim was old-fashioned and sweet, the sleeves just bizarre enough to be appropriate in a gathering like this. Her hair was arranged in a demure Gibson-girl style, her pink-polished lips forming a dangerously welcoming smile.

"How lovely that you're here. We don't usually see you at gatherings like this." She gave a light laugh, indicating with a depreciating flick of her wrist the surrounding scene. Her eyes were as cold as ice.

Mallory managed a cool smile but declined to reply.

Jeannine said, gallantly coming to the rescue, "Mallory, someone is waving to you from across the room. Will you introduce me?"

Evelyn followed the direction of her gaze, where anyone could have been waving to anyone, then she returned to look at Mallory, the smile never faltering. "Well, my dear," she said pleasantly, "I won't keep you. I only wanted to thank you for a wonderful story."

Mallory could not keep the small dart of puzzlement and alarm from shooting across her features. "Don't worry, you'll see it in tomorrow's paper. I'll have a copy sent by special delivery," Evelyn supplied with a brilliant smile as she turned to go.

Mallory felt a cold knot of dread settle in her stomach as she watched the small figure glide across the room and eventually fasten onto some other hapless victim. Colt. It had to be something about her and Colt. Mallory didn't think she was up to that yet. . . .

Jeannine looked at her sympathetically, but she did not know what to say. Besides, she had just spotted Byron going up the winding staircase and she had been separated from him long enough. She didn't want to desert her friend, but. . . .

"Look, Mal," she said, twining her arm through Mallory's and giving it a bracing squeeze. "Ignore her. Parties are for having fun. You do remember how to do that, don't you?" Then she grinned. "This place alone is enough to keep you laughing. Have you been to the bathroom yet? They've got rose petals in the john! And there's this big room upstairs that's all decked out like a casino. Come on," she said, tugging on Mallory's arm. "Let's go check it out. You've got to meet Byron anyway, and I just saw him go up. Let's do some serious partying!"

Mallory appreciated what Jeannine was trying to do, but she didn't think she could face a casino at that moment. "Thanks, but I see Sky Danson over there." Sky had won his fame as Garth in Mallory's trilogy, and they had gotten to the stage of casual acquaintances over the years. "I suppose I'd better go say hello."

Jeannine, looking relieved, gave Mallory's arm a final pat before releasing it. "Good girl. Loosen up. I'm going to find Byron. Don't forget you've got to meet him before you go."

Mallory managed an almost enthusiastic smile. "Can't wait."

"And don't forget to check out the john!" Jeannine called with a grin over her shoulder just before she too disappeared into the crowd.

Mallory managed a rather weak smile, and then she turned and fortified herself to make meaningless conversation with Sky Danson.

JEANNINE GOT SIDETRACKED by a former lover and his latest playmate, both of whom, made garrulous by previous indulgence in party favors, wanted to talk. Jeannine was surprised at how little they had to say and how quickly she became bored. In fact, the entire party seemed a little dull without Byron. Once she would have enjoyed this sort of thing whole-heartedly—much in the way she was encouraging Mallory to do—but now she only found it superficial and a bit sad. . . just as Mallory did.

Byron was not in the casino upstairs, and when she mimed a question to the man with whom she had seen him last—the music was too loud to talk— he gestured toward a doorway down the corridor and tried to slip his hand under her skirt. Jeannine thanked him and stepped out of his embrace.

The bright glare of two overhead chandeliers made her blink as Jeannine opened the door the man had indicated, then she took a step back. On the rumpled king-size water bed, illuminated in perfect detail by the incredibly high wattage of the room, were a nude man and woman. With a silent grimace of apology, she started to pull the door closed behind her when the man looked up.

Byron.

It would have been merciful had Jeannine not remembered anything after that. In fact, she remembered every slow, cold detail. Byron swore softly—in irritation, not alarm—and sat up. The woman, with an annoyed expression, looked from Byron to Jeannine and swung her legs over the side of the bed, beginning to pull on her panties. She was beautifully proportioned, blond and tanned all over. Jeannine felt ill.

She should have raged; she should have screamed. She should have thrown something. Perhaps the old Jeannine would have. But the new Jeannine, the one capable of having a dream and watching it crumble to dust before her, just stood there, staring. She did not feel angry; she did not feel outraged. All she felt was a dark and creeping acceptance of the truth.

The woman, tying an unbuttoned silk shirt into a low knot over her jeans, tossed Byron a quick wink as she reached the door. Incredibly, Byron returned a grin. Jeannine had never noticed before the satanic quirk of his brow when he grinned. Both Byron and the woman, Jeannine realized slowly, were high.

The door closed firmly, and she was alone with Byron.

"You son of a bitch," Jeannine said slowly. Her cheeks felt cold, and so did her fingers. Her voice sounded very calm.

Byron looked bored as he reached to the night table for a cigarette. Jeannine had never seen him smoke before. "Come on, darling," he drawled. His cultured accent grated on her ears. "Don't affect that outraged morality with me. You can't pretend you haven't done much the same thing in places like this. Party drugs, party sex...." He shrugged as he lit the cigarette, leaning back against the headboard. "That's what it's all about, isn't it?"

Yes, thought Jeannine dully. *That's what it's all about*. Play out the fantasy, go for the good life, take it while you can... and never mind when everything turns to ashes because nothing lasts forever in the land of tinsel.

"I never expected this of you," she said.

And why not, she wondered. Just because he dressed in three-piece suits instead of leather and chains, because he spoke in a refined accent instead of in trendy slang. That was all appearance, and she should have learned by now that nothing is ever what it seems.

Byron merely lifted a quizzical eyebrow. "I'm not sure I understand."

For the first time Jeannine found herself capable of movement, but even then just a small, rather helpless turn of her wrist. "I believed in you." Her voice sounded expressionless and calm, but inside something was slowly beginning to break—and she was afraid it was something that could never be mended. "It would have been different if you had been like all the rest. . . but you said you wanted to be real for me. You said you wanted to be part of my life."

He relaxed with a smile. "Darling, I am real, and this is all a part of your life. Don't you see that's why we're so perfect for each other? We both like the same games, and we both play them so well."

Jeannine felt a twinge of sickness tug at the pit of her stomach. Perhaps, she thought, once. . . once I knew how to play the games. But not now. It wasn't enough anymore.

"What about the woman you're supposed to be engaged to?" Her tone did not reveal much interest. In fact Jeannine did not even know why she asked the question. Somehow it seemed important, though. "How does she fit into all this?"

Byron shrugged his shoulders. "Not at all, actually. After we're married, she'll live in England for the most part and I'll stay here, just as I've always done."

Perhaps that was the first time Jeannine had admitted to herself that she really had been thinking in terms of marriage to this man. Marriage, fidelity, lifelong commitment.... She had expected him to leave his fiancée for her. She had almost believed he had already done so.

But the things she had imagined she had seen in him—things like integrity and fidelity—really hadn't been there at all.

"So much more uncomplicated that way," he continued easily, drawing on the cigarette again. "She has no interest in the kind of life I lead, and I'm not particularly fascinated by hers. You and I, however, can continue as we've always been—"

Jeannine did not hear the rest of his plans. She turned and closed the door quietly behind her.

She should have known, she thought as she made her way downstairs to retrieve her wrap.

MALLORY FINALLY SAW HER HOST after she'd been at the party for two hours. By that time the noise and color and frenetic activity were making her temples pound like a scream bursting to get out.

A laser show had begun on the back lawn, and Mallory recognized some of the special effects that were used in her films. A computer console directed beams and flashes of light perfectly synchronized with the music, whirling colors across the lawn. The natural beauty of the artistically landscaped garden faded beneath this display, and the guests danced with abandon beneath the rainbow of snapping electric colors and the thunder of sound. Mallory almost found the scene frightening, watching as she was from the edge of the partially enclosed terrace. The thirsty quest for self-gratification gone out of control and magnified by all the power of modern technology.

Mallory had tried to appear to be enjoying the festivities, but the strain was wearing on her. Ironically, when she had written *Day of the Last* she had exposed a culture she knew about but had never experienced firsthand. Since then, the truth of the imaginary world she had created in the pages of her script had come back to haunt her in so many ways... with Colt, with her own brush with Evelyn Bouchard, and especially tonight at this party, where every nightmare could come true....

"Something to see, isn't it, Mallory?" Gabe Newall, her producer, stood proudly beside her and looked out over the festivities. "The technicians are on loan from the studio. Had the computer flown in from France, though. Amazing what those Frenchies are doing with microchips these days. That's who we've got to keep our eye on for the next space race, if you ask me."

"It's spectacular, Mr. Newall," Mallory agreed politely. Also ostentatious, and overdone, like everything else there. Like the guests themselves, all competing with one another and trying to outdo one another for the most bizarre costume, the smoothest line, the greatest degree of careless sophistication....

Mallory was suddenly very tired.

"Not to bring up business at party time, babe,"

Newall said, clicking ice cubes together in his nearly empty glass with a swirling motion. "But we're ready to start production in two weeks, and we've got to have your signature on Collins's contract."

Zeke Collins was the best of all possible candidates to direct her film. Or at least everyone told Mallory he was the best. He was young, talented, filled with new and adventurous ideas, and the studio was pushing him. Mallory could not fault his previous work, although it wasn't exactly to her taste. Collins was at his best with the comedic absurd, with vicious little tongue-in-cheek stabs at convention and society. He had never before directed a serious film. Worse than that, he didn't have the experience or the sympathy with the subject matter that Mallory felt was a prerequisite for any director she chose. He didn't really care about what she was trying to say, not as she did, not as. . . .

But she had to stop thinking about Colt. He was no longer a part of the picture. In all truth, he never had been.

Throughout the evening, Jake had never been far from Mallory's sight. She did not know whether he had arranged it that way or she had, but whenever she happened to glance up he was just across the room, standing head and shoulders above the rest of the crowd, sleek Stetson pushed back casually, engaged in careless conversation with someone, relaxed and reassuring her with his mere presence. Mallory was not surprised when he strolled over to rescue her now.

"Some setup, Gabe," he drawled in his best

country-boy-come-to-town manner. "Cost you a pretty penny too, yessiree. How much do you reckon one of those dancing fountains like that one there would set a fellow back? Pretty thing, isn't it? Kind of reminds me of—"

Mallory, enormously grateful, excused herself and slipped away.

She knew she had to make a decision about Zeke Collins. She knew the studio was probably right. They wanted him—why fight it? Simply letting them have their way and forgetting about it would be so easy. She had made her grand stab at asserting her rights when she had won the choice of director. Why push her luck? It hardly seemed to matter anymore.

When she tried the bathroom door, it was locked. She started to turn away, but it opened almost immediately and a man and a woman came out, arm in arm, giggling and looking very pleased with themselves. Biting back a twinge of disgust, Mallory went inside.

The bathroom was huge, with a vaulted glass ceiling and hanging plants suspended from the beams. The tiles were mirrored and the fixtures were black. There was a sunken tub surrounded by a garden of flowering plants and the carpet was plush and red.

Mallory stood there for a long time, her own figure in the white gown reflected a thousand times in broken miniatures around the walls, listening to the hiss of the automatic air freshener and the whoosh and gurgle of the Jacuzzi controls. She wondered dully and distantly if there had not come a point in the lives of every one of these people when nothing seemed to matter anymore.

She washed her hands and dampened a scented guest towel, pressing it to her neck. Her eyes in the enormous mirror over the sink seemed remote and unreadable, almost as though they did not belong to her.

When she left the room, Jake was waiting for her. She did not have to tell him she was ready to leave.

Chapter Fifteen

"So, Peaches, was it so bad?" Jake tossed his hat on the glass-topped coffee table and lounged back on the sofa, watching her.

Mallory smiled a little as she brought him his drink—bourbon, straight, no ice. "Pretty bad," she admitted.

She poured a sherry for herself and sat down beside him, tucking one foot beneath her as she settled back into the curve of his arm. "I guess I didn't feel much in the mood for celebrating tonight, that's all," she amended. "You know how those parties always depress me. It's like being center ring in a three-ring circus."

"Always has been, always will be," Jake agreed as though unbothered by the fact. His finger smoothed an errant strand of strawberry-blond hair behind her ear almost absently. Mallory found the unexpected but tender gesture soothing. "About time you got used to these things, don't you think?"

Mallory nodded, though without much conviction, and stared into her glass. She could feel Jake's caring gaze upon her. The solid warmth of his arm around her shoulders was comforting, good and real and strong, after the bizarre playground she had just left.

"They're really pushing me about Zeke Collins."

Jake took a careful sip of bourbon before replying. "You wanted the responsibility, peaches."

She sighed. "Yes. I know."

"What is it again that you've got against this young buck who, by the way, has only won two Oscars and been nominated for a third?"

Mallory tilted her head back to rest against his firmly muscled arm, staring unseeingly at the far corner of the room. Why was she making this so hard on herself? Chances were, the studio was right. Collins would probably do a good job. His name certainly couldn't hurt box-office sales. And if he blew it, so what? She had nothing to lose. Whatever happened to the film once it went into production was not her responsibility. Her only mistake had been in caring too much about this project. She should have learned by now that quality was not a prerequisite for anything in this business.

What was it Colt had said? Integrity. Yes, integrity. A very luxurious commodity.

"I don't know, Jake," she said slowly. "I'm just . . . uneasy with Collins. He doesn't really have a feel for the script. I have this awful feeling that if I give in to what the studio wants, I'll be making a big mistake."

Jake leaned forward and put his drink on the table. Forming his words thoughtfully, as always, he said, "You delay much longer and you'll be in breach of contract. I'll tell you the truth, honey, this deal is held together with Scotch tape and good intentions as it is. You start screwing around now and I wouldn't be a bit surprised if the studio turned all its guns loose on you. They've let you flex your muscles, but there's a limit to their patience. You're coming close to blowing your reputation in this business. So let me ask you again." His tone was precise and deliberate. "What have you got against Zeke Collins?"

"Nothing," she sighed. "It's simply that he's not—"

"Colt Stanford."

The flatness of Jake's tone made Mallory look at him in surprise. The grimness she saw on his face was totally unexpected. His normally pale eyes were dark with a force she had never seen there before, and he met her startled gaze levelly.

"Now you listen to me, Mallory." He could not be silent any longer. It was about time he interfered in this, the most important decision of Mallory's—and perhaps his—life. His words were clipped and firm. "You should've gotten that man out of your system weeks ago. He was no good for you, professionally or personally. He was dangerous—an instigator and a troublemaker. You don't need that. Look what he did to his own career. Do you want the same thing to happen to you?" Jake shook his head impatiently. "You've got it made now. All you have to do is ride with the tide. The last thing you ever needed was a man like Colt Stanford messing up your life."

Mallory looked at him for a moment, completely stunned. She had never heard Jake speak so adamantly on any subject. In the wake of her startled silence, Jake's eyes softened; he brought his hand up tenderly to touch her face.

"Ah, Mallory," he said softly. The light stroking pressure of his thumb against her temple was soothing and adoring, and the sweet light deep within his eyes took her breath away. She had looked into those eyes a thousand times and had never seen what she was seeing now...had never even imagined it. "Sometimes I think you get so caught up in weaving your dreams you can't see what's right before your eyes. Like me," he said, and dropped a gentle kiss on the edge of her eyelid. "Here all these years, waiting for you...."

Mallory did not know what to say, or do, or even think. Yet something instinctive responded to what he was saying, and what she saw in his eyes...as though she had known it was there all along. Jake, so strong and secure and always there, taking care of her....

He did not rush her. His hand cupped her face warmly, fingers nudging back tendrils of hair, his expression showing his tolerance of her surprise. He smiled at her, and though there might have been a trace of hope in the smile, it was also a little sad. "You never guessed, did you?" He let his hand drop, briefly caressing her shoulder. He averted his eyes.

A wry grimace deepened the groove along his cheek. "I didn't mean to spring it on you like this," he said simply. "I guess I just figured it was high time you knew." Then he looked at her soberly. "Maybe you're not completely over Stanford. Maybe this isn't the best time, and maybe that's the chance I'm taking. But then again, maybe it's best you take a good look around you. I'm what you need, Mallory. Not some fly-by-night pretty boy who doesn't know a good thing when he's got it."

How like Jake. No pretty phrases, no practiced seductions, no clever persuasions. She felt a rush of tenderness for this man she had loved and depended on for so long. She touched his arm, her eyes softening. "Oh, Jake. . . ."

"No." He held both her arms, and the openness and the vulnerability in his look made her ache inside. "No hasty words tonight. I only wanted you to know and. . . to think about it. I want to take care of you, Mallory," he said, before he kissed her.

She wanted him to kiss her. It was exactly what she expected, and needed. Filled with gentleness and care, the kiss spoke of the simplicity and the strength of the man, the careful, unpretentious predictability of him, the core of something stable in a precariously rocking world. Jake—sturdy, reliable. . . .

She closed her eyes and leaned against his shoulder, holding him, and thought about how safe she felt in the haven of his arms. Perhaps he was right. Perhaps this was what she needed, to be loved by someone whose future was secure. Perhaps it was what she had always sought.

Then he pushed her gently away. She looked up at him, wanting to say something to let him know her gratitude for his love and the support he'd given through the years. But he stopped her with a finger laid across her lips. "Not tonight. I want you to think about it, and to be certain."

So unlike Colt, who had given her no chance to think, but who had been so very sure. Colt, impulsive, reckless, careless of the consequences. He was everything Jake was not.

Mallory was glad Jake had not given her an opportunity to speak. She did not know what she would have said.

Jake let himself out quietly, but Mallory remained on the sofa alone for a long, long time.

THE NEXT AFTERNOON Mallory sat by the pool, the open script in her lap, and looked at Jeannine helplessly. Mallory wished she knew what to say to make her friend feel better. And she wished Jeannine, usually so prompt with the magical advice, could say something, anything, to help Mallory find her way out of the tangled mess her own life was becoming.

When Mallory had called Jeannine that morning she realized her friend sounded strange. Foolishly Mallory had attributed it to a hangover. She had wanted to talk to Jeannine about Jake and about the film. Now Mallory felt a twinge of guilt at how ready she always had been to burden Jeannine with all her problems, never imagining the depth of Jeannine's worries. For the woman who sat across from Mallory now bore little resemblance to the flighty, exuberant and carefree girl Mallory had always known.

"Jeannine, I'm so sorry," she said at last, her voice

filled with aching sympathy. It sounded inadequate. She had listened with only half an ear all these weeks while Jeannine extolled the virtues of her latest Prince Charming, never once imagining that this time Jeannine might be truly in love. Mallory was as sorry for her own insensitivity as anything else.

Jeannine looked at her, and her eyes were surprisingly thoughtful and calm. "I'm not so sure I am." She smiled wanly. "I guess no one grows up without a few scars. I think it was important to me to find out what I want...even if I didn't get it this time."

Then, with another quick smile that was meant to be reassuring, she scooped up her oversize quilted purse and got to her feet. "Anyway, I just wanted to let you know I'd be out of town for a couple of weeks. I've got plenty of good people to take care of the shop and I could use a vacation. I thought I might drive out to Sedona. It's so peaceful up there I'll have plenty of time to think."

She started to leave, then she turned with a flash of the more familiar grin. "You know what else? I thought maybe this fall...." She shrugged a little, uncomfortable. "Well, I've always been a bit jealous of how dedicated you are to whatever project you take on and how rewarding your job was when you were teaching.... So I thought I might go back to school, get a few courses and try my hand at being a teacher for a while. I've always liked kids," she said a little wistfully. "It's time I did something worthwhile."

"I think that's great," Mallory said sincerely, getting to her feet. Jeannine would make a great teacher. She would be marvelous at anything she decided to do, once she settled down to do it. Jeannine was the perfect example of turning adversity into opportunity, and Mallory wished she could be more like her.

Jeannine passed off the declaration with an impish grin. "It was either that or have my hair styled into a mohawk cut and dyed purple."

The two women laughed, then moved into an embrace. "You're going to be fine," Mallory whispered. Suddenly her throat was thick with emotion.

"You too." Jeannine stepped back, holding her friend's shoulders firmly, and despite the evenness of her voice there was a bright film of tears in her eyes. "You just take one last piece of advice from your old friend. If you ever do find the real thing, don't let it go. You hold on for all you're worth."

Mallory nodded. "We both will."

They hugged each other again, briefly, then Jeannine turned quickly to leave.

MALLORY SPENT THE REST OF THE AFTERNOON sitting by the pool, trying to reread the script, but mostly her thoughts plodded in a circle. She wanted to call Jake, but restrained herself. She couldn't mislead him. And she wasn't sure of her feelings, though she did not know why. Jake was one of the very few people in her life she could depend on. She trusted him, and certainly the affection she had built up for him over the years should count for something. But reliability, understanding, affection...were they enough?

She did not think she could deal with any decisions about her personal life when her career was nearing such a crisis point. Why had she fought so hard for the right of approval on this particular film? She should have known that when it came right down to the crunch, she wouldn't have the stamina to see it through. She was being manipulated by the producers into doing what they wanted her to in the first place, and she was buckling under just as they knew she would. She did not have the courage to risk her reputation on one film. There would be others.

Besides, if she couldn't have Colt Stanford, it really didn't matter who else she chose as the director.

Mallory did not realize how long she had been sitting, staring unseeingly at the battered script before her. Evening shadows were beginning to lengthen, and, impossible as it seemed for August, there was actually a hint of chill in the air. Mallory slipped her arms into the sleeves of her lavender terry cover-up and reached for the evening paper on the wrought-iron table beside her. The housekeeper must have put the paper there before she went home. Mallory shook her head in weary amazement. She had to get herself together. A whole afternoon lost, and nothing to show for the time.

She closed the script and replaced it on the table. She noticed how quiet everything was, how unearthly still. It was as though every animal and bird had scurried into its respective burrow and nest, leaving her the only living creature on the planet. Even the traffic sounds were muted. It was spooky, and Mallory did not want to sit outside any longer. She decided to read her paper inside, under the reassuring glow of lamplight, and maybe even see what Mrs. Horscht had left her for dinner. . . .

She unfolded the paper and stopped on the threshold of the patio door, her brow puckering in confusion. This was not the *Los Angeles Times*. It was a trade journal, and a note was paperclipped to the front. "Mallory," it said in red ink, "most people in your position are more careful how they dispose of their trash. Thanks for a great story! E. Bouchard."

Mallory did not have to look long or far for the article. Nor was she particularly surprised by the content. The only thing that did amaze her was that such a relatively uninteresting story should have rated a place on page three.

The photograph of Mallory took up almost half a column. "Profile of a genius: dark past gives birth to multimillion-dollar monster."

There it was in black and white—her secret, her private horror, her life disclosed for all the world to see. Mallory scanned the article as she walked slowly inside, waiting for the pain, the sense of exposure that would leave her feeling terrified. The whole story was there, a complete analysis of Hollywood's mystery lady, from her humble beginnings in a rural Mississippi town, through her struggling college years, to explicit details of her marriage and its ending with one near murder and a suicide. Oh, the piece was startling, dramatic, powerfully written. Yellow journalism at its very worst, it had the desired effect on Mallory.

Everything about the final nightmare was noted. The agony of that endless thirty-six hours, the terror, the helplessness, the humiliation. The time Mallory thought she could never live through again she now was living in the span of ten minutes while she sat at her kitchen counter on a dusky August afternoon five years later. She could still vividly remember the heat, dust and sweat. She could even recall hearing the sirens and the bullhorns, the maniacal laughter that shook the body of the stranger who held her captive. She felt the cold circle of metal pressing into her skull. She relived the terror of being convinced those were the last minutes of her life, relived also the sorrow for and helpless confusion about a perverted love that had reached its crazed finale.... She felt stripped, she felt outraged, she felt frightened and angry. She read the words and silent tears were rolling down her cheeks when she finished.

Then it was really over. She'd faced it all one last time; she'd cried one last time. And it felt good. Perhaps that was what had been necessary to really free her. To confront the demons from her past and to know they had no place in her present life, to realize once and for all, that she had no more reason to fear them. She could let go now. The trauma of those thirty-six hours would always be with her, but it would no longer have the same power. She had thought Bouchard's column was the worst thing that could happen, but Mallory had faced the publicity and found it to be, after all, little more than a shadow. The worst was over. Mallory felt cleansed, renewed and strengthened.

She was almost smiling as she wiped away the last of her tears and placed the paper on the kitchen counter. This was what she had been so afraid of? She should have been angry, she should have felt threatened. . . but what she felt, she realized with slowly dawning surprise, was relief.

Mallory had been terrified that the unleashing of the ghosts of her past would threaten the security she had built for herself today. But the telling of the story had not changed anything. She was who she was — a woman with a scarred past and the strength to overcome, and there was no shame in that. She had lived through the actual event. Why had she ever been so frightened of others knowing about it? That was all over, and she had walked away from it. It simply did not matter anymore.

She smiled a little as she glanced at the handwritten note. "Most people in your position are more careful how they dispose of their trash." She remembered Colt as he'd carried a box filled with memories and nightmares to the trash can, and ironically, she remembered the conversation they had had so long ago. . . about the people on the fringes of one's life, the maids and the waiters and the delivery boys. Or had it been a gardener or a meter reader that Evelyn had hired? Who would have guessed, and what could Mallory have done to have prevented the article even if she had wanted to?

Nothing, that's what. And Mallory was glad. Sometimes it was good to be reminded that nothing is ever as bad as you fear. How odd that Evelyn Bouchard, with no good intentions whatsoever, should have been the one to free Mallory from her long imprisonment.

Colt, Mallory thought, would be proud of her.

She left the paper on the counter and wandered over to the sink, filling a glass with water as she stared out the window. A strange, science-fictionlike twilight had fallen, yellowish green and phosphorescent. It looked like the backdrop lighting for one of her films. The script lay where she had left it, still and impotent on the patio table. And that was the way it would remain, words without life, a story without meaning, unless. . . .

This revelation was not startling. Mallory had known for the past six weeks and suspected even longer. Until this moment, she had not had the courage to admit to herself that there was only one person who could direct this film. Colt Stanford.

There was no point in hiding from reality any longer.

The three steps that separated her from the telephone were the longest Mallory had ever taken in her life. She could not believe she had the nerve. After what she had said to him, the way she had treated him, how dared she ask him to do her a favor? He would laugh in her face. He would hang up as soon as he recognized her voice.

No. This was business. He might hate her now—
he had every right to—but he loved the script almost as much as she did. He was an artist just as she
was, and he knew the creation must prevail at whatever cost to the creator. He would not let personal
feelings cloud his judgment. It was obvious he was
the only person who could bring this story to life,
and he would accept the responsibility.

He had to.

Mallory realized she could be making a decision
that would be disastrous to her career. She was
aware of the risks involved in presenting Colt Stanford to the studio. But wasn't her film worth that
risk?

Wasn't Colt?

Mallory's hands shook as she fumbled for the
phone. And what about herself? What would it do
to her to hear the sound of his voice again? How
would she be able to stop herself from crying out the
words he once had wanted so badly to hear? How
could she keep her heart from closing up her throat,
her yearning from reaching out to him over the telephone?. . .

But this was business. She could not ask him to
forgive her, any more than she could stop loving
him, but she had no intention of making him a victim. She would call him and conduct herself professionally. Who knew? Maybe something could be
salvaged of their friendship, their mutual professional respect for each other. . . .

Her fingers were icy as she punched the buttons;
her heart was pounding and the muscles of her

throat constricting. Maybe it would be better if Jake called him.

No. With a deep, somewhat unsteady breath, Mallory firmly pushed the last button. She was calling because she wanted, and needed, to do this herself.

His telephone began to ring.

Mallory's breath caught and everything within her went weak as his voice spoke into her ear. "Hi, this is Colt Stanford—"

Colt. Her entire being was flooded with such love and need that she couldn't speak, she couldn't move, and for a moment even the sound of his voice was blotted out. She stood, her eyes closed against all the things she had to say and could not, her hand tightly gripping the telephone receiver, and everything within her crying out to him. Colt. Colt. . . .

"You just missed me, but don't despair, I'll be back shortly, at which time I'll gladly return your call. Don't forget to leave your number!"

An answering machine. Slowly, her breath returned to her body, her vision cleared, her muscles relaxed. This was her chance. She could hang up now and he would never know. The idea had been a foolish one. She couldn't ask him.

A tone sounded in her ear. She took a breath and spoke carefully into the machine. "Colt, this is Mallory Evans, and I need to talk to you."

No, she couldn't speak to him over the phone. She couldn't spend the rest of the night waiting for him to return her call, wondering if he would, taking the chance that he might not. She glanced at her watch. "The time is seven thirty-five and I'm leaving right now to come over. If you get this message before I arrive, the trip will take me about half an hour." And if he did not, she decided as she hung up the phone, she would surprise him. If he wasn't home, she would wait. She had to see him. And she was going to see him tonight.

Mallory took the time only to change into jeans and a sweater and grab her purse. The telephone began to ring almost as soon as she replaced the receiver and continued to ring until she was out the door, but she ignored it. It was probably just someone wanting to commiserate with her about the Bouchard article, and Mallory simply wasn't interested.

She hurried to the car and fumbled impatiently with the door lock, then had a moment of frustration as she tried to remember how to work the seat belt. She drove the car so rarely none of its parts were very familiar to her. She got the seat belt fastened and shifted into gear carelessly, leaving a rubber skid mark on the drive.

Mallory's mind was racing as she took the back roads to Colt's apartment. If she let herself stop and actually think about what she was doing, she would lose her courage. So she let her thoughts take their own convoluted course, focusing on the implications and not the act. Jake would be horrified. He would say that Colt was using her. . . . And Mallory would reply that she didn't care. Maybe for once she needed someone to take control of her life, and how could she be manipulated into something she already wanted? Why, oh why, hadn't she realized that before?

The producer would be horrified. The studio might even find a loophole to back out of the deal. But she had the contractual right of final approval of the director, and the only director she would approve was Colt. If the step she was about to take meant losing the film entirely, so be it. Colt had once said she was a born risk taker, and gambles did not mean much unless something big was at stake.

A genuine dusk was falling now, and Mallory fumbled on the dashboard for the headlight switch, experiencing a moment of pique as she always did with the car that was too complicated for the average person to drive. At that moment she noticed a slight shimmy in the wheel beneath her hands.

Immediately all other thoughts gave way to panic as she took her foot off the accelerator and concentrated on keeping the car under control. That was all she needed—a breakdown on this nearly deserted road in a thirty-thousand-dollar Porsche, miles away from the nearest gas station or telephone.

The shaking became worse, jarring her teeth and pulling at her muscles as she tightened her hands on the wheel. She had slowed to a mere crawl, but the car did not respond to the lessened speed or her grip on the steering wheel. It actually seemed to be rocking beneath her.

That was when Mallory noticed the tops of the trees were shaking. The utility poles were swaying. A low, ominous roaring sound filled her ears.

Then the very asphalt before her began to crack and peel away like old paint, giving way to the heaving, breathing earth beneath. The car lurched and tilted, and with a muffled scream, Mallory slammed on the brakes. The car did not stop moving, but slid slowly sideways down a newly created hill. A geyser shot upward through the undulating pavement before her as a water main broke beneath the earth and wires danced and writhed like snakes, spewing electrical sparks in every direction. A cloud of dust blurred the scene before her. Everything seemed to be moving in slow, slow motion.

A sharp cracking sound split the air like a shotgun blast and slivers of wood pelted the side of the car and splashed on the windows. Mallory watched in frozen fascination as the huge telephone pole above her seemed to teeter and sway for that brief instant that is forever before it came crashing downward, filling her vision. She screamed a scream that never escaped her lips, both hands clutching the back of her neck and head, her knees drawn up swiftly toward her chest. The shock of impact jarred her forward, the locking seat belt snapped her backward, the sound of breaking windshields and the ripping of metal tore at her ears as small round nuggets of glass rained inward. The back end of the car lifted high into the air, pulled by the weighted front, then came crashing down, bouncing violently on the rear suspension.

The air was filled with smoke and the dancing light of fire and water, the landscape heaved and shifted and tumbled and fell; the earth rumbled and twisted and erupted its discontent in showers of dust and rock. Inside a small crumpled Porsche pinned to the uncertain ground by the weight of a utility pole, one woman sat, unable to move, unable to scream. There was nothing she could do but sit helplessly, silently, and watch the world come to an end.

Chapter Sixteen

AFTER A LONG, LONG TIME, the chaos finally came to a halt. The earth ceased to move; the air no longer groaned. There was nothing now but the crack of an occasional falling branch or the tumbling of a pile of stones, the gushing of water, the muffled explosion of a power transformer down the line. Mallory leaned back against the headrest and tried to breathe deeply. She was bathed in cold perspiration, and her entire body still vibrated from the violence of a splitting earth. Her heart was a slow, heavy timepiece somewhere in the center of her chest. It was only then that Mallory truly realized what had happened. An earthquake.

After a long time she was able to open her eyes. The safety glass surrounding her had shattered and formed an opaque screen; she could see nothing before her. There were gaps in the side windows but through them nothing was visible but patches of haze. The acrid smell of electricity and faraway woodsmoke drifted in on the heavy air. Mallory had to sit a moment more, trying to calm her breathing and will strength into her muscles. She had to think what to do.

The first thing was to get out of the car. She

reached for the door handle but it wouldn't work. In confusion, she looked for the release button, finally found it on the dashboard and remembered it was automatic. The engine was stalled but the auxiliary-power indicator still glowed red on the control panel. She tried the handle. She turned to put her weight against the door but was pulled back by the cutting strap of her seat belt. The door was obviously jammed, but she could push the remaining glass out the window. . . .

Her hand fumbled for the seat-belt release, her movements clumsy from shock. She couldn't find the catch. With another calming, shaky breath, she twisted against the restraint of nylon and tried again. The passenger seat had shifted during impact, wedging the metal release in an awkward position next to the floor. Although she flattened her hand, the clasp was out of reach. She pulled and she tugged but it did not budge. She struggled until beads of perspiration dotted her face and made her hands slippery, then she sat back, breathing hard, exhausted. There was nothing she could do. She was trapped.

The sirens began, wailing and fading, rising again. A minute later, the Civil Defense alarm began escalating to its full screeching pitch, and the irony of that almost made Mallory smile. Too little, too late.

Mallory tried to make out the numbers of the luminous dial of her watch. She listened to the fading sirens and counted the beats of her heart. She did anything but think about being forcibly confined in her car on an empty road in the aftermath of an earthquake.

Was Colt all right? Where had he been when it had struck? According to the sound of the sirens, the major damage must have been concentrated to the west...toward her house, but away from Colt. *Please God, let him be all right. Let me get out of this so I can tell him....*

She squeezed her eyes shut against the sudden wave of burning tears that rushed for release. If she started crying now she would never stop. He had to be all right, she had to find him....

She wondered how long it would be before rescue teams started searching this road. It could be hours, days...no, she would not be that long...away from Colt. Someone would rescue her.

She thought about wasted time. She wanted forever, but six weeks would have been enough. Six weeks that she had been apart from him, lost to her stupid fears and insecurities.... Six weeks could be forever, when that was all you had.

She listened to the beat of her heart tick away the minutes, trying not to think of time passing and time already passed that she could not reclaim, trying not to worry about Colt...trying not to think it might already be too late.

She did not know how long she had been there. Minutes or hours, it was a piece of eternity. Then, so quickly it almost could have been an optical illusion, she saw a flash of light swing across her shattered windshield. She held her breath, widening her eyes as though by straining to see she could clearly

make out what was on the other side. Then again—
far away but longer this time—the beam of a car's
headlights coming toward her.

The light dipped and disappeared. With a racing
heart, Mallory leaned on the horn. Someone had
come. "Help me!" she shouted, having no idea
whether or not her voice would carry through the
car. "I'm here—help me! Someone!" She pressed the
horn again and held it, sending out a single, endless, blaring cry for rescue through the night.

The sound was deafening yet somehow empty, as
it is when one calls out, uncertain whether anyone
will hear. The noise blotted out reason but left
hope. Mallory held the pressure until her hands
began to ache and the blast grew weaker with the
draining battery. No one came. But somebody was
out there, she was sure.

Then, over the fading volume of the horn she
thought she heard a human voice. She thought she
heard her name. She released her hand and in a
moment she heard the call again. "Mallory!"

Colt. It was Colt.

Her lips moved to form his name but no sound
came. It wasn't possible. She was hallucinating. . . .

"Mallory, I'm here! Hold on a few more minutes. . . I'm coming. . . ."

Footsteps crashing through undergrowth and
slipping on pebbles. Then the shadow of a human
form fell over her, and the car door shook as he
grabbed it.

"Colt!" she cried. She tried to twist around to
reach him, to see him. Colt! He was here, he was

alive, he had come for her and miracles were possible.... "Colt, I—"

"It's all right, darling." He was breathing hard. "I'm here. You're going to be all right." His voice was calm and commanding. He was in control, just as he always was. She tried to restrain the wild cavorting of her heart, tried to stop the dizzy spinning of her mind, tried to calm the ecstasy that transported her out of a nightmare and into possibilities too magnificent to be dreamed of. She tried to listen to him, to concentrate on what he was saying.

"The door is jammed." Every word was precise. How she loved that voice. How desperately she depended on the man to whom it belonged...just as she always had. He was there when she needed him, as he had always been. "I want you to lean as far to the right as you can and cover your head and face. I'm going to have to push the window in."

She did as he instructed, doing what she could to protect herself. The window fell inward with a single crunching sound, scattering scraps of safety-coated glass over her lap. She felt his hands upon her, and she turned with a muffled cry into his embrace, drowning in his strength, inhaling his scent, tasting his skin and hearing his murmured words mingled with the incoherence of her own, "Thank God...thank God you're all right...."

For an endless time they held each other, clutching and strengthening the embrace. Mallory tasted the salt of her tears on his neck and felt the moisture of his breath on her cheek and she loved him. He was there, he was real, and her world was filled with him. She could ask for no more.

At last he moved reluctantly away, and Mallory became aware of the cutting pressure of the seat belt. Her hands lingered on his arms, unwilling to let him go, and her tear-blurred vision was filled with his face—beautiful, adoring, intense, looking at her, touching her. She stammered, half crying and half laughing, "My...seat belt. It's stuck. I can't—"

His hand caressed her cheek. When he straightened up, her hands trailed after him but in a second he was beside her again, a pocket knife swiftly and efficiently ripping through the nylon. Then strong arms were pulling her through the window, setting her on solid ground, holding her tightly.

They must have kissed. They must have touched and held each other with the frantic desperation of those who have found something long after hope had been abandoned of ever rediscovering it. Mallory remembered none of the details of the past several hours. She only knew that Colt was there, that his love enfolded her and hers reached for him, that they were together and nothing would separate them again. The time they were locked in each other's embrace was endless, and within their physical communion were all the certainties words could not relay.

But there were thoughts that had to be voiced, questions that had to be answered—the rites that would solidify the miracle. Mallory looked up at him, her hands stroking his arms over and over again, constantly reinforcing the assurance that he was really there, that he was not merely a figment of her imagination. Her eyes were blurred with trying to take him all in at once. "Colt, what...how... how did you...?"

He brushed his lips across hers to still them. "I heard your message as I was walking in the door. I called you right back, but apparently you had already gone."

She shook her head slowly. "I heard the phone ringing, but I had no idea it would be you."

"When the quake hit...." He closed his eyes as though against a great pain, and she felt a shudder run through the muscles of his arms. "God, Mallory, you don't know what it did to me, knowing you were on the road...not knowing...." He stopped, and Mallory shared his dark memories. She understood because she had gone through the same agony over him.

"The damage on my side of town is relatively light," he continued in a moment, "but the freeways are a disaster area. I know how much you hate to drive that Porsche—" he spared a rueful glance for the crumpled ex-status symbol "—so I could only hope you had taken the back roads. Still, it took me over an hour to get this far. There were a lot of accidents, with people panicking when the first tremors began, and emergency vehicles blocking the way... I had to leave my car about a quarter mile back, where the road started to crack. There are a lot of downed trees and utility poles. I was beginning to think I'd never reach you, or worse, that you hadn't left the house after all."

But Mallory did not want to think about that now, about what might have been or what almost was. It was enough that he had found her, that despite the disaster they were together. She wrapped her hands around his arm and held on tightly. "Let's go home," she whispered.

He looked at her with an expression that was troubled with sympathy and regret. "Mallory," he said quietly, "I'm afraid the damage in your neighborhood was pretty extensive. I heard on the radio that they have the entire area barricaded off."

She smiled and only tightened her hold on him. Did he really think she cared? After all this, what did it matter? "Anywhere that you are is home," she said softly. "Let's go."

COLT HAD INSISTED she soak in a hot tub to ward off shock and the aches and pains from bruised and pulled muscles she had undoubtedly sustained during the accident. Now somewhat restored, Mallory sat curled up on Colt's sofa, wearing one of his comfortable cotton shirts, her eyes fixed in numb disbelief on the television set, where film clips of the destruction were just now being telecast.

Colt pressed a glass of brandy into her hand. Not removing her eyes from the screen, Mallory murmured, "It's incredible."

Colt stood beside her for a moment, watching the telecast, then he stepped forward and abruptly switched off the set. "I think that's enough of that," he said, and his face was grim when he sat beside her.

Mallory shivered involuntarily, the havoc aired on the news and the tight look on Colt's face reminding her all too poignantly of the nightmare just past. . . her near escape. Immediately Colt's arm went around her shoulders, and she could feel the straining of his arm muscles in an embrace that wanted to crush.

"Thank God, Mallory," was all he said, his voice hoarse. "Thank God."

Mallory let the prayer wash over her and penetrate her being. She tried to believe that she was safe and there with Colt. That it was Colt's arm around her, Colt's breath warm against her neck. Colt's heart beating strong and sure next to hers.

He straightened, loosening the pressure of his arm slightly. There was both wonder and uncertainty in the depths of those warm brown eyes. "When I think. . ." he said, and his voice still sounded a little uneven. "When I think how close I came to losing you. . .forever. . . ."

But he hadn't. He had searched for her. He had wanted her, he had found her, he had brought her home. Her hand came up and stroked the clean smooth plane of his cheek. There was a slight tremor to the movement, but neither noticed it. "I'm here now, Colt," she whispered, "for as long as you want me."

He smiled, but it was a rather strained gesture as he gazed at her hungrily, urgently, trying to observe everything of her presence, still not quite believing her words. "How about forever?" he suggested huskily, and mutely she nodded.

He took the glass of brandy from her unprotesting fingers and set it on the table. He kissed her very gently and with restraint, as though she were a fragile creature who had to be treated with the utmost care.

And she touched him in the same way, her fingertips exploring the fringe of dusky hair that fell across his forehead, the bone structure of his cheeks, the softness of his lips. Just to touch him, just to see him and breathe again his familiar scent.... Her senses were filled to the bursting point, trying to capture and retain every nuance of him.

Colt's fingers traced a thin line on the curve of her thigh where it was exposed beneath the hem of his shirt, his eyes following the movement. He smiled a little at himself when he saw his hand shake. "I've missed you," he said inadequately. Every day, every night he had dreamed of this, of having her near and touching her. Every movement had been filled with memories of her and needing her, never believing he could ever really have her. Even he was now not able to completely believe she'd made the commitment.

Mallory's eyes were full of longing. "It's been too long." So much wasted time filled with the absence of him, and time was so precious. What lay behind her was gone, and she could never reclaim it, but as for the future.... "I'll never throw away our time together again," she promised softly, searching his eyes. "Please let me stay with you, Colt."

He gathered her into his arms, holding her tightly, closely. "Just try to get away," he murmured.

But she didn't. She wrapped her arms around his neck and offered him her lips.

There was so much they needed to talk about and to say to each other. Colt wanted to know how this miracle had happened, and why she had come to him. He wanted to tell her about every agonizing moment he had spent apart from her, and that he had never stopped loving her. He wanted to give her promises and ask promises of her and he wanted to plan the future with her. But already their bodies were moving into the natural symbiosis of love, and the words that should have been said were overshadowed by what their hearts and minds and souls were already communicating so perfectly.

His hand caressed the smoothness of her waist beneath the shirt and the gentle curve of her breast. His breathing was shallow, his skin was flushed, and though he wanted to savor every moment, he could barely make himself go slowly. Her fingers were tugging at his own clothing, and soon Mallory and Colt were lying side by side on the sofa, naked in an embrace, just as they had done so long ago.

Her gaze was raw and urgent, her face was dewed with the delicate flush of passion. Colt kissed her cheek, stroked the tousled fall of strawberry-blond hair. He wanted to worship every inch of her. He wanted this to last forever, but the demands that were pulling his body to hers were too powerful to be ignored. With a small and apologetic smile, he whis-

pered somewhat raggedly, "Would you mind . . .
very much . . . if we made love now, and talked
later?"

She shook her head, the urgency of her hands
upon his shoulders confirming the gesture as she
pulled him down to her. "But there is one thing I
wanted to tell you," she said, and he looked at her.
She had wanted to say the words so long, she had
thought them to herself so many times, and her
throat ached with needing to say them. Simple
words, but meaning so much. . . . "I love you," she
whispered.

And that, after all, was the only thing he wanted
to hear.

Outside, the world lay in ruin, but wrapped in
each other's arms, they made their own world.
Through the night they loved each other, and the
dream that had begun so many weeks ago was finally theirs to hold.

THE NEXT DAY they walked through the rubble of
what once had been one of Los Angeles's most exclusive residential areas. It was a sobering experience. They had to leave the car five blocks away and
pass around a tightly secured barricade. National
Guardsmen patrolled broken streets. Cleanup crews
went about the grim business of clearing away fallen
trees and broken glass. Tendrils of smoke still curled
from piles of ashes where electrical fires had
destroyed buildings in a matter of minutes. Mallory
offered quiet sympathy to neighbors who were meth-
odically sifting through the remains of their houses in

hope of saving some valuables. Multimillion-dollar mansions lay like so many broken toys, tilting into the streets or reduced to piles of scattered planks and crumbled bricks. Mallory's home was one of them.

They stood in the street while Mallory took one last look at what was left of a lifetime of dreams and five years of dedicated ambition. Ashes to ashes and dust to dust.

Colt's arm was around her, his strength comforting her. He was obviously expecting her to feel much more than she did over the loss of all she possessed. At one time Mallory too would have been surprised to feel so little sorrow at the sight. But last night, in Colt's arms, she had discovered that the only thing she had ever really had of any value was intangible. And no one could ever take that from her.

At last Colt asked softly, "What are you going to do?"

She looked up at him with a rueful smile. "Build again, I suppose."

She saw the slow light of admiration and respect in his eyes; he turned her into his arms and he kissed her. "I love you."

Mallory cupped his face in her hands. That wonderful, adored face, the face she wanted to wake up to and go to sleep beside every day for the rest of her life. "The feeling is mutual," she murmured, and they embraced for a long, long time.

Then Colt looked down at her, the lazy light of contentment playing in his eyes even as a half-puzzled smile formed on his lips. "I never did ask you—why did you call me last night?"

Mallory stepped back a foot, looking up at him. What a world lay between then and now. "I called to ask if you would be interested in directing my film. At least that's what I told myself. I think the real reason I called had very little to do with the film."

But even as she spoke a cloud of reluctance began to form in his eyes. His hands slipped slowly from her arms. "Mallory, don't do this," he said carefully. "Don't do it to us, or to your film. Don't you realize the only reason I stayed away from you all this time was because I could see what your association with me was doing to your career? The gossip was starting, and maybe you were beginning to believe it a bit yourself." She shook her head violently, but he lifted a finger against her protest. "It would have gotten worse. People were saying I was using you to get back into films. If the studio starts to believe the talk, it will back away from you entirely." His smile was regretful but gentle. "Face it, darling, I'm a dangerous man to have around in this business."

She looked at him unflinchingly. "You're the only one who can give my script proper direction, Colt. You could spend the rest of your life trying to convince me there are others just as qualified as you, and both of us would know it for a lie. No one else has lived it, Colt—no one else cares as much as you do." She saw reluctant acknowledgment in his eyes, and she pressed her advantage. "Maybe this will be the key that will set you free from your past too," she persuaded. "It's about time, don't you think?"

He looked at her for quite a while. "You could lose it all."

She looked up at him soberly. "Will you still love me?"

His face softened as he reached for her. "Darling, you know I will."

She slipped her arm around his waist; they turned and began to walk away from the ruins. "Then," she said, leaning her head against his shoulder, "I have nothing to lose."

Epilogue

THE HOUSE WAS FILLED TO CAPACITY. Tuxedoed men and glittering women occupied every available space, sat on the stairway, crowded the hallways and spilled out into the moonlit garden, all of them laughing, talking, drinking, shouting congratulations, embracing. It was a typical Hollywood party, and the three guests of honor sat smugly on the mantelpiece. All of them were short, gold and bald, and all of them were named Oscar.

The film was *Day of the Last*, written by Mallory Evans, directed by Colt Stanford. The awards were for best film, best screenplay and best director.

The home belonged to Mallory and Colt, though it was not to be their permanent residence. Already they had purchased a piece of prime canyon property and had promised themselves to start building as soon as their current film was completed. They were in no hurry; time was on their side.

Mallory accepted hugs and kisses, returned jokes and made reckless social commitments. All the while her heart was swelling with love and admiration for the man across the room. This was his night, so much more than hers. He had fought a hard battle against prejudice and suspicion and emerged the victor. He had made this film see its full realization. For three long years he had nurtured the project, drawing every ounce of perfection from all involved, insisting on nothing less than each person's ultimate potential. Through it all Mallory had been by his side, learning and growing, finding more about him to love every day.

Jeannine slipped an arm around Mallory's waist and hugged her briefly. "You look radiant."

Mallory's dancing eyes swept over her friend. "And you look. . . sedate!"

Jeannine was dressed tonight in a brilliant red caftan woven with a gold-spangled floral pattern, dangling rhinestone earrings and a half-dozen bracelets on each arm. Nothing was sedate about her but the expression on her face, which was more peaceful than subdued. Jeannine had matured during the past three years. She had learned contentment with herself and harmony with life. Her buoyant nature was still present. Her effervescent personality had not dimmed, but she seemed to Mallory a happier woman now than she had ever been.

Jeannine laughed and made a dramatic curtsy. "Only the best for *the* social event of the season!" She looked at Mallory, her eyes glowing with quiet pleasure, and said, "Oh, Mal, I don't see you enough anymore. It's good to be here."

Mallory squeezed Jeannine's hand in silent agreement. Since Jeannine had sold her shop and begun teaching fashion design at a small private school in the northern part of the state, the only time they saw each other was on an occasional weekend...or when Jeannine came to L.A. to shop. Their phone bills, however, were tremendous.

"I thought the only reason you moved north was to get away from these wild Hollywood parties," Mallory teased.

"Are you kidding?" Jeannine scoffed. "The only reason I keep coming back is for the wild Hollywood parties. Besides, you and Colt couldn't give a wild party if I wrote you a step-by-step outline. Speaking of whom—" her eyes wandered over Mallory's shoulder, to where Colt and Jake stood engaged in conversation "—how are the two men in your life getting along?"

Mallory followed the direction of her gaze. It still bothered her, knowing that she had had to hurt Jake, even though she knew he understood they were better friends than lovers. She sometimes wondered if knowing that had made the situation easier for Jake, and if he was still in love with her. She supposed she would always feel awkward around him, even though he never did or said anything to make it so. Since she had been living with Colt, her relationship with Jake had returned to what it always had been—professional, friendly, concerned. Jake would always hold a very special place in her heart.

"I don't know," Mallory said, her smile just the slightest bit troubled. "Why don't we wander over and find out?"

"I guess you've been taking pretty good care of her," Jake was saying.

Colt nodded. He knew how Jake felt about Mallory—he had always known—but he did not feel threatened. He could never resent anyone who loved Mallory, and he understood that Jake's feelings for her were far more fatherly than anything else. "I'm doing my best."

Jake saw Mallory approach with Jeannine. "She doesn't appear to be suffering any harm," he admitted. Then he looked at Colt intently. "I only want her to be happy."

Colt met his eyes evenly. "So do I."

The two men regarded each other for a moment, not as adversaries, but as respectful equals who had achieved an understanding. A moment later Mallory slipped her arm around Colt's waist.

"What is all this serious talk?" she asked. "Don't you know business is for business hours?"

Colt smiled at Jake in private communication, then drew Mallory against him in an easy one-armed embrace. "We stand corrected," he assured her.

The bell-like tinkle of a spoon against a champagne glass brought most, if not all, the celebrants to attention. Jeannine, a born toastmaster, lifted her glass to the couple standing before her. "To the most talented partnership in Hollywood," she sang out. "Long may they reign!"

There were cheers and applause and the sound of clinking glasses, and Mallory burst into laughter of sheer delight as Colt leaned down and sealed the toast with a kiss. Then Jake, resplendent in white tie and a black Stetson designed expressly for the occasion, stepped forward and cleared his throat.

"I have just one thing to say," he began and Mallory and Colt gave him their attention. "You two have been living in sin for the past three years—any thoughts on making this partnership a little more permanent?"

More cheers and some good-natured, ribald comments, and Colt looked down at Mallory with twinkling eyes. "I'm willing if you are."

The music and the laughter, the lights and the glitter all faded away like a dream as Colt's hand closed securely around Mallory's, and hers entwined with his. This time, they had found something real, and they were not about to let it go.

THE STORY BEHIND THE STORY

The behind-the-scenes developments that went into the creation of *Dreamweaver* are intriguing and, admittedly, at first a little confusing. Every good book needs a good author. But who is Felicia Gallant? Viewers of the daytime television serial "Another World" know she is the world's most popular romance writer, who in turn is actually actress Linda Dano.

Felicia is an outrageous, lovable, sensuous, caring, witty woman with a flair for flamboyant clothes and the budget to pay for them. Her sequined outfits, flowing boas, sparkling jewels and daring hats have become synonymous with Felicia's tough yet tender femininity. And as Linda Dano the actress has discovered, Felicia has garnered a large, faithful following since her first appearance in "Another World" on January 6, 1983.

Fans often think of the two personalities as one individual. Because of this, Linda suggested the creation of a real romance novel that could be purchased in stores. "My fans constantly ask me about my writing career. So it occurred to me that I really *ought* to write a romance. I approached the producers of 'Another World,' and the show's sponsor,

Procter & Gamble. We agreed that since Felicia Gallant is such a successful romance novelist, her book should be published by the world's most successful romance publisher. We all said 'Harlequin' at the same time."

The project met with an enthusiastic reception at Harlequin; many of the staff members had rearranged their lunch break so they could watch "Another World." Harlequin was also excited at the prospect of having Felicia/Linda collaborate with one of its most experienced authors—Rebecca Flanders. The two women first met in New York City to iron out the details of the characters and plot for Felicia's first "real" best-selling novel. The writing was made even easier by the fact that Rebecca's mother had already converted her to a faithful watcher of "Another World."

Although Felicia is a relative newcomer to the show, "Another World" has been on the air for twenty years. It premiered May 4, 1964, as a half-hour program. The format was expanded to a full hour in January 1975 and shortly thereafter won an Emmy award for Outstanding Daytime Drama. "Another World" has maintained a tradition of excellence over the years and currently has a daily audience of nearly five million people.

In May, Linda flew to Harlequin's headquarters in Toronto, Canada, to review the progress of the cover and sales material with her new publisher, W. Lawrence Heisey, Harlequin's chairman, and to brainstorm with Rebecca Flanders.

The publication of *Dreamweaver* was first announced at Tavern on the Green in New York City. The party was later aired on "Entertainment Tonight," and the project as a whole has received tremendous media attention.

Harlequin hopes you have enjoyed *Dreamweaver* as much as the company has enjoyed the experience of its creation. As Larry Heisey said, "We are delighted to publish a best-selling novel and to celebrate the Felicia Gallant name."

ABOUT FELICIA GALLANT

Felicia Gallant is a daytime TV character who is portrayed by actress Linda Dano. As a television novelist, Felicia has written many best-selling romances that have been previously published by the fictitious Cory and Winthrop. Her first smash hit was *Island of Passion*, followed by *Lust in the Kremlin, For Love of Poppy, Forbidden Passion, Desire under the Banyan Tree, Flames in the Night, Riviera Moonlight, The Deadly Camellia, Gone with the Dawn, White Snow in Hell, Passion's Progress, Moonlight Desire* and *To Love and Have Not*. Also among her writing credits is the Felicia Gallant romance exercise book. (None of these titles are available in bookstores.) Currently she is working on her favorite project, a new love story. *Dreamweaver* is her first book with Harlequin.

Felicia takes her writing very seriously and spends considerable time on research before ever jotting down one word. Beneath that glamorous exterior is a keen businesswoman who is a co-owner of Winthrop Publishing.

When she takes a break from her writing, she might elect to go out to buy a new hat or research her favorite topic—men. Then there are other moments when she would really prefer to eat a hot dog, with everything on it, or settle down in front of the fireplace with a bowl of homemade stew. For Felicia Gallant is really the pseudonym of Fanny Grady who comes from the back streets of Ohio.

Her penchant for travel has led her to live in Europe for several years — "Paris is so passionate." This is where Felicia was last in residence before coming to Bay City. It was her love of Los Angeles, however, that inspired her to choose this exciting city as the setting for *Dreamweaver*.

Some readers may find a resemblance to Felicia herself in the character of Jeannine, yet there are also similar personality traits in Mallory. Many of the males in the story are loosely based on men Felicia has known, but Colt Stanford is the type of man she would still like to meet.

ABOUT LINDA DANO

Linda Dano, who enacts the role of Felicia Gallant on NBC-TV's daytime drama "Another World," started her career gracing magazine covers as a top fashion model.

Following a familiar route from model to successful actress, Miss Dano landed the lead in an NBC-TV prime-time show, "The Montefuscos," and made numerous television appearances on "The Rockford Files," "Charlie's Angels" and "Barney Miller."

Even before Miss Dano joined "Another World," she was familiar to daytime fans for her two and one-half years as a character in "One Life to Live" and a year in "As the World Turns."

Miss Dano operates a fashion-consulting firm and spends her spare time restoring her landmark eighteenth-century Connecticut residence.

ABOUT REBECCA FLANDERS

It's hard to believe that Rebecca Flanders's first Harlequin novel was published in March 1983. Since then she has written more than twenty other books for Harlequin Romance, Harlequin Presents, American Romance and Intrigue. Interestingly her first story was rejected by Harlequin because it did not fit into any of the existing series, but was later picked up when the American Romance series began.

If Rebecca seems prolific, that quality is the result of her dedication and hard work. She normally writes anywhere from nine to twelve hours a day, every day. She has developed the habit over the years, having first expressed an interest in writing at the age of nine. At college she studied journalism and psychology.

Harlequin asked her to collaborate on *Dreamweaver* because of her proved skill as an author and because of interests shared with Linda Dano/Felicia Gallant. Both women have a fascination for the entertainment world and fashion design. Rebecca also enjoys hobbies of oil- and watercolor painting, as well as composing and listening to music and rollerskating.